PRAISE FOR MAIA CHANCE

THE BODY NEXT DOOR

"*The Body Next Door* is one of those deeply riveting, read-in-one-sitting kind of books. Like a riptide, Chance dragged me down into the chilly depths of cult life with its twisting dynamics of power and victimhood, only to shine her light on the human heart itself, in all of its fragility and resilience. Moody and hypnotic at times, sharp as a scalpel at others, this book is a darkly mesmerizing kaleidoscope of voices that will spin you dizzy all the way to its heart-aching conclusion."

—Jenna Satterthwaite, author of *Made for You*

"A twisty, surrealist cult story . . . full of secrets, betrayal, and deception, *The Body Next Door* kept me guessing until the very end."

—Allison Buccola, author of *Catch Her When She Falls*

"Maia Chance's *The Body Next Door* is a psychological thriller that seizes you by the collar from the very first page and refuses to let go until the very last. Told from the multiple points of view of the residents of Orcas Island, each character is more twisted and unreliable than the one before, leaving you grappling to unfurl every single secret. Chance demonstrates a mastery in pacing and suspense here and her mythic prose has a haunting, poetic quality to it that only underscores the eeriness of this small island town. If you think you have it all figured out by the end—you don't. This is by far one of my favorite thrillers of the year."

—Emily Smith, author of *You Always Come Back*

"*The Body Next Door* is one part mystery, one part speculative fiction, and total intrigue. Chance's novel checked all the boxes for me: compelling characters, atmospheric setting, and the convergence of past and present to solve a fascinating mystery. The Pacific coastal island setting combined with a missing person and a creepy cult made me turn the pages late into the night."

—Kristen Bird, author of *Watch It Burn*

"Moody and mesmerizing, *The Body Next Door* takes readers on a twisty, creepy, and compelling ride through family dysfunction and betrayal. This original cult thriller delivers unexpected turns as it builds to an emotional and breathless end that lingers long after you're done reading."

—Darby Kane, internationally bestselling author of *The Engagement Party*

"Maia Chance thrills readers with a compelling tale, cast with fascinating characters, entangled in page-turning intrigue until the very last page."

—Rick Mofina, *USA TODAY* bestselling author

"Seamlessly blending a cult-centric murder mystery with magical realism, Maia Chance has crafted a one-of-a-kind story set in the enchanting backdrop of the Pacific Northwest. Heart-wrenching, twisty, and wondrous, *The Body Next Door* unfurls like a wildflower, delicately unraveling the intricacies of each character's life, exploring how ultimately each of our pasts—the good and the bad—can echo in our hearts forever."

—Katie Garner, author of *The Night It Ended*

"*The Body Next Door* is packed with twists, lies, and secrets tied together with an unexpected surrealist element that creates a truly unique thriller unlike anything I've read before. With multiple rich POVs spanning Washington's elite to a survivalist cult, Chance's characters will keep you guessing until the very last chapter."

—Amanda Pellegrino, author of *The Social Climber*

"*The Body Next Door* is a compulsive page-turner with a fresh spec twist and bombshell reveals. Chance piles on the lies, secrets, and twisted timelines, leaving you breathless and utterly hooked until the final page."

—Lisa M. Matlin, author of *The Stranger Upstairs*

"*The Body Next Door* is a chilling page-turner that presents a cast of compelling characters and then forces us to reconsider everything we thought we knew about them. I absolutely loved the lush Pacific Northwest setting, and I was fully absorbed in the mysteries of family, place, and community that unspool over the course of the story. Highly recommended!"

—Polly Stewart, author of *The Good Ones*

THE RAVINE

OTHER TITLES BY MAIA CHANCE

The Body Next Door

DISCREET RETRIEVAL AGENCY MYSTERIES

Come Hell or Highball

Teetotaled

Gin and Panic

Naughty on Ice

FAIRY TALE FATAL MYSTERIES

Snow White Red-Handed

Cinderella Six Feet Under

Beauty, Beast, and Belladonna

AGNES AND EFFIE MYSTERIES

Bad Housekeeping

Bad Neighbors

THE RAVINE

A NOVEL

MAIA CHANCE

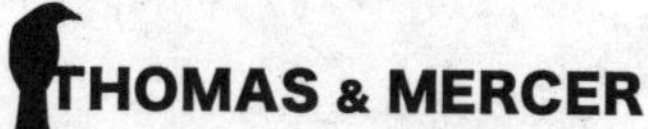

This is a work of fiction. Names, characters, organizations, places, events, and incidents are either products of the author's imagination or are used fictitiously. Otherwise, any resemblance to actual persons, living or dead, is purely coincidental.

Published by Thomas & Mercer, Seattle
www.apub.com

EU product safety contact:
Amazon Media EU S. à r.l.
38, avenue John F. Kennedy, L-1855 Luxembourg
amazonpublishing-gpsr@amazon.com

ISBN-13: 9781662535109 (paperback)
ISBN-13: 9781662535093 (digital)

Cover design by Shasti O'Leary Soudant
Cover image: © joe daniel price / Getty; © PATSTOCK / Getty

Printed in the United States of America

THE RAVINE

1

If I hadn't found that dead girl's head in the ravine, what would've happened to us?

There was definitely no hope after that. Looking back, it almost seems like some kind of over-the-top metaphor: our marriage, sacrificed, slowly rotting into the mossy earth.

When I first glimpsed the island from the ferry deck, I didn't like its stealthy approach, vaporous and dark even on a warm September day. I didn't like how the string of houses along the shore resembled bad teeth.

But why didn't I feel the wrongness before that? Before the island? Why didn't my skin crawl when my husband suggested, out of the blue, that we uproot our lives and try to grow our family on the other side of the country?

Why didn't I notice there was something just *off* at the clinic when Dr. Zakarian, the best in the business, said, *Motherhood takes sacrifice*?

◆ ◆ ◆

I sat in the flimsy gown on the examination table, goose bumps needling up and down my arms, and Dr. Zakarian told me what unexplained infertility meant.

It's pretty much what it sounds like. You could've set your watch to my twenty-eight-day menstrual cycle. My organs and hormones and blood work were on point. Sex was happening on the right days of the month with a husband whose sperm was Olympic swim team quality.

And yet, one full year of trying and no second line on the pregnancy pee stick.

I wasn't quite desperate. But my husband was, and I think it was starting to rub off on me.

The fertility clinic was in a townhouse on a leafy street near Central Park, the kind of place with nothing but an engraved brass sign by the intercom to announce its presence. It was several steps up from a regular clinic. The lighting was flattering, and the air smelled faintly of fresh roses.

"What I've seen during my time in clinical practice," Dr. Zakarian said, sitting on his rolling chair with a clipboard in his hands, "is that once women reach a certain age—"

"*A certain age?* I'm only thirty-four," I said.

"Yes. You'll be thirty-five in November, correct?"

I resisted the urge to drop my gaze. "Well, yes, but I—"

"In terms of reproduction, thirty-five and up is considered advanced maternal age."

"*Advanced maternal age?* You're kidding."

"I'm not."

I looked at this man who appeared to be about the same age as me, with his sleek dark beard, the lines on his forehead, and thought about how he'd be able to father babies until he dropped dead of old age but somehow *I* was already out of time. It was so freaking unfair.

"Once women reach a certain age, the stress in their lives starts to take its toll on their ability to conceive," he said. "I understand that you have a stressful job, Mrs. Sullivan?"

"I'm used to it."

"You work long hours?"

"I'm a researcher at a cancer lab. Memorial Sloan Kettering."

"That's a yes?"

I straightened my glasses and nodded.

"Do you sleep eight hours every night?"

I gave a laugh that sounded too shrill. "Does anyone?"

He tapped his clipboard. "I noticed you have a prescription for Ambien?"

"I'm an insomniac."

"Well, stop with the pills. They aren't your friend. No alcohol, either. And I'm guessing your nutrition could be better."

"Actually, I drink a green smoothie every morning."

"You're on the low end of the BMI for your height."

"I'm built like my dad. Genes, you know? You can't escape them."

"Are you eating enough protein? Good, grass-fed red meat?"

"Well, I—"

"You should be eating it rare. Still bleeding. For the heme iron. And you should consider introducing organ meats."

I imagined biting into a hunk of something dripping red and raw, and my stomach turned.

"How much caffeine do you consume?" Dr. Zakarian asked.

"Does caffeine affect fertility?"

"The little things add up."

"I drink two cups of coffee a day." A lie. I drank four.

"Do you exercise?"

"I'm a runner. And I go to spin."

"Think about sticking to gentle exercise. Yoga. Walking."

"Wait—what?"

"You seem inclined to argue, Mrs. Sullivan."

"Well, I *am* a believer in the scientific method. Rigorous skepticism and all that?"

Dr. Zakarian didn't smile at my attempted humor.

I cleared my throat. "It's just that—"

"Look. I can soft-pedal this for you. Make some recommendations about vitamins and sleep hygiene. I know your career is important to you, but you need to face facts. The world tells women that you can have it all, but you really can't. Not all at the same time, anyway."

Okay. I knew how I appeared to him. He thought I was one of those women who was addicted to their career, and suddenly they woke up and they were turning thirty-five and ticktock, bitch.

Fine, that *was* me.

But he was acting like I didn't care. Like I didn't have Pinterest boards filled with baby nursery ideas—the perfect soft rugs, the safest cribs, the cutest swaddling blankets and strollers and nontoxic teething rattles. Like I didn't scroll through Instagram during work breaks, hypnotized by that syrupy-dark opiate of pain and pleasure, scanning the mommy-and-me outfits, the flour-dusted cookie-making sessions, all those chubby cheeks and baby bumps and sun-dappled backyards. Images like razor-bladed candies endlessly pouring from a million elsewheres.

I looked directly at the doctor. "I want a baby. I—we, my husband and I—we *really* want a baby."

"There's always IVF."

"We want to try to conceive naturally." This was important to my husband, so it was important to me, too.

Dr. Zakarian leaned back in his chair. It squeaked softly. "Okay, well, if you want my honest opinion, you need to eliminate the stress in your life. *All* of the stress. My advice is scale back at work. Stop working altogether if you can. Not forever. Only for a time, so your body can get back to equilibrium and you have at least a shot at conceiving naturally." He got to his feet. "I'm sorry there isn't an easier answer for you. I really am."

I gave a disbelieving little laugh. "I can't just, you know, quit my job. Who does that?"

"Motherhood takes sacrifice." Dr. Zakarian had his fingers on the door handle. "You need to ask yourself, Are you willing to do whatever it takes to have a baby?" Without waiting for my answer, he left.

I sat there, cold and alone, and said to the door, "Yes. I *always* do whatever it takes."

2

A black Prius was at the curb when I emerged from the clinic.

It had to be the Uber my husband, Gregor, had said he was taking straight from JFK. He'd been in LA for a few days, meeting with a record label. He'd already texted to say the meeting came to nothing. They wanted him to sell out.

The car's rear door opened. Gregor got out, moving with the taut elasticity of the very fit. He wore his usual jeans, hoodie, and sneakers with an inborn elegance. Sunlight burnished the gold of his shoulder-length hair.

My heart gave a familiar heave.

He was younger than me by a few years, gorgeous, talented, charming, and rich. And we were crazy about each other.

"Babe?" he said. I couldn't see his eyes behind his aviator sunglasses, but I heard the worry, the love, in his voice.

I went down the steps and straight into his outstretched arms, and love gushed through my veins like a drug.

Whenever Gregor touched me, I became beautiful. I blazed to life. It was like his touch had some magical power to light up my cells, to transfigure me, to make me something glowing and complete.

I tried to explain this to him once, early on, tangled up in bedsheets and his warm limbs, and he'd frowned in confusion. "But you *are* beautiful, Harlow," he'd said, running his palm slowly over my hip. "I don't have anything to do with it."

He had everything to do with it.

The truth was, I was a plain woman, unimpressively built, A-cupped, burns-never-tans, dishwater blond, with brown eyes, a slightly too-big nose, and a phobia of contact lenses.

I'd done my utmost with what I'd been born with, of course. I kept fit. My makeup was understated yet flawless. My teeth had been lasered to the whiteness of printer paper. The pale highlights in my long, straight hair were realistic. My bifocals were Tom Ford.

Gregor, though—he drew beauty out of me, body and soul, the same way he pulled music like iridescent threads out of his guitar. He didn't know how empty I felt when I was away from him, hunkered over my microscope, poring over my computer screen blackened with numbers. When I was away from him, I was colorless. Aching to be brought back to life.

"What did the doctor say?" he asked, pulling back a little from our embrace so he could look at me. "Is it . . . are you . . . ?"

"No bad news. Not . . . not exactly." My throat tightened. "Can I tell you in the car?"

"Oh God, yeah. Sorry."

We settled into the Uber's back seat, and the driver rolled the car forward. I would've liked to go out to a dim bar somewhere with my husband and drink enough Sancerre to make me forget the hollowness inside me.

But Dr. Zakarian had told me not to drink, and we were heading to our airy condo in Nolita where Gregor's five-year-old son would be waiting with his nanny, Rosa.

Family first, Gregor always said.

I'd legally adopted Sam, so even though he was another woman's child, a dead woman's child, I thought of him as, well, *mostly* mine. Sam called me *Harlow*. I called him *my stepson*. It worked for us. And if—*when*—I had a baby, Sam would be a big brother, and the four of us would be inextricably knitted together.

As we inched through the late-afternoon traffic, I told Gregor the doctor's diagnosis.

"Unexplained infertility?" he said. "But isn't that what we're paying him for? To *explain* it?"

We were holding hands on the seat between us. He'd started squeezing too hard, so I gave my fingers a wiggle. His grip loosened. I could feel the thick calluses on his fingertips from the guitar strings. His body was practically vibrating with tension.

"Sorry," he said. "I just . . . I thought he'd have the answers."

"Well, I mean, he did. Sort of. He told me . . ." I took a deep breath through my nose. Let it out through my mouth.

"What?" Gregor turned to face me. He'd pushed his sunglasses to the top of his head, and I could see the urgency in his sea-blue eyes.

"He said I'm not getting pregnant because I'm too stressed out."

"Okay. And?"

"And he recommended that I take some time off work."

"See? That's what I've been saying all along, babe. I mean, you don't need to work."

"I know." I watched the sidewalk slipping past. We'd had this conversation before. Gregor was a semi-well-known musician, not pulling in a fortune, but his family owned millions of acres of forest land and about half the lumber and paper mills in the Northwest. Gregor had a substantial trust fund. He would inherit Pacific Crest Lumber someday.

Money wasn't an issue for us. But I wanted to work. *Get educated,* Mom had repeated again and again after Dad left us. *Then you won't need a man to make your life complete.*

"Do you believe in fate, Low?" he asked. He was squeezing my fingers too hard again.

I turned back to him. "What do you mean?"

"Do you believe that some things are meant to be? Like, that every now and then all the stars line up exactly the way they're supposed to, and something magical happens?"

"I mean . . . maybe?"

"Like you and me, for example."

"Well, yeah." I tried to keep it light. "*Obviously* you and me."

He smiled. "I got a call a few days ago. Out of the blue. And I wrote it off as a stupid idea, but now . . ."

"Tell me," I said.

"Well, my buddy from when I was a kid, this guy I had a band with back when we were teenagers, he called me and asked if I'd be interested in making an album with him."

"Okay." I couldn't guess where this was leading. Gregor was always doing projects with other musicians. He was a talented guitarist and songwriter, with a voice like gravel and brown sugar.

"He moved back to the island five, six years ago—he and his wife and their little kids. He asked me to come out for a few months—well, maybe more like six months—to do it. He's on leave from his job, and he connected with these two musicians who are also living on the island now, the fiddler from the Sail Aways—I actually know her from way back, Ruby Watts—and this banjo player who toured with Scotty Gerard."

I nodded, even though I still didn't know all the names in the folk-pop scene. "Okay," I said slowly. "You're talking about *the* island? In Washington state?"

When Gregor smoked weed, he'd start talking about this *amazing* island in Puget Sound where he'd spent boyhood summers at his family's cottage. I hadn't been there. We'd been together for only nineteen months—six months of dating, thirteen of marriage. Sometimes I woke up next to him and wasn't sure who he was at first. We were that new.

"Yeah," he said. "That island. And, well, it's sudden, but doesn't it also feel kind of perfect? I mean, you know I've been worried about Sam, how all he wants to do is screen time and how he has basically no nature in his life, and it would be so great for him on the island. It's all forests and fields and beaches. And if the doctor thinks you should be taking time off work, and with me between projects . . . it kind of feels like the universe is telling us something, don't you think?"

I heard the ache in Gregor's voice, the want. I was stabbingly aware that more than anything else in the world, what I wanted was for *him* to get what *he* wanted.

So even though I grew up in a farming town in Iowa and islands and forests kind of freaked me out, I heard myself saying, "Okay. Yeah. Let's see if we can figure it out. And if I can get leave at work."

"Wait—really?"

"Really." I loved the boyish smile that lighted his face. "I'm sure my boss will be understanding."

Gregor drew me closer and kissed me, and the emptiness inside me was filled back up again.

3

We figured out how to make a six-month stay on the island work. We could live at Gregor's family cottage, and there was a preschool with an opening for Sam. But my boss, the director of my research program at Memorial Sloan Kettering Cancer Center, was *not* understanding.

Yes, it was short notice. But Gregor happened to have this window of time between other projects, and so did the other musicians on the island.

My boss played hardball, pointing out that our single-cell DNA sequencing project was both high profile and behind schedule, and he couldn't spare me right then. I told him I couldn't wait. He said he was surprised that I was willing to jeopardize an almost guaranteed promotion. Instead of getting my hoped-for family leave, I ended up resigning on the spot. I was really sorry, I explained, and I hoped he'd consider hiring me back at a later date.

Even though it wouldn't be a financial problem, I worried, as I walked to the elevator with a cardboard box of personal items in my arms, that I'd just sacrificed myself. And for what, exactly?

I'm the daughter of a man who ran an Ace Hardware. Our town's tallest structure was the water tower, and the people there never seemed to talk about anything except soybeans, corn, and high school football. All I ever wanted was to get out. To go to a good college, to get a PhD, to move to a big city and have an important job. *This* was never part of the plan.

I stepped into the elevator and pressed the button for the lobby. The doors slid shut.

My three closest New York friends treated me to a goodbye-for-now brunch at the place in the West Village that served my favorite French toast.

Sitting on the patio in the late-morning light, listening to the chatter of my kind, intelligent, and accomplished friends, it seemed insane to leave, even if it was only for six months. My life in New York was perfect.

Well, it would be if I could only get pregnant.

As if reading my mind, Owen—my friend since the day I started at the lab—lifted his Bellini.

We were all on our second Bellini at this point. I'd given myself permission not to follow Dr. Zakarian's advice for a day.

Owen's eyes twinkled as he said, "To our beloved Harlow. I'll desperately miss her snark, and her notes on the whiteboard about expired food items in the break-room fridge, and her incredible wingwoman skills—oh, and her brilliant analytical mind, of course. Cheers."

"You're making it sound like I'm *dead*," I said, laughing as we clinked our glasses.

"To Harlow," Phoebe said, dangly earrings swishing around her pretty face. Phoebe and I had been roommates in Boston, back in our MIT days. Now she was a Wall Street trader and killing it. "I'm going to miss you *so incredibly much*. And also, if Adi hasn't popped the question by the time you're back, will you *please* have Gregor give him adulting lessons?" She lifted her glass. "Cheers, sweetie."

We touched our glasses again.

"Harlow," Cherie said, thrusting out her bottom lip dramatically—because hey, she *did* work on Broadway, as a costume seamstress. We'd met a few years earlier when we'd both been volunteers at a 5K charity run. "I don't know how I'm going to survive the torture of six a.m. Saturday spin class without you. Also, are you going to eat that?" She made a lascivious face at the bacon on my plate. "Oh, and cheers!"

"You guys, I'll be back in a few months," I said. "And I plan to go back to the lab, too. I'm not throwing away my entire education just to sit around filing my nails." I hadn't told them about trying to get pregnant. It felt too private.

"Oh my God, you will *not* be back to the lab," Cherie said, taking a bite of my bacon. "You're going to come to your senses and realize that being pampered by your rich husband is *way* nicer than, like, squinting at mitochondria."

"No, she'll get bored of being pampered," Owen said. "I give her one month on that island, and then she's going to be looking for ways to stir up shit."

"*Thank* you," I said, bumping my shoulder against Owen's. "Someone who truly understands me."

"If *I* had this chance," Phoebe said, "I'd jump at it. Also, I'd be a complete liar if I said I wasn't a teensy bit jealous. You're living the fairy tale, Harlow."

"There's no such thing," I said with a smile. But secretly, I believed there was.

Gregor, Sam, and I weathered a days-long flurry of packing up our lives into three big suitcases. Our housekeeper was going to keep coming once a week to deal with our mail and houseplants, which was a luxury I didn't take for granted.

Then, on September 29, Gregor, Sam, and I arrived on the island.

4

We were picked up at the ferry dock by my mother-in-law's boyfriend. Douglas parked a huge, boxy black Mercedes-AMG G-Class in a buses-only zone and climbed out. He was lanky, silver-haired, and sun damaged, in a pink polo and jeans.

When Gregor was fifteen, his dad had drowned in a sailboating accident. He'd told me his mother had no intention of marrying Douglas—who she'd been dating for three years—and diluting the family fortune. It was unclear whether Douglas knew this or not. Not that he was a gold digger or anything—he was a retired Microsoft executive.

"Welcome," Douglas said with a veneered grin. He gave Sam and me hugs and clapped Gregor's shoulder. "Pauline couldn't come." He lifted one of our suitcases into the SUV's cargo area. "She's dealing with the steaks. You don't mess with that."

We climbed into the car—Sam and me in the back seat and Gregor up front—and rode up a steep, curved road and into the heart of the island.

"I understand it's your first time on the island, Harlow?" Douglas asked over his shoulder.

"Yes," I said.

"It used to be truly rural, you know, with berry farms, chicken farms, that kind of thing. In the seventies, the back-to-the-land hippies discovered it, but now it's a funny mix of the old island families, homesteading types, artists, and commuters with Seattle jobs."

"And retirees," Gregor said. "And people with weekend or summer homes, like Mother."

"Correct," Douglas said.

We followed a two-lane highway for maybe six miles, then took a disorienting series of turns. The roads were bounded by bleached fields or dense trees. I glimpsed the occasional glitter of water. The car windows were down, and the air smelled of green things and salty air.

And it *was* idyllic. I'm not saying it wasn't.

But even from a distance, from the ferry deck, I'd felt uneasy about all the fir trees. Now, from the car, I could see how they encroached, almost like they were straining to meet over the road and smother it.

I'm a prairie girl, okay? I need to see the horizon.

Sam—small, tender, and incredibly cute—sat on his booster beside me. His skinny brown legs dangled, clean sneakers touching at the toes, iPad on his lap. His brow was furrowed in concentration as he poked his fingertip against the screen. He was playing a game that involved feeding cats bowls of kibble, fish, and steaks. I didn't think he'd taken a break from the game since the car left our house in New York early that morning.

"Hey," Gregor said, swiveling to face Sam. "Buddy. That's enough screen time. Put it away."

Sam didn't answer.

"Hey," Gregor said, more loudly this time. "Earth to Sam. Turn it off. Now."

"Why?" Sam asked. He didn't sound whiny. Even though he was five, Sam always sounded remarkably composed and reasonable.

"Why?" Gregor repeated. I felt his energy shift from *we're having a family adventure* to frustration. "Because I—" He stopped himself. Took a breath. "Because, number one, this island is beautiful—"

"Gorgeous!" Douglas said.

"I don't like it," Sam said, punching his finger on the iPad. "It's weird."

"Fine," Gregor said. "You can think the island is weird. But this is where your family comes from. It's important." He reached back and grabbed the iPad. Sam clung to it for a moment, but Gregor yanked it free and tossed it into the cargo area behind us.

I stared at Gregor. What had gotten into him? He was usually so laid-back. Was he nervous about seeing his mom?

Sam's big hazel eyes widened. "You'll break it, Daddy," he said.

"Good," Gregor said. "Look out the window."

◆ ◆ ◆

When we reached the gates of Himmel Cottage, Douglas tapped a code on a security touch screen. The iron gates swung slowly open. We drove down a long driveway, first through a sunny orchard and then between more of those tall, strangling trees.

How am I going to last six months stranded on an island, buried by all this vegetation, with nothing to focus on except my uterus? I thought with rising panic.

But then I thought, *No. Stop it. This is going to be good. Like a vacation. It'll bring Gregor and Sam and me closer together.*

The driveway opened out onto a circular sweep.

"Here it is," Douglas said as he parked behind an Audi station wagon. He unbuckled and climbed out.

"My great-grandfather Jakob Himmel built this house," Gregor said as he unbuckled, too. "That's your great-great-grandfather, Sam. He said he built the house he saw in his dreams. So. What do you think, Low?"

"About . . . ?"

"About the house. The island."

Um, I feel like all these trees want to murder me?

I forced a smile. "I love it." Lying to Gregor felt wrong. But when I saw relief soften his face, I thought, *Worth it.*

The three of us got out.

The house really did look like something out of a dream, three rambling, chunky stories of dark shingles and cream-painted gingerbread, massive stone chimneys, deep porches, fat pillars, heavy eaves, and ivy. The grounds were lush and well tended. I saw a smooth sheet of water beyond the house.

My mother-in-law, Pauline, appeared on the porch, waving and saying something to Douglas, Sam was running toward the water, and I thought, *No turning back now.*

Gregor took my hand. "It's going to be okay, babe," he said softly. "Breathe. We're in this together."

"Thanks," I said.

"For what?"

"For being so sweet to me."

"I'm not that sweet."

"Yes." I lifted his hand to my lips and kissed it. "You are."

"Wow, look at that," he said. "God's gift to the Pacific coast."

"What?" I said, scanning around. I thought he was referring to the house.

"No, down there." Gregor pointed to the ground. A hedge curved alongside the driveway, growing out of damp mulch.

"Honey," I said. "What are you talking about?"

"Hello!" Pauline called. She was coming closer.

"These." Gregor gestured with his sneaker to something in the mulch, under the shade of the hedge. "*Psilocybe cyanescens.* Wavy caps."

Then I saw them: a cluster of caramel-brown mushrooms with warped-looking caps and skinny white stems.

"It's magic mushroom season, baby," Gregor said with a grin.

"I'm not going to eat random wild mushrooms, and neither are you," I said.

"They aren't random. I know exactly what they are. Eat two caps and three hours later you'll be staring into the face of God."

I rolled my eyes, but I wasn't really concerned. Drugs had never been a problem for him, and he didn't ever do anything in front of his son.

As for me, I was a lightweight. I stuck to the occasional glass of wine or fruity cocktail, especially now that I was trying to conceive.

Gregor crouched and picked a couple of the mushrooms. They slid easily from the ground, dirt clumped on their stems. He put them in his hoodie pocket and stood up.

Curling his arm around me, he gave me a squeeze. "That'll take the edge off dealing with my mother," he whispered.

"Oh my *God*," I whispered back, half laughing, and then Pauline reached us, and I plastered on a Hallmark Channel smile.

5

Pauline lived in Seattle most of the time, but she was as well preserved as an Upper East Side socialite. She was tall—inches taller than me—and bone thin, with an ash-blond bob and an expertly done facelift. Her eyes were a penetrating blue.

She wore navy slacks, pristine white leather sneakers, a navy-and-white striped top, and chunky gold jewelry—a very nautical, I-own-a-sailboat look. She smelled like Chanel No. 5.

She embraced her son, and then she turned to me. "Harlow," she said in her throaty NPR voice as she held out her arms. The hug was stiff, but that was both of our faults. We'd met only twice before, at our Manhattan engagement party and then our wedding at a historic farm in upstate New York. "So lovely to finally see you again." She stepped out of the hug. "Taking time off from that grueling job of yours is going to do you a *world* of good." Her gaze slipped down to my pelvis and back up again.

Oh God, I thought. *How much has Gregor told her?*

"Thanks so much for letting us stay here," I said. "It's all so lovely."

"Oh, it's the *family* home. It's yours now, too. Come on. Let me give you the grand tour."

The house was objectively amazing. More amazing than I'd been led to believe after hearing Gregor refer to it as a *summer cottage.*

First of all, Himmel Cottage was four or five times bigger than the split-level ranch I grew up in. And even though it was a hundred years old, it was obvious that Gregor's family had sunk a fortune into maintaining it. Dozens of clean windows glittered in the sun. The hedges growing along the porches were perfectly clipped. A recently mowed lawn sloped gently to a seawall, piles of silvery driftwood logs, and a strip of pebbly beach.

The view of the island's inner harbor was surreal, with tree-mounded hills and white boats dotting the blue, blue water.

To be honest, it was a little claustrophobic. The view, I mean. You couldn't see the horizon because the hills were in the way. It felt like I was missing something, just over the hills. Something wild that could sneak up on me.

The house's cool interior was all wide plank floors and casual (yet obviously expensive) coastal-chic furnishings. White linen slipcovers. Seagrass rugs. The scent of sweet lemon on the air. The kitchen was to die for with its massive cream-and-brass Lacanche range, the expanse of marble island flanked by rattan stools, the breakfast nook, the hanging copper pots, the French doors opening onto what Pauline called *the veranda*.

The one thing that wasn't perfect was the wallpaper. It was old fashioned. No, actually—it was just *old*. Yellowing. Bubbling and curling, with faded florals and stripes and medallion patterns. *Odd choice.*

Pauline caught me eyeing it. "My grandfather chose all the wallpaper when he built this house. It was imported from France. I couldn't bear to have it removed. I think of him every time I see it."

She must really love her grandfather, I thought.

In the kitchen, Pauline introduced us to the live-out housekeeper, a sweet-faced fiftysomething woman named Emilia. She, Pauline told me crisply, would keep the house spotless and do all the cooking we wanted Monday through Friday.

In New York, a housekeeper cleaned our place once a week. This was next level.

Pauline led Gregor and me through the rest of the house. There was a den with a huge sectional couch and an enormous TV. There was a wood-paneled library with green leather chairs and a rifle hanging over the fireplace. ("Purely decorative," Pauline said when she saw me notice the gun.) There were several bedrooms at the top of the sweeping stairs, including the largest bedroom facing the harbor, to which Gregor's and my luggage already had been spirited.

"What's up there?" I asked Pauline, peering up another flight of stairs. "The attic?"

"My suite," she said. "I love it up there because you can see Mount Rainier. Come on—let's go outside. I'll show you the swimming pool and the new exercise studio in the pool house—Gregor, Douglas put in a Peloton."

We toured the grounds and then somehow, I was alone with Pauline on the porch. She poured me a glass of water from a pitcher clinking with ice.

"Oh. Thank you," I said, accepting the water. I was thinking, *Where the heck did Gregor go?* Being alone with Pauline made me jumpy.

"Forgive me for being blunt, Harlow," she said, "but surely the honeymoon is over. Isn't it high time you had some babies?"

I felt a flicker of anger. Or maybe it was defensiveness.

"I do wish Gregor hadn't left it so long," she added. "And I was surprised when he . . . Well, you're thirty-five, aren't you?"

"Thirty-four," I said weakly.

"You don't have a lot of time left. I'd like to have grandchildren before I'm too old to enjoy them." Her lipsticked mouth peeled away from bleached teeth.

"You do have Sam," I said. I sounded breathless. I couldn't believe she was actually *saying* this stuff.

"Yes, well, you know, Sam isn't really . . ." Pauline looked down to the lawn, where Gregor and Douglas had come into view. Douglas was pointing to something in the harbor, and Gregor was nodding. Then Sam streaked past.

I frowned. "Sam isn't what?"

"He doesn't really *know* me that well."

"Oh. Right." I felt my face flushing, and I prayed Pauline couldn't guess what I'd *thought* she was going to say, which was, *Sam isn't really the right kind of grandchild.* Because of his brown skin. Because of his dark curls. Because his dead mother had been Black.

Gregor didn't talk much about Josephine. They'd been married for only a few months when she'd died in a skiing accident. It had been her first time skiing, Gregor had told me. She'd crashed into a tree and broken her back.

It's my fault, he'd whispered to me, his voice thick with grief and guilt. *If I hadn't insisted that she learn how to ski, she wouldn't have died.*

You can't blame yourself like that, I'd whispered back. *You aren't responsible for random acts of fate.*

Sam was two when Josephine died. He'd been born a year before Gregor and Josephine got married.

"Cubby—Gregor's father—was the love of my life," Pauline said, "and I just want the same thing we had for you two. The experience of bringing a child into the world, a perfect little baby who's the embodiment of your love—there is no more precious gift."

"We want that, too," I said.

"*Do* you?"

"Yeah." I tried to make my tone say *back off.*

Pauline sighed. "Sam doesn't even have the Himmel nose."

"Excuse me?"

She pointed to her nose with a manicured nail. "Haven't you noticed it?"

"Um . . . no?"

How rude would it be, on a scale of one to ten, if I left for the bathroom right this second? I wondered.

"Gregor has it," Pauline said. "The high bridge? The distinctively curved nostrils? We all have it. All of us pure-blooded Himmels.

Gregor, me, my father, and of course, my grandfather. I'd love to have a grandchild with the Himmel nose."

"What exactly are you doing here?" I said before I could stop myself. "Putting in an order for your grandchild's face? This isn't, like, Amazon dot-com."

"Goodness." Pauline's eyes hardened. "The little mouse *bites*."

I felt my face going hot. "And also, my theoretical baby isn't going to be a pure-blooded Himmel, because half of their genes would be mine, and half of their genes would be Gregor's—who's a Sullivan, not a Himmel, right? With half of *his* genes from his dad? And you know there's no such thing as *pure blood*, right? From a genetics standpoint, it makes zero sense."

"That's right, you have that *wonderful* MIT degree. And you're of good German and Norwegian stock, too, aren't you?"

"Stock?" I repeated. I thought, *As in livestock?*

"It's too bad your hips are so narrow," Pauline said, "but that's why we have cesarean sections, isn't it? I suppose you'll have to do."

"Excuse me," I said tightly. "Would you remind me where the powder room is?"

6

In the downstairs powder room, I washed my hands, did some breathing exercises to calm down, and then texted my sister, Audrey.

She was two years older than me—thirty-seven—my only sibling, and she already had two tweens and one teenager. She'd married her college sweetheart, and they'd moved to Audrey's and my hometown after Luke finished his medical residency in Des Moines.

Me: Made it to the island. This house is insane. It's not a cottage, it's basically a mansion. Only also kind of like a cuckoo clock on steroids? Is it wrong to think it's kind of creepy?

To my surprise, Audrey texted back right away.

Audrey: If it's creepy, it's creepy. Is the monster-in-law there?

Me: Oh yes. And she's already put in her order for one grandchild/clone.

Audrey: Are you joking?

Me: I wish. Apparently she's surprised Gregor married such an old lady. Oh and she thinks my hips aren't fit for childbearing.

Audrey: WTF? I hope you told her to jump off a bridge?

Me: Well she technically has a point about my age.

I also typed And she's not the only one who can't figure out why Gregor married me, but I deleted it.

Audrey: Nope she does NOT have a point and don't let that witch bully you.

◆ ◆ ◆

"Honey?" I said to Gregor later, when we were alone in our guest room to, as Pauline had put it, *freshen up for dinner*. Sam was in his own room across the hall, unpacking his toys. "Can I ask you something?" I sat down on one of the armchairs by the cold fireplace.

Gregor flopped onto the bed, sending decorative cushions bouncing to the floor. "Ask away, babe." He put his hands behind his head.

"You didn't . . . does your mom know about . . ."

I watched him. The thick hair swept back from his forehead, his eyebrows furrowed to his high-bridged nose. It *did* look like Pauline's nose—*the Himmel nose*.

I wished I could unsee that.

"Does your mom know we're having trouble conceiving?" I said.

"What? Of course not. Low. Jesus. That's private."

Something unknotted inside me. "I didn't think you would. But she said some stuff to me. About popping out babies. And some pretty outdated ideas about genetics."

"Aren't all older women like that?"

"Like what?"

"You know, obsessed with grandchildren?"

I thought of my own mother, who'd died a few years earlier of cancer. I remembered how when I was thirteen she told me, blowing a sidelong stream of Parliament Lights smoke, *Never have kids, Harlow. They'll screw up your whole entire life.* That was after Dad had left, though, so maybe it had been the vodka talking.

"Yeah," I said to Gregor. "I guess they probably are."

He'd gotten up off the bed and gone to a window. "Pests," he muttered.

I went to his side. Two deer, a doe and her fawn, were walking gingerly across the lawn below.

"I think they're cute," I said.

"No." Gregor shook his head. "They're parasites. Breeding and breeding, out of control, no predators—"

"You're so mean. The little one looks exactly like Bambi."

Gregor snorted. "You need to toughen up." He slid his hot hands up the back of my T-shirt and jerked me tight to him. I arched instinctively into his hard center. He pushed me to the bed, and for a while I forgot about the deer, and my bitchy mother-in-law, and my own disaster-zone mom, and about all those horrible trees.

Pauline and Douglas made dinner for us, red wine–marinated steaks with charred broccolini, which we ate in the dining room with its French doors overlooking the harbor.

Douglas was halfway drunk in that loud golf-bro way, and he, Gregor, and Pauline carried the conversation.

Pauline was pointedly ignoring me. My punishment for losing my temper with her earlier, I assumed.

Sam and I were mostly silent. Sam had refused the steak, so the housekeeper, Emilia, magically produced a steaming bowl of macaroni and cheese.

Outside, the sun sank behind the hills. Emilia came out of the kitchen to pull curtains across the French doors, blocking out the encroaching night.

Pauline said something in brisk Spanish. It sounded like she was scolding Emilia.

Emilia dragged open the curtains again and retreated.

"Silly woman," Pauline said. "She hates the full moon."

I glanced outside. The first thing I noticed was the moon, pearly and round, surfacing over sawtooth trees.

Pauline went on, "She's, you know . . ."

"Peasant mentality," Douglas said loudly. He was bleary eyed with booze. "She's from a little pueblo in Mexico." He pronounced it *meh*-hee-co with an affected accent.

"It's important to be culturally sensitive," Pauline said. "Her worldview is so different from ours. She's very . . ."

"Catholic," Douglas said, dumping the last of a bottle of malbec into his glass. "In that wonderfully *colorful* Aztec-virgin-sacrifices-meet-the-Virgin-Mary kind of way."

"I'm pretty sure I read somewhere that the Aztecs didn't actually sacrifice virgins," I said.

"Why does she hate the full moon?" Sam asked. "Is she scared of werewolves?"

"What do you know about werewolves, buddy?" Gregor said.

"Nothing like that," Pauline said. "I think she told me once that the light of the full moon can curdle milk, or something to that effect. Presumably a superstition she imported from her homeland."

"Everyone has their superstitions," Gregor said, sawing at his meat. "For example, Mother, *you* quote-unquote *don't believe in* vaccines." He spoke with a hostility that surprised me. But then I remembered him mentioning once that he hadn't had his childhood vaccinations.

"That's not a superstition," Pauline said. "I happen to adhere to the scientific principle of the survival of the fittest."

"Not a scientific principle, my love," Douglas said. "It's pseudoscience at best, an adulteration of Darwin's theory—isn't that right, Harlow? Pauline, Harlow's a scientist. Let's hear what she thinks about—"

"And anyway," Pauline said, still addressing Gregor, "aren't you sending Sam to that forest preschool? They're all anti-vaxxers there, you know."

"I don't need to agree with all of their beliefs to send Sam there," Gregor said.

"Oh, really? Just the beliefs that are convenient for you?"

"Yeah, basically. Sam's had all his shots. If the other parents want their kids to catch totally preventable diseases, what do I care?"

Gregor and Pauline locked eyes. Something I didn't understand passed between them.

Pauline was the first to look away. "Anyway," she said, "it's not as though I'm being *condescending* about Emilia's superstitions or the fact that she's an immigrant. I mean, our family were immigrants once, too."

"Here we go," Douglas muttered into his wineglass.

Pauline turned to me, her eyes bright. "Has Gregor told you about his great-grandfather, Jakob Himmel?"

"Of course," I said. "The founder of Pacific Crest Lumber? He was from Germany, right?"

"Württemberg, to be exact," Pauline said. "He set out for America when he was only twenty—he was from a very poor farming family. When he landed in New York in 1880, he had nothing but the clothes on his back and a wood-cutting axe. He made his way west, working for logging companies, and he eventually ended up right here on this island. He was just a lowly logger boy with no education to speak of, and yet he managed to—"

"Sorry about this," Gregor whispered to me across the table. "Mother thinks her grandfather was the second coming of—"

"You can mock me all you like, Gregor," Pauline interrupted, "but the fact of the matter is, if it weren't for Grandpa Jakob's incredible foresight and resourcefulness, we would have *nothing*." She turned to me again. There was a crimson fleck on one of her front teeth. Lipstick, I thought. Or blood from the steak. "He saved up enough money from his wages to buy out the local shingle mill when the owner went bust. He turned the mill around, made it a huge success, and kept on growing his fortune from there. He really was a remarkable man. An example of true American spirit."

"Speaking of American spirit," Douglas said to Gregor, "are you following the Mariners at all this season? That Dominican fellow is *tremendous*."

After we finished our lemon rosemary sorbetto (which Sam also refused, to be swiftly replaced by Emilia with vanilla pudding), I claimed to have a headache and went upstairs before everyone else.

7

I showered in the guest room's spacious marble en suite, brushed and flossed, and did my skin-care routine.

Then, as I'd done every day for the past year, I checked the fertility tracking app on my phone. Not that I needed to. I was hyperaware of my cycles by this point. Sometimes I thought the best thing about pregnancy would be getting to take a break from thinking nonstop about my menstrual cycle.

The fertility app said I was due to ovulate the day after tomorrow, on October 1. Just to be sure, though, I did a urine-based ovulation test. I'd brought a hundred-pack of test strips in my toiletry kit.

As expected, the test was negative. One line only. No LH surge yet. I dropped the used test strip in the wastebasket.

I padded around in my fleece robe, unpacking my suitcases and Gregor's, hanging things up in the walk-in closet and folding other things away into drawers. After that, Gregor still hadn't come, so I changed into my pink-striped pajama set and got into bed.

I picked up my phone and looked at my screen saver with a smile. It was a loved-up-looking selfie of Gregor and me on our honeymoon in the Seychelles. Gregor has his sunglasses on, and he's smooching my cheek while I gaze directly at the camera. I adored that picture.

I scrolled through Instagram for about an hour. I studied pictures of other women's kids splashing their little boots in puddles and piling apples into a bucket. That gave me a gnawing emptiness under my ribs, so then I skimmed articles about using meditation to boost fertility. After that, I watched a YouTube video called "Fertility Success! How We FINALLY Got Pregnant Naturally!!"

Gregor still didn't come.

For the next hour, I floundered around in Reddit's "Getting Pregnant Over 35" quagmire.

Still no Gregor.

Normally, I would've simply gone downstairs to see what was taking him so long. But the idea of encountering Pauline made my stomach hurt.

Dr. Zakarian had said not to take Ambien, but I knew for a fact there was no evidence that it was problematic if you were trying to conceive. I'd done deep dives into the medical literature.

To be safe, though, I googled it again.

Ambien was fine. Totally fine. And anyway, this was the span of time after my period but before ovulation when I could be 100 percent certain I wasn't pregnant.

I went to the bathroom, dug the bottle of Ambien out of my toiletries case, and swallowed one with a glass of tap water. Then I climbed back into bed and waited.

Thirty-five minutes later, my brain hit the brakes. My body was growing deliciously heavy as I removed my glasses, switched off the bedside lamp, and lay down.

Once my eyes adjusted to lights out, I noticed that the room was icy with moonlight. I turned onto my side and watched the round moon out there in the black sky, and it seemed to throb slightly.

It's like a ripe egg, I thought drowsily, *drifting along a fallopian tube of sky.*

I smiled about this as my eyelids grew heavier and heavier, and I was gone.

◆ ◆ ◆

My eyes popped open.

Something had woken me, some sound.

The moon wasn't in the window anymore, but the room was still pale with its light.

I sat up, fumbled for my glasses, and pushed them on. I was alone in the bed. The pillow and duvet beside me were rumpled, but Gregor wasn't there. I checked my phone, plugged into its charger on the nightstand. 1:21.

Where was Gregor?

I sat still for a few minutes, unsure of what to do. I wanted to go and find my husband, though I hated the idea of running into Pauline. But there was no way she'd be awake. I forced myself out of bed, taking my phone with me.

First, I peeked into Sam's bedroom. It was the most likely place for Gregor to be because sometimes Sam had nightmares.

I made out Sam's small form under a quilt. I heard his steady breathing.

No Gregor.

I silently shut the door.

I went down the staircase into the entry hall, illuminating the way with my phone's flashlight. I passed through the living room, the dining room, the library, and the den.

All the rooms were dark. No one was up. The house seemed alien in the night, infinitely large, and the wooden floors and beamed ceilings, the banisters and the paneled walls, all seemed to exhale the astringent odor of tree sap.

In the kitchen, I looked out the French doors. The lawn was frosted with light. A moonbeam streaked the surface of the harbor. Lights from other houses twinkled along the far shoreline.

I couldn't imagine where Gregor had gone. There was no way he'd be up on the third floor with his mother and Douglas, would he? Especially not in the dead of night. Did this house have a cellar? But why the heck would Gregor be in the cellar?

The most likely scenario, I decided, was that Gregor was outside. It was easy to picture him sitting in the dark beside the pool, smoking weed and playing his guitar. This suddenly seemed so likely that I could almost hear the thrum of his guitar and the papery crackle of the burning joint.

I tried the door handle. Unlocked. I pulled the door open and stepped outside.

8

Cold, damp air swished around me and fogged my glasses. I rubbed the lenses clear with my cuff. Hugging myself for warmth, wishing I was wearing more than thin pajamas, I walked slowly down the long porch. I passed the silhouettes of rattan chairs and chaises. They were all empty.

I went down the steps onto the lawn. Dew from the grass soaked the hems of my pajama bottoms as I walked toward the swimming pool. My bare feet grew numb.

I knew from Pauline's tour that the pool was set off to the side and concealed from the house by a hedge. And when I circled around that hedge, I fully expected to see Gregor with his guitar and a joint, just like I'd pictured, even though—*Jesus*—it really was way too cold to be hanging around outside.

I stopped. The surface of the pool reflected the weak light of the sky. All the chaises around the pool were empty.

Confusion hit me then, so strong it was physical. I staggered over to the nearest chaise and sank down on its edge. I was full-on shivering now.

Then I heard it: the whisper-soft shuffle of someone walking on wet grass on the other side of the hedge.

I lifted my head, straining to listen.

Whoever it was, they were coming closer.

I pictured myself standing up and going to look around the hedge, but I was paralyzed. I imagined myself calling out *Gregor?* but the syllables died in my mouth. I just sat there, shivering, unsure if I was cold or terrified. I watched the end of the hedge, waiting for whoever it was to appear, and when the shuffling of the grass was *right there*, I stopped breathing—

and waited—

and a figure appeared. A man.

Gregor.

The first thing that registered was all the bare skin, pearl gray in the moonlight. He was stark naked.

His penis—impossible to miss—was semi-erect, like he was a little aroused, or had been very recently. And I thought with a sickening shot of jealousy, *Who?*

He walked to the edge of the swimming pool and looked down into the rippled water. Was he watching his own reflection? Or the reflection of the sky? Whatever it was, he was transfixed.

The breeze lifted his hair. And his hands, dangling beside his muscled, bare thighs . . . what was that dark stuff on them? No, it wasn't only his hands that were smeared with it, but also his belly and his buttocks and his chest. It wasn't shadow—

Oh God. It was *blood. My husband was covered in blood.*

But wait—*no*. It was mud, near-black, viscous.

What the heck have you been doing? I thought, but failed to say aloud. *Rolling around on the ground?*

"Gregor," I whispered.

He swung his head to face me. His eyes were hidden in eye socket shadow, but I saw the crease of his brow, the slackening of his jaw, as though he was surprised. Or frightened, even.

"Gregor," I said again, more loudly this time. "What are you doing?" Then everything snapped into place. "Honey—did you take those mushrooms?"

He stared at me like he couldn't understand. Then he ran. I saw the shadowed divots of his working glutes and quads. I saw his penis bobbing. He disappeared behind the hedge.

I bolted to my feet, which was a mistake because I was woozy from the Ambien. I grabbed the chaise headrest for balance. My head felt like it was stuffed with batting. I pictured it leaking out of my ear like I was a ruined stuffed toy.

After a few moments, I felt steady enough to go to the end of the hedge. I looked out across the sweep of moonlit lawn.

Gregor had vanished.

I stood there shakily for a while, trying to figure out what to do. Should I try to find him? He was clearly as high as a kite. I considered waking up Pauline and Douglas but then dismissed the idea. They didn't need to get involved in Gregor's magic mushroom trip. It would only embarrass him.

I decided to go find him.

I crisscrossed the lawn. I went down to the beach. I went to the driveway, but it was so dark on that side of the house, under the trees, that I told myself there was no way Gregor would venture there.

I was crossing the lawn for the third or maybe fourth time when I noticed that one set of doors on the porch, the ones leading to the kitchen, were standing open.

Did *I* leave them open? I couldn't remember.

Or had Gregor gone inside?

I went up the steps, along the porch, and inside. I shut the doors but left them unlocked in case Gregor was still out there somewhere. I went upstairs.

As soon as I opened the door of our dark room, I heard the rush of a faucet. A slice of yellow light glowed under the en suite bathroom door.

I sighed. He was back.

I plugged my phone into the charger on the nightstand. I pulled off my pajama bottoms with their dew-drenched hems. I climbed under the duvet and took off my glasses. I was shivering spasmodically.

The light blinked out under the bathroom door. The door swung open and a figure crossed the dim room. The mattress bounced as Gregor got into bed.

He snuggled up close to me and draped an arm over my waist. He felt so warm.

"You okay, babe?" he mumbled. "Jesus, you're ice cold."

"How are *you* so warm?" I mumbled back. "Did you take a shower?" Stupid question. Of course he'd taken a shower, because the last time I saw him he'd been filthy. "Are you okay?"

"I am now. Now that you're here."

I was finally getting warm again, and I'd found my husband, and that was enough for the Ambien to pull me back down into its pit.

9

When I woke up it was a sunny morning. Gregor was coming out of the bathroom again, this time with wet hair and a towel around his waist.

I struggled upright. I felt hungover. I knew there was something wrong, something *off*, but I couldn't remember what.

We're here in this house, I thought, *this creepy-ass house. Himmel Cottage. We're here on the island with too many trees. Then there's my mother-in-law—her pale eyes drilling into me, that Cruella lipstick—but—that's right, thank God, she's leaving today.*

So what's wrong?

Then I remembered. Gregor, buck naked and aroused and smeared with mud in the moonlight.

"What were you doing last night?" I asked him. My voice sounded scratchy.

He had his back to me, rifling through a chest of drawers. "Babe, where did you put my boxer briefs?"

"Top drawer. Wait—you took *another* shower?"

"Huh?"

"Never mind. Honey. Last night—did you do those mushrooms?"

He opened the top drawer, took out a pair of blue boxer briefs, and then turned to look at me. "What?"

"I saw you. Out by the pool. In your birthday suit, covered with—well, I think it was mud?"

He was looking at me like I was insane. "Mud," he repeated flatly.

"Did you . . . are you hurt?" I scanned his body, what I could see of it. No visible injuries.

"I'm fine."

"You were super high last night. You don't remember?"

"You saw me," he said flatly. "Outside." He glanced past me, to the windows.

"Uh, yeah?" I was getting annoyed. "I just wish you would've given me some kind of heads-up. That you were going to do the mushrooms? I was really worried, first when I couldn't find you, and then, after I saw you. It was like . . . it didn't seem like you even recognized me, you were so messed up. And then you took off running. I was afraid you were going to hurt yourself."

As I told Gregor all this, his expression shifted from confusion, to realization, to . . . what was it? Fear?

But why would he be *afraid*?

"I was up late drinking with Douglas," he said, letting the towel drop to the floor and pulling on the briefs.

I averted my eyes, but I couldn't help remembering what he'd looked like last night by the pool.

"He brought out this amazing small-batch bourbon," Gregor continued, "and I guess it went down a little too easy because after he went to bed it seemed like a good idea to eat those two caps I picked."

"It was like you were in another dimension," I said. "I don't think you could even understand me when I was talking to you."

"Well, you know, that's psychotropics for you." Gregor crawled across the bed, bare chested, shoulder muscles working. He moved his face very close to mine, and I could smell Scope, and shampoo, and his own delicious skin. "Are you mad at me?" he murmured.

"No." I traced the stubbly line of his jaw with my finger. "I'm not mad."

"Good." He nuzzled his face into the crook of my neck, inhaling noisily. "Oh my God, you smell amazing, babe. Are you ovulating?"

Before I knew Gregor, that would've made me wince. But he was deeply in touch with what he called his *primal nature*, and I was getting used to it. "I don't think so," I said. "But really soon. Maybe tomorrow?"

With his face still against my neck, he said, "I saw your bottle of Ambien out on the counter."

I frowned, pulling back a little. "What?"

He sat back on his heels. "Did you take Ambien last night?"

"I couldn't sleep lying in bed in this strange place wondering when my husband was going to decide to show up—"

"I was talking to my *mother*, Low. Who I haven't seen in a year because of *your* work schedule."

"I thought you said you were drinking with Douglas."

"Yeah, but before that I was talking to my mother. What is this? A courtroom? I have to have my story perfectly straight or you—"

"Sorry. No, it's fine. I get it."

"Awesome. And it's just . . . Ambien can make people kind of high, right? So maybe that influenced your perception of me last night?"

"I guess so, yeah."

"And anyway, since we're trying to conceive you probably shouldn't be taking it at all. Just to be safe."

"It's okay. I've read the studies."

"But we should be extra careful, right?"

"Right," I said, thinking wearily of all the sleepless nights ahead.

"Glad we're on the same page," he murmured, crawling closer again. He unbuttoned my pajama top with a serious expression on his face. He leaned down to slowly lick my collarbones and then my nipples, and that was the end of the conversation.

Gregor went downstairs first, while I was still getting dressed after my shower. Then I tidied our room, fully aware that I was procrastinating because I didn't want to see Pauline. Which made me feel like an ingrate because she was letting us stay in her gorgeous house for six months, with full use of her luxury car and her housekeeper. But instead of making small talk with her over coffee, there I was dumping dirty clothes into the bathroom hamper.

I plucked Gregor's hoodie from a chairback. It was the green one he'd been wearing yesterday. I dropped it into the hamper.

I hesitated.

I picked it up again and slid my hand into one of the pockets. Empty. I slid my hand into the other pocket and felt something cold and rubbery. I pulled out two brown-capped mushrooms with dirty white stems.

My heart started to pound. Obviously Gregor hadn't eaten these *exact* mushrooms, but there had been more where he'd picked them. There could be thousands out there on the grounds.

Except . . . hadn't he said something about eating, specifically, the two mushrooms he'd picked in front of me?

I wasn't sure. I wasn't sure what he'd said, and I wasn't sure what I'd seen the night before. I'd been on Ambien. Gregor was right—*I'd* been high, too.

I threw the mushrooms in the wastebasket, dropped the hoodie back into the hamper, and washed my hands. I dabbed on a little blush and mascara, pulled on a sweater, and went downstairs.

There was breakfast in the kitchen and a walk along the shore, with Sam climbing through driftwood and running on seaweed-caked sand. And then, after lunch, Pauline and Douglas got into their Audi station wagon, and we all waved goodbye with promises to see each other again on Thanksgiving.

I breathed a secret sigh of relief.

10

I called my sister later that day, while Gregor and Sam were kicking a soccer ball around on the lawn.

"He was *naked*?" she said when I'd finished describing the events of last night. "Seriously?"

"Yeah," I said. "I mean—I think? If I wasn't hallucinating from the Ambien."

"Has it made you hallucinate before?"

"No. But there's a first time for everything."

I'd left out the part about Gregor having been semi-aroused. I shared most things with Audrey, but even that was too intimate. It also felt, somehow, humiliating to *me*.

"It sounds like a safety issue," she said. "If he's running around in the dark, out of his mind and naked, he could hurt himself. Are you going to talk to him about it?"

"We already talked about it. I'm not going to bring it up again. He doesn't need me nagging him all the time."

"Harlow. You're his *wife*. You have a right to discuss his recreational drug use with him."

"Half of marriages end in divorce. Maybe if more people gave each other the benefit of the doubt, they'd—"

"That's what you think you're doing? Giving Gregor the benefit of the doubt?"

"That's exactly what I'm doing."

"How is it that you're a complete smart mouth with everyone but him?"

"Because I want to stay married?"

"But you're not being *yourself*."

"Maybe I'm being someone better."

Audrey sighed. "This is about Mom and Dad, isn't it?"

"What? *No.*"

"Look. There's a difference between having open communication with your husband and nagging and bitching at him until he packs his suitcase and leaves."

"Is there?" I said. "I'll bet it all sounds the same to the husbands."

Our mom was all about drama, and emotions, and making sure our dad knew precisely how unhappy she felt at any given moment and why it was all his fault.

Before she drove him away, that is.

My theory was that he couldn't take it anymore. That he wanted to have a beer and watch the White Sox in peace.

One afternoon when I was twelve, Audrey and I came home from school to find our mother sobbing on the kitchen floor. Tears and Revlon mascara made sooty tracks down her cheeks. Her hair, usually flat-ironed to Jennifer Aniston perfection, was a frizzy disaster. She was wearing her favorite pink Old Navy sweats, but they were matted with cat hair from the floor. And she couldn't stop crying.

"Mom?" Audrey said. She and I stood, frightened, in the kitchen doorway. "Mom, are you okay?"

"Of course I'm not okay!" She imploded with more sobs. "It's your damned father!"

Audrey and I exchanged wide-eyed looks.

"What happened to Dad?" Audrey said.

"Nothing *happened* to him. He left."

"What do you mean?" Audrey's voice wavered like she was going to cry.

"He packed his suitcase and left. He's gone. He's not coming back. He's moving in with someone else."

"Who?" Audrey said. "Grandma Susan?"

Mom cackled, smearing viciously at her nose with the back of her hand. "Grow up, Audrey. He's moving in with another woman. Some slut from Palmer. She's got kids. Two daughters. Cheerleaders at the middle school, if you can believe it. So I guess I'm not the only one he needed to replace."

When Mom said that, something rooted itself in my belly. A poisonous little seedling began to grow.

Dad didn't want me.

Was it because I was a knobby-kneed dork who preferred softball and chemistry sets to Barbies? Was it because I wasn't pretty? If his new daughters were cheerleaders, they'd be really pretty, and no way would they be dorks.

Now, at the age of almost-thirty-five, that thing was still living inside me. Sometimes I thought it was only a threadlike little sprout, struggling to survive in the dark. Other times, though, it felt like it had flourished and grown so large that it *was* me: I'm not good enough. I make men leave.

I knew, too, that I was supposed to be angry at Dad. Mom was. Audrey was. But I wasn't. I was still angry at Mom, even now that she was dead. It was all *her* fault.

If she'd known how to do things the right way—being a mother, being a wife, being a woman—and if she'd taught those things to Audrey and me, Dad never would've left.

◆ ◆ ◆

Gregor would be meeting with the new band on Monday, in a barn studio on the property of Ben Blakeley, the guy who'd proposed the whole album idea to Gregor in the first place. Ben's property was right across the road, so Gregor would be able to walk there every day.

Next weekend we'd be hosting a get-together with the entire band and their significant others, but that seemed like an eternity away.

Gregor, Sam, and I spent Saturday afternoon driving the Mercedes around the maze of narrow roads that cut across and circled the island in a way that seemed entirely illogical to me.

We braked for honor-system farm stands selling fresh eggs and dahlia bouquets and the last of the year's peppers and cucumbers. We drove into the island's only town, a few-block cluster of shops, restaurants, an IGA, a pharmacy, a library, an old-fashioned movie theater, a post office.

We went into the pharmacy to buy toothpaste for Sam. We'd forgotten to pack the bubblegum-flavored kind that he liked.

"Well *hello*, Mr. Sullivan," the cashier said when it was our turn to pay. "It's so great to see you back on the island." She was a wrinkled woman with a white bun, and she looked at Sam and me with bright, curious eyes. "Is this your family?"

"Yep," Gregor said, grinning at her. "My wife, Harlow, and my son, Sam."

"Welcome," the woman said with a warm smile.

I felt a glow. In New York, even if someone did recognize you, half the time they'd pretend not to anyway. *This is actually nice,* I thought. *I could maybe like it here.*

"Who was she?" I asked Gregor when we were outside again, walking back to the car.

"No idea," he said.

I frowned. "But it seemed like she knew *you*."

"Of course." Gregor opened the back door of the Mercedes. "I'm a Himmel." He looked down at Sam. "Hop in, buddy."

"So, what, you're like island royalty?" I said in a playful voice.

"Basically." Gregor was buckling Sam into his booster. "I'll show you."

We drove the short distance to the town library. Gregor double-parked in front, idling the engine, and pointed to the façade of the pretty old redbrick building. "See? Jakob Himmel Memorial Library. And see the statue?"

I nodded, taking in the life-size bronze statue of a bearded man near the front doors.

"That's him. My great-grandfather."

"Wow," I said with a smile, reaching out to ruffle the back of Gregor's hair. "Does this make me a princess?"

"He basically *made* this island," Gregor said, driving forward. "Before him, it was nothing."

11

I asked Gregor if we could stop at the coffee shop, a clapboard building with a rickety porch on the edge of town. He parked in the potholed lot out back and we went inside.

It was busy, all the tables full, the air heavy with the aromas of roasting coffee and baked goods. It had a cozy vibe, and I saw a lot of muddy boots and Patagonia fleeces. A cluster of old-timers sat around a tabletop placed on a wooden barrel. At another table, a young woman fed two flaxen-haired toddlers something from a bakery bag.

We got in the short line at the counter.

The barista, a young blond woman, was covered in tattoos. Her bare arms were inked with creeping vines and the phases of the moon and some symbols I didn't recognize. Probably Celtic runes or something. I saw a mushroom on her forearm, too, red, with spots on its cap, and I tried not to think about the previous night.

The barista's belly was swollen taut with her third trimester, and I felt a jab of envy in my own belly.

She caught me staring. I looked away, my cheeks warm.

I read the notices pinned to a corkboard. Massage, knitting instruction, a children's llama club, sound healing, a Styrofoam recycling drive, farm-sitting, a string quartet performance, a tool exchange, and a local production of *The Taming of the Shrew*.

The bell on the door jangled as more people entered, including another blond woman. She had a tiny baby strapped to her chest in a fabric sling.

"Exactly how many blond hippie moms with little kids live on this island?" I said to Gregor when we were back in the car with our coffees and a hot chocolate for Sam.

"What?" Gregor said.

"Didn't you see them all?"

"See what?"

"All the blond moms with the little blond kids. There were, like, at least three families."

"Babe. Don't worry. It's going to happen for us, too."

"I'm not *jealous*," I said, stung. "It was just an observation."

Well, maybe I was a little jealous.

Gregor started the engine and put the car into reverse. "A lot of the original settlers of this island were from Scandinavia," he said. "It makes sense that you'd see a lot of blond hair. Heck, even I was white blond when I was little. Hey—that gives me an idea. We should call the band the Settlers. What do you think?"

I sipped my almond-milk latte. "It has a nice ring to it," I said.

My ovulation test came back positive Sunday morning. I showed it to Gregor when he was sitting on the chilly sunlit porch, strumming his guitar. Two plum-colored stripes on a flimsy ribbon of paper, but to us it may as well have been the Dead Sea Scrolls.

He pushed his sunglasses to the top of his head and grinned. "Yeah, baby," he said, setting aside his guitar. "Where's Sam?"

"Glued to Netflix."

"Meet you upstairs."

Then it was Monday.

The day that reality was supposed to set in, our new schedule where Sam was going to go to his new preschool, someplace called KinderWild, Gregor and the band were going to start jamming and writing, and I was going to figure out how to chill the heck out enough to get knocked up.

Unless . . . Unless maybe I was *already* knocked up. Because Gregor and I had definitely had sex, lots of it, over the weekend, and now I was officially in what women who are trying to conceive call the "two-week wait."

Don't think about it, I told myself, knowing full well that I would think about it. A lot. That I was going to obsess for the next ten days, trying to decide if maybe my breasts were slightly tender, if maybe I felt *something happening* inside my uterus.

I was going to obsess until I could start doing early-result pregnancy tests—which supposedly can work five days before your missed period. I had no firsthand knowledge of that because I'd never missed a single period since my very first one when I was thirteen.

But this could be it. This could be the month.

Emilia made us breakfast. Scrambled eggs and pancakes for Gregor and Sam, coffee and a green smoothie for me. Then Gregor set out on foot for rehearsal at the Blakeleys' barn.

I watched him walk out the mudroom door with his worn leather messenger bag over his shoulder and his guitar case in his hand. I wanted to rush after him for one last kiss.

"Bye, honey," I called.

"Bye, babe," he called back.

The door thumped shut.

I turned to Sam, who was chewing pancake. I tried to remember the last time it was him and me, without Gregor or the nanny. I couldn't recall. I'd been working such long hours at the lab, and for so long.

I smiled brightly. "It's just you and me," I said.

Sam gazed at me serenely. He sipped his milk. "And Emilia," he said. Emilia was at the kitchen sink, scrubbing the griddle.

"Well, yeah."

"And that guy." Sam pointed outside, where a landscaper was buzzing across the grass on a riding lawn mower.

Sam had milk on his upper lip. He was so cute it hurt.

It took me ten minutes to get him to brush his teeth and another ten to cajole him into the car. I typed in the address for KinderWild in the Mercedes's GPS, and we headed out.

I'd explored the KinderWild website when we were still in New York, after Gregor told me he'd enrolled Sam there. I'd clicked through a homemade-looking site filled with pictures of small kids crouched in the mud, climbing trees, that sort of thing, and a mission statement about "preparing the child for the path, not the path for the child."

The website even had an entire page devoted to something called "nature-deficit disorder." This condition was supposedly a result of modern kids' lack of immersion in nature, and—supposedly—it led to a host of behavioral problems.

The whole thing seemed New Agey to me, but Gregor was dead set on it, and it was only for six months. And who knew? Maybe Sam would love it. It couldn't be *that* different from his Montessori preschool in the East Village.

The GPS talked me around the harbor and up and down a few hills and then onto a gravel road that seemed to disappear into green murk.

Convinced I'd taken a wrong turn, I pulled over and double-checked the map. Nope. This was it. I drove forward again.

"This is a bad place," Sam said behind me.

"It's just . . . different," I said. "Different from what we're used to."

"I hate it," he whispered.

I was hating it, too, but I kept that to myself.

After about a quarter mile of increasingly rutted road, we arrived at a gravel lot clogged with parked cars. I saw children and women getting out of muddy Subarus and pickups and Teslas.

I managed to squeeze the huge Mercedes into a spot next to a vintage blue Volvo station wagon and switched off the engine.

I didn't see a school. I didn't see any buildings. Only a parking area ringed by fir trees.

"Okay!" I said, forcing cheerfulness for Sam's sake. "Here we are!" I got out and opened his door, and that's when he started to cry.

"Oh, Sam," I said. "Baby. It's okay."

"It's a bad place," he said again.

If it had been completely up to me, I would've buckled him back up and driven him home. But obviously I couldn't make a decision like that without Gregor's input.

"Sam, it'll be okay," I said. "I promise. You just have to give it a try. There's going to be trees to climb, and maybe some . . . some birds? Or squirrels, or something? And the day will be over before you know it."

"I want to go home," he said through his tears. "I miss Rosa."

"She'll be there when we go back to New York."

"I miss her *now*." Sam stuck his thumb in his mouth and started sucking.

I'd never seen him suck his thumb before. Was it some regressive behavior?

"Sam," I said. "Listen to me."

He screwed up his eyes tight and kept sucking his thumb. It made a wet clicking sound.

I had no idea what to do. I glanced around, limp with helplessness.

Across the parking area, three women emerged from an opening in the trees. The woman in the middle carried a baby on her hip, and she was holding hands with a small child. The other two women didn't have children with them. They both tipped their faces toward the middle woman, like plants bending toward a sunny window.

I turned back to Sam. "Sweetie," I said to him, "it's only for a little while. And Emilia packed your lunch box! She said there were some yummy surprises in there for you."

Something made me glance over my shoulder again. Two of the women had peeled off, heading, I assumed, to their cars. The third woman, still carrying the baby and leading the small child, was making her way slowly across the parking lot toward Sam and me.

Just my luck, I thought. *The blue Volvo must be hers.*

12

"Let's go see the school, okay?" I said to Sam. I needed to get him out of the car before Blue Volvo Lady arrived and wanted out of her parking spot.

Sam grunted in disagreement, still sucking his thumb.

"Um, excuse me?" someone called behind me.

I turned.

The woman had stopped behind the Volvo. "I don't think I can open my door?" she said, frowning. "You parked way too close."

She was startlingly pretty, suntanned and large eyed, with a long white-blond braid laid across her shoulder. She was wearing a flowy, ankle-length floral dress, a brown knitted cardigan, and flat leather boots. Her children had wispy white-blond hair, too, and they were dressed in shades of brown and cream. The three of them had an out-of-time *Little House on the Prairie* quality.

"I'm so sorry," I said. "Hold on—I'll move my car."

"That would be *amazing*," the woman said.

Well, she was a girl, really. She appeared no more than twenty-five, although clearly she'd been busily reproducing for years. In New York I would've assumed a woman her age with kids in tow was the nanny, not the mother, but the baby and the toddler matched this girl like a boxed set.

Plus, the baby was now rooting their face against the girl's shoulder. And then, to my astonishment, the girl pulled the collar of her dress down, exposing her breast, and the baby latched on to her nipple and vigorously began to suckle.

The girl met my eye. There was a challenge in her expression, an *I dare you to have a problem with this* I'd seen on other breastfeeding moms' faces. But something else, too: the faintest glimmer of malice. I quickly looked away.

"Wait," she said. "Are you Harlow? Harlow Sullivan?"

I turned to her again. "Um . . . yeah?"

"I'm Kirsten." She said it decisively, like I'd know exactly who she was. "I didn't realize it was you."

"I'm sorry," I said falteringly, "I don't think we've . . ."

"Kirsten Blakeley?"

Blakeley, I thought. *Why does that sound familiar?*

Then it hit me.

"Oh, of course," I said. "You're . . . is Ben your husband? The . . . he's a drummer, right?"

"Yeah." Her expression had darkened. "Gregor didn't mention me?"

"Well, no—I mean, yeah. Yeah, I knew Ben had a wife and that you guys are close neighbors, and Gregor is there today, in your barn. But I . . . I guess he just didn't mention your name." *Or*, I added inwardly and with a twinge in my gut, *that you are stunningly gorgeous.*

"Well," Kirsten said, "welcome to the island. You guys are going to love it here."

"Some of us have our doubts," I said wryly, glancing at Sam inside the car. He had stopped crying, probably because he was curious about the new people.

"You know, I'm pretty sure I can squeeze my car out," Kirsten said. "It's no problem." She opened one of the rear doors, unlatched the baby from her breast, and buckled them into a rear-facing car seat. Then she circled around the car with the other child so they were right next to me.

Her eyes were grass green with coppery spokes. She smiled, and I realized I'd been wrong. There was no malice in her. Only sweetness.

"How are you settling in?" she asked. "It's so hard, isn't it, getting used to a new house?"

"It's all right. I mean, I don't think . . . we don't plan to stay for more than a couple months."

"I thought it was six months?"

"Oh. Yeah. Six."

"That's smart," she said with a knowing nod. "The longer the better, right? Urban environments are really toxic—spiritually and physically."

Part of me marveled at the audacity of her doing the Wise Woman thing. I mean, I was about a decade older than her, for Pete's sake. But I also felt an annoying little glow because she'd called me *smart.* Since when was I so hungry for the approval of strangers?

"Gregor said you were a scientist?" she said over her shoulder, now buckling the child into a car seat.

"Yes," I said. "I am."

She straightened and shut the door. "You'll see that on this island, what your job was, where you went to college, stuff like that, it doesn't matter." She smiled again. "Nobody cares."

I blinked, unsure if I'd been slighted or not.

"Hey," she said, "I have a ton of stuff going on today, but would you and Sam like to come over tomorrow after school? He's the same age as my oldest, Magni. We can have some tea and cookies and get to know each other a little better."

"Oh," I said, taken aback. She knew Sam's name and his exact age? Just how well did she know my husband? "Sure, that would be lovely."

"Great!" Another flash of smile. "Okay, I've got to run, but I'll probably see you here this afternoon at pickup." She gave a little wave as she circled around to the driver's seat.

13

By the time Kirsten was driving away, Sam had calmed down. I managed to coax him out of the car, and we went into the woods by the path I'd seen the others taking. He was still sucking his thumb, but he finally seemed willing.

It was cooler in the shade of the trees. Birds cheeped, and a breeze ruffled the boughs high overhead. After a few twists in the path, we came upon a dirt-packed clearing where about two dozen small children and two women were sitting on logs arranged in a circle. One of the adults was speaking, but she stopped when she saw Sam and me. Everyone stared.

The first thing I noticed was that all of the children were white. So were the women. Before Sam was in my life, this wasn't something I probably would've noticed. But I'd started to feel uncomfortable on his behalf if he was the only brown-skinned person in a given situation.

Here at KinderWild, not only were all the kids white, but almost all of them had blond hair. This struck me as statistically impossible. But then, the majority of the little kids I'd seen so far on the island had also been blond. This wasn't New York.

One of the women circled around the logs to meet Sam and me. She was about my age, deeply tanned, with hennaed dreadlocks, jeans, hiking boots, and a blue fleece vest over a short-sleeved T-shirt.

"Hello," she said with a smile. But her hushed voice implied, *You're late, and let's not disrupt the others.* "I'm Teacher Terra." She looked down at Sam. "You must be Sam?"

He nodded up at her, eyes wide, thumb in mouth.

Terra focused on me. "And you must be Sam's mama, Harlow?"

"Stepmom, actually," I said.

"It's so nice to meet you. Make sure you bring Sam on time from now on, okay? We start at nine o'clock."

"Right," I said. "Sorry."

"Come on, Sam." Terra took his hand. Her T-shirt sleeve rode up, and I saw a tattoo on her upper arm, two cojoined X's, one stacked on top of the other to form a diamond. I had the sense I'd seen the symbol before, but I couldn't think where. "You'll sit with me today," she said to Sam, and she led him away.

When I returned to Himmel Cottage, I heard the drone of Emilia's vacuum. I didn't want to get in her way, so I went out to the pool, settled onto a teak chaise in the thin autumn sunshine, and opened the internet browser on my phone.

I typed *kirsten blakeley* and tapped "Go."

An avalanche of results filled the screen. Most of the hits were from Instagram, all tagged with the handle IntoTheWoodsWeGo. I opened an image search to find an ocean of Kirsten photos.

Kirsten in a folksy-looking dress, her pale hair braided around her head, milkmaid-style.

Barefoot Kirsten standing tiptoe on overgrown grass, pinning white garments onto a clothesline.

Kirsten bending her head gracefully over a bowl, stirring something with a wooden spoon.

A selfie of Kirsten (although could she really have taken it herself?) gazing pensively past the camera lens, sunlight illuminating her poreless tan skin, her freckled nose, her green-and-copper eyes.

Kirsten in an old-fashioned white nightgown with long sleeves, a high, lacy collar, and a row of tiny mother-of-pearl buttons down the bodice. The caption read **Full moon's out! Anybody else having a hard time getting their beauty rest? #foreverlove**

Kirsten in a short video, dancing with her baby, laughing with her head thrown back and her long dress fanning out.

In another video, Kirsten dicing bloodred chicken livers and chatting about how to make them into country gravy.

Then there were Kirsten's children—there seemed to be three, including the baby—in homespun-looking outfits, posing in a cottage or a garden, hugging chickens and cats, biting into plums with pink juice dribbling down their cheeks, piling rocks at the beach.

What am I even looking at? I thought.

I opened my Instagram app and found IntoTheWoodsWeGo.

845,822 followers.

Okay, I thought. *Wow. So she's some kind of influencer?*

Her bio said:

> **I'm Kirsten, wife of musician Ben Blakeley and BLESSED BY GOD with 3 (and counting!) forest-schooled free-range littles. I post about mothering, heritage homemaking, and learning how to claim your God-given fertility on our tiny slice of island paradise in the Pacific Northwest.**

I scrolled methodically through Kirsten's Instagram account, starting with the most recent post, from yesterday: a from-above shot of an apron heaped with apples. The caption said:

> **People don't get that I don't WANT to be the breadwinner in my home. Being the nurturer, the nourisher, the giver of comfort and the maker of beauty—THAT is my calling. Instead of being a "girl boss" today I spent my morning in the orchard, gathering up only the most beautiful apples in my @willowtreeprovisions apron to take home to my family. I have my GOD to thank, the God of apple trees and wild grass meadows and growing baby bumps and my three precious, sacred littles running free in the sun. #masculinefeminine #stayathomemama #traditionalliving #autumnvibes #blessed**

Sure, the religious messaging was heavy-handed—and that's coming from someone raised in small-town Iowa. Also, Kirsten was clearly making money by promoting baby carriers, organic makeup, lanolin nipple balm, teething biscuits, herbal supplements, and, most of all, the indie fashion brands that made the retro-folk clothing she wore so well.

It was all one big advertisement, basically. I knew how momfluencers operated.

But the *images* . . . they were hypnotizing. As I scrolled, something stirred in my chest, something hard and deep and painful. It was longing, I realized. Longing for a different time and place without the horror of mass shootings and climate change and microplastics and Elon Musk. And it was homesickness, too, for a home I'd never been to but to which I wanted so, so badly to return.

Which was nonsense. I knew that. My genes didn't hold memories of wooden houses and sourdough starters and babies in handknitted sweaters.

But scrolling through Kirsten's Insta feed, it sure as heck *felt* like they did.

14

I scrolled through IntoTheWoodsWeGo for hours, inspecting each photograph as carefully as a forensic analyst before moving on to the next. There were thousands, a treasure trove, because Kirsten had been at this for more than five years. It would take me days to see them all.

I finally forced myself to stop. I had some lunch, changed into workout clothes, and did thirty-five minutes on the elliptical in Pauline's pool house. I texted Audrey, and then Owen and Phoebe back in New York. None of them responded right away, though. Of course not. They all had busy—no, *hectic*—lives.

No one told me being a lady of leisure was going to be so lonely.

I got back on Instagram.

Then, somehow, it was 2:45. Time to leave to pick up Sam.

"How was it?" I asked Sam once we were buckled into the car and rolling away from KinderWild. "Was it fun?"

I hadn't seen Kirsten anywhere. I felt disappointed by that, which in turn made me feel foolish and kind of gross. It wasn't normal to look at someone else's social media for an entire day, was it? I told myself it was only because I wasn't working, and I had no friends on the island and very little to occupy my time. I told myself I wouldn't do it again.

Sam didn't answer my question.

I glanced in the rearview mirror. He was sucking his thumb. Mud flecked his forehead, and his hair looked wild.

I tried again. "What did you do?"

There was a long silence while I navigated an extra-bumpy stretch of road. I'd decided Sam wasn't ever going to answer when he said, "Some of the kids played on drums, and the rest of us were supposed to dance."

"That sounds fun. Did you dance?"

"I started to, but I was doing it wrong, so I stopped."

"There's no *wrong way* to dance, sweetie."

"Teacher Terra said I was doing it wrong."

"What?" I glanced in the rearview at Sam again. His thumb was back in his mouth, and he was scowling out the window.

That witch, I thought. *What is wrong with her?*

"Why haven't you ever mentioned Kirsten Blakeley to me?" I asked Gregor that evening, keeping my tone light. Sam was asleep, and Gregor and I were in the bathroom together, standing at the his-and-her vanity sinks.

"What do you mean?" he said. He flipped open the toothpaste cap.

"Well, I met her today in the KinderWild parking lot, and she seemed to know all about me, but I couldn't remember you ever mentioning her."

I had debated with myself for hours whether to bring this up with Gregor. In the end, curiosity won. I'd decided to ask him, but to be careful not to make a big deal about it.

"I'm sure I mentioned her to you, babe," he said, smearing toothpaste onto the bristles of his Sonicare. He stuck it in his mouth and switched it on to a muted buzz.

"I would've definitely remembered you mentioning your bandmate's internet-famous wife."

"What do you mean?" he said around foaming toothpaste. "She's internet famous?"

"Are you telling me you don't know?"

"I mean, Ben mentioned she had a big following on . . . is it TikTok?"

"Instagram. She has almost a *million* followers."

"None of that shit is important to me. You know that."

"She's also really beautiful," I said. Immediately, I regretted it. It made me sound insecure.

Gregor switched off his toothbrush and spat foam into the sink. "Babe."

Was he going to pretend he hadn't noticed Kirsten's beauty? I wasn't sure if I wanted that.

He swiveled the faucet on and blasted the toothpaste down the drain. He swiveled it off again and looked at me. "Beauty is in the eye of the beholder."

"Please," I said on a groan.

"Fine," Gregor said. "You want to know the truth?"

"Always."

"I didn't mention Kirsten because she has three kids, and I thought . . ."

"What?" Something inside me went cold and still.

"I just thought maybe you'd be a little . . ."

"A little what?"

"I thought you might be jealous."

"Jealous," I repeated flatly.

"Of her, you know . . . her fertility."

"I'm a grown woman, honey," I said.

Shut up, I told myself. *Just shut up.*

But words kept on sliding out of my mouth as though they had a life of their own. "I have a PhD from a top-tier school. Until very recently I was doing research at one of the most prestigious cancer centers in the country. And you're afraid I'm going to be jealous of some girl because she popped out a bunch of babies so young she's going to be a grandma by the time she's forty? Gee. Thanks."

Gregor stared at me. I couldn't blame him. I'd *never* talked like that to him before. God. I sounded as bitchy and unhinged as my mom.

"Whoa," he finally said. "Are you . . . done?"

"I'm sorry. I'm just tired."

"Kirsten may not have a college degree, but it sounds like she's pretty successful at the influencer stuff."

"I know," I said. "Sorry. I don't know why I said all that."

"It's okay." Gregor planted a toothpaste-scented kiss on my forehead. "Let's get you into bed."

I didn't say anything else as I left the bathroom. Gregor was right—I *was* jealous of Kirsten. Of her beauty, her internet fame, and, yes, I was jealous of her fertility.

I curled up in bed, sick with self-loathing. I felt old, and used-up, and mean-spirited. It had taken me till the age of thirty-three to find a man who wanted all the same things I did, a man who loved all of me, and here I was jeopardizing it because I couldn't keep my insecurities to myself.

A minute later, Gregor got into bed, too, and switched off the light. He didn't say anything. He didn't reach for me.

A reel of images flickered past my mind's eye. Brown leather boots and yellow chickens and purple plums and white-blond hair.

15

Sam informed me the next morning that he didn't want to go back to KinderWild. He said it quietly, around a bite of Puffins cereal.

Later, after Sam had gone to get dressed, Gregor came downstairs. I took a deep breath and told him what Sam had said. I hated to stir things up after we'd gone to bed not speaking. But I owed this to Sam.

"It's predictable, right?" Gregor replied, pouring cream into his coffee. "We switched up his school after the school year started. Kids hate that. He needs to get a thicker skin. Which means *you* need to stop coddling him."

"He also told me the teacher said he was 'dancing wrong.'"

"I love the Mama Bear thing, Low, but—"

"I'm not being a—"

Gregor silenced me with a soft kiss on my mouth, our first physical contact since our unpleasant exchange about Kirsten Blakeley the night before. "You're going to make a great mom," he murmured.

Aren't I already a mom? I thought. *Or a stepmom, anyway?*

But his touch, his scent—after being without them for so many hours, I could've wept with relief.

◆ ◆ ◆

I'd hoped to have a word with Teacher Terra that morning. But this time, the KinderWild teaching intern—Gilda, a brown-haired, sad-eyed wisp of a girl in a long dress and hiking boots—led Sam away by the hand into the Gathering Place.

After that, I drove to the coffee shop we'd visited on Saturday, more to kill time than anything else. I mean, there was a state-of-the-art electronic espresso maker at the cottage.

The pregnant barista with the tattoos was working again. Once again, she was wearing a tank top so her inked-up arms were on display. And once again, the spotted red mushroom jumped out at me first. It looked poisonous. It also reminded me uncomfortably of Gregor's little adventure the other night.

Then I noticed the tattoo beside it: two X's, stacked vertically and conjoined so they formed a diamond between them. It made me think of surgical stitches, or fish scales.

And, come to think of it—didn't Teacher Terra have the exact same tattoo?

When it was my turn, I ordered an almond-milk latte. Then I said to the barista, "I'm sorry if this is rude, but I couldn't help noticing your tattoos—they're so amazing—and I was just wondering, What does the symbol with the two X's mean?"

She frowned down at her arm, then back at me. "It doesn't mean anything. I thought it was pretty. Why?"

"Oh," I said. "It's just . . . I saw someone else with the exact same tattoo, here on the island, so I thought it might be—"

"I forgot," she interrupted. "Did you say you wanted almond milk or oat milk?"

All righty, then, I thought. *I guess we're not talking about the tattoo anymore.* "Almond milk," I said. "Please."

I wasn't surprised that Sam hated the idea of going to the Blakeleys' house for tea and cookies after I picked him up from KinderWild.

"I want to watch *PAW Patrol*," he said. This was his favorite cartoon.

"After we visit the neighbors." I was parking the Mercedes at Himmel Cottage. Sam and I could walk to Kirsten's house since it was so close by.

"Magni is mean," Sam said. He didn't sound sulky. He sounded matter-of-fact.

"What did he do?"

"Do we have to go?"

"Sweetie. What did Magni do?"

"He makes mean faces. And he sometimes spits."

"At you?"

"At everyone."

I got out of the car, opened Sam's door, and unbuckled him. "I know you're tired, sweetie, but it's important that we get to know Magni and his family," I said. "Daddy plays music with Magni's dad now, and besides, they're our neighbors."

It was disingenuous, putting it to Sam like that. Because it wasn't with a sense of neighborliness or wifely duty that I set out for the Blakeley house, but with a ravenous curiosity.

Sam and I walked down our own driveway, through the orchard and the gate, and across the main road. I'd noticed the Blakeleys' mailbox before: battered metal on a post, with the address painted in fanciful lettering. Their gravel driveway went uphill and around a bend.

Then I saw Kirsten's perfect little house. It had weathered shingles, white trim, and a rusted metal roof, and it stood in a sunny clearing carved from the forest. I recognized the deer-fenced garden and the small greenhouse from Kirsten's Instagram. Also the flower beds, the cream-painted chicken coop, a couple of small outbuildings, and, standing aloof from the house, the rustic barn of silvery wood.

As we walked closer, I caught the briefest glimpse of someone darting behind the corner of one of the outbuildings—a tumble of brown hair, the swish of a long dress.

Not Kirsten. Someone else.

My neck prickled, but I shook it off. *It's none of my business.*

Muffled music throbbed from inside the barn. Gregor was in there, and I missed him with a sudden pang.

We went across the overgrown lawn and up the creaking porch steps. I knocked on the green door.

Even the door was familiar—Kirsten routinely shared photographs of it on Instagram—and I felt ashamed. I shouldn't have known so much about a stranger's private life.

On the other hand, she'd put it all out there for the world to see. She *wanted* an audience.

It still felt wrong, though. Off-balance.

You'd think the balance would've been tilted in my favor since I knew a thousand times more about her life than she knew about mine. But somehow, *I* felt like the powerless one, waiting there on her porch. In her mid-twenties—at an age when I'd still been flailing around in grad school and bar crawls and going-nowhere relationships—Kirsten had her life completely together. She'd cracked the code.

I guess secretly I'm a terrible person because all I wanted right then was for Kirsten's life not to be as perfect as it seemed online. I wanted to find a weak seam and rip it wide.

The door opened.

"Hi!" Kirsten said, smiling and showing her white teeth. She was wearing a ruffled apron with tiny flowers in shades of rust and peach. "Come in, you guys. The muffins are in the oven."

"They smell delicious," I said. "Sam, don't the muffins smell good?"

"I don't want muffins," he said. He plugged his thumb in his mouth.

"You might change your mind," Kirsten said. "They're blackberry. Alder and Magni picked the berries themselves." She led us along a tiny center hallway, past a cramped staircase, and into a small kitchen. She was barefoot, I noticed. And I wondered how she'd tied her apron bow so perfectly.

In the kitchen, I felt like I'd walked onto a television set, or maybe into the pages of *Country Living* magazine. Everything was in shades of white and cream and wood tones, with drying herbs strung from the ceiling and open shelves arranged with glass jars of spices and dried beans and flours and nuts. A brick fireplace took up one wall. Over it hung an old-fashioned axe. A vase of white dahlias sat on the mantel shelf.

A plank table stood in the middle of the room, and that's where Kirsten invited Sam and me to sit. The baby—*such* a beautiful baby—was sitting in a high chair, wearing nothing but a cloth diaper and mashing avocado into their mouth.

Of course, I'd seen it all before, on Instagram. But to my dismay I saw that it was even prettier in real life.

16

Kirsten went to the stove and did something with a steaming teakettle. "Magni and Alder are upstairs," she said over her shoulder.

A series of thumps overhead confirmed this.

"Would you like to go and play with them, Sam?" Kirsten asked.

Sam quickly shook his head.

"I think these first days of school are tiring him out," I said.

"Oh, totally. There's definitely an adjustment period for new children at KinderWild."

"How old is your baby?" I asked, watching the chubby little one smear avocado across the high-chair tray.

"Six months. Her name's Barri. She's just starting to experiment with solids—oh my gosh, she *loves* making a mess."

"Barri?" I said. "That's an unusual name. Isn't it a town in Italy?"

"Is it? For us, it's way more personal than that." Kirsten turned her back to pour the boiling water, so I assumed she didn't want to elaborate.

Kirsten served cups of chamomile, and roasted nuts of a variety I couldn't identify, and hot buttered blackberry muffins. It all tasted strange, herbal and a little musty, but then that's what the entire house smelled like.

She was chatty, and our conversation flitted from one topic to the other, mostly homes and child-rearing and the weather. She told me about her plans for an over-winter greens garden and how she wanted to build a rabbit hutch in the spring. She mentioned a women's circle she belonged to, and how she made her own goat-milk soap and sauerkraut.

She refilled my teacup without my ever having to ask for more, and gradually I relaxed. The kitchen took on a strange haze, like a Photoshop filter, and languid well-being stretched through my limbs. Even Sam seemed more relaxed, munching through his second muffin.

She never mentioned her momfluencer gig, and neither did I. I kept wondering, *Does she know I know? Does she assume? Or is she trying to keep it a secret?*

Presently, Kirsten wiped the avocado from Barri with a wet cloth, settled her on her lap, and pulled out a breast. The baby latched on with the decisive suction of some kind of sea creature.

Sam was staring. I wasn't sure if he'd ever seen breastfeeding before. I didn't think Gregor would object if he found out, but I still silently prayed that Sam wouldn't mention it.

"Sometimes I feel like our entire family life revolves around my breasts," Kirsten said with a sigh. "You'll see, when you have children."

Her condescension chafed. I turned my head, feeling my cheeks heating up.

The kitchen sink window overlooked a stretch of tall grass and a shadowy wall of trees. Kirsten had recently posted a photo on Instagram of herself holding hands with her two little sons, walking toward those trees.

In the photo, she's glancing over her shoulder at the photographer with a mysterious smile. Her hair fans loose in a real or manufactured breeze. She wears a long brown dress. The little boys are in denim overalls and T-shirts. All three of them are barefoot. The caption reads **Into the woods we go, to lose our minds and find our souls.**

What that meant, I had no clue.

My eyes kept straying to that wall of trees, though. I imagined I could make out a parting in the grass, an opening in the undergrowth.

"Do you want to go out there?" Kirsten asked. She'd followed my gaze.

"What? Oh. No, not really. I don't . . . To be honest, the woods kind of freak me out."

"Oh my gosh, really? I *love* the woods."

"Well, I'm originally from Iowa." I forced a laugh.

"There's a path," Kirsten said. "Can you see where it begins? It leads to this beautiful, magical forest, like no place you've ever seen." She kissed the top of her baby's head. "It's literally heaven up there."

I laughed again. I was sounding like a nutjob. "I'll have to take your word for it, because no way am I going in there."

"You'll come around," Kirsten said. "Everyone does."

Suddenly, all I wanted was to get away from her. From her perfect little house, her beautiful children, her sweet, milky, self-satisfied atmosphere. I told her I needed to get going, that I needed to start dinner—even though Emilia was probably cooking it right that second.

"Come again tomorrow?" Kirsten asked me, tipping her head. "I still haven't shown you around the homestead."

I heard myself saying, "Yeah. Yeah, that sounds great."

That evening, I didn't mention to Gregor that I'd visited Kirsten. I told myself it was simply too unimportant to discuss.

17

The next afternoon after KinderWild, Sam and I walked over to the Blakeley homestead for the second time. It was another sunny, warm day, and I was in cropped jeans, a white T-shirt, and green flip-flops.

Once again, I could hear music inside the barn as we walked past. Kirsten answered the door in a peach apron over a gauzy white dress. This time, she was baking hazelnut-oat cookies, and while she gave Sam chamomile tea again, the tea she placed in front of me was dark brown and smelled like dirt.

"Try this," she said. "It's a blend with pennyroyal—amazing for the feminine cycle. Oh my gosh, why are you looking at me like that?" She bit her lower lip. "Gregor told me you guys are trying to conceive and that your body needs a little encouragement?"

I'll kill him, I thought.

"It's okay," Kirsten said. "Lots of women in their late thirties have a hard time conceiving. It's like you have to wake your body up and remind it about what it's made to do."

I'll kill her, too.

"Thanks," I said in a dry tone.

"You're welcome. I'll put some more of the blend in a jar for you to take home, okay? Everyone in my women's circle swears by this stuff."

Kirsten started bustling around with the oven and a tray of cookies, giving me a chance to compose myself. But I mean, what the *heck*? My husband was talking to Kirsten—practically a stranger—about my fertility issues?

So much for it being *private*, like he said.

I tried to put it out of my mind. Kirsten wanted to be nice. She was just kind of tactless.

I took a sip of the tea and grimaced. It tasted even worse than it smelled—bitter, earthy, woody. But hey, maybe it would help me get pregnant.

The conversation turned to how Sam was liking KinderWild so far (not much) and how I was filling my days now that I had time off work (internet-stalking Kirsten, but I obviously didn't mention *that*). Sam hadn't wanted to play with Alder and Magni outside, but Kirsten showed him where the children's bookshelf was in their bedroom, and I assumed he was contentedly looking at books.

"Why haven't you mentioned your social media thing?" I asked Kirsten after a lull in the conversation.

Her eyes widened. "Oh, I guess I just . . . I didn't know if you even knew about that part of my life? And I didn't want it to, you know, get in the way of us being friends. Is . . . sorry, is that dumb?"

"No, it's not dumb, but . . . why would it get in the way of us being friends?"

"Well, I mean, you're this fancy scientist from New York City. And I'm just a mom who didn't even finish college. I was worried you'd think it was kind of . . . shallow?"

"I think it's interesting," I said. "It's really . . . you're an entrepreneur, you know. I admire that." I meant to sound encouraging, but instead I sounded condescending.

But Kirsten was smiling. "Okay. Well, thanks. That means a lot."

"Does your husband take your photographs?"

"Ben? Oh my gosh, no." Kirsten laughed. "Gilda does."

"Gilda?"

"The teaching intern at KinderWild?"

"Oh, right." I pictured the sad-looking girl in her hiking boots and long dresses.

Maybe that's who I saw yesterday disappearing behind the outbuilding, I thought.

"Ben doesn't like the whole social media thing," Kirsten said. "He thinks it's 'nontraditional.' But he doesn't complain about the income I get from my brand collaborations, so." She lifted a shoulder. "You're lucky. With Gregor's family money, I mean. You guys don't have to worry."

How did she know about that? Never mind—of *course* she knew about it. It was public knowledge. "Yeah," I said vaguely, and averted my eyes from Kirsten's too-bright gaze. "Sorry—would you mind telling me where the bathroom is?"

Following Kirsten's instructions, I found the tiny main-floor bathroom, off the central hallway. I took my time in there, even though it reeked of patchouli.

Was it too soon to go home? Because like yesterday, I had suddenly maxed out on this entire situation. Kirsten had boundary issues.

When I stepped out of the bathroom, I heard voices in the kitchen. Kirsten's, and a male voice.

Wait.

Gregor's voice.

I approached the kitchen slowly. I wasn't exactly *sneaking*, but I wasn't making a point of being noisy, either.

I paused just outside the doorway.

Gregor and Kirsten were standing in front of the kitchen sink, and Gregor was holding Barri. They were both gazing down at the baby, the early-evening sun lighting up all of their golden hair like a shared halo.

"Man, she looks just like you," Gregor was saying softly. There was a gravelly awe in his voice, and his big, suntanned arms cradling the tiny baby . . . it felt like I was being forced to look at something precious that I couldn't have.

No—it felt like a hatchet to the rib cage. And then it felt like I was standing there trying to keep my hemorrhaging heart from falling out of my chest.

18

"Her hair," Gregor said softly to Kirsten, gazing down at the baby. "Her eyes. Does she . . . yeah, she even has your dimple, Mama."

Mama? I thought. *MAMA?*

"I wish I could get a photo of this," Kirsten said. "It's such a waste."

I dimly thought it might be a good idea to retreat, or to clear my throat or cough or whatever, to give them time to rearrange themselves in a less intimate way.

But I couldn't take it anymore.

I stepped into the kitchen. "Hey!" I said too loudly. "Gregor!"

He turned, his startled expression morphing into guilt before landing on a smile. "Low. Hey. I didn't know you were here." He threw a quick, questioning glance at Kirsten and then carefully handed the baby to her. "I just . . . we decided to stop a little early today. The band, I mean. I—we—were thinking of having a beer on the porch. We came up with a really awesome, special song today. I think it's going to be huge."

I nodded and smiled mechanically, a dashboard bobblehead. "Great," I said. "That's so great."

"Where's Sam?" Gregor asked. His Adam's apple worked.

"He's looking at books upstairs."

"Oh. Great."

I didn't look at Kirsten. I just couldn't. But I was sure I could feel something like victory radiating off her.

Then the back door opened and a man appeared, and I thought, *Thank God.*

"Hello, my love," Kirsten said to the man. "Harlow, this is Ben. My husband."

It was only in that moment that I realized Ben was never pictured in any of Kirsten's Instagram posts. She mentioned him in the captions—**my shoulder to cry on, my rock, man of my dreams, world's sweetest papa**—and in the videos. But no photographs.

"Hi," I said to Ben. "It's so nice to finally meet you."

"Hey," he said, eyes skimming over me.

He was wiry, dark-haired, not much taller than I was, in cuffed jeans with suspenders, a green flannel shirt, and work boots. Full-on lumbersexual cosplay to match Kirsten's cottagecore thing, I supposed. He had sallow skin, bloodshot eyes, and a bushy beard.

"Did you finish your chores?" he asked Kirsten.

"Yes," she said, eyes on the floor.

Ben frowned at the kitchen table, which was untidy with the remains of our tea and cookies. "Doesn't look like it."

What is this? I thought. *Besides incredibly messed up?*

"I got distracted," Kirsten said. "Talking with Harlow."

"About what? No, never mind—whatever it was, it'll be all over the internet by tonight." Ben's eyes toggled to me. "You know that saying, if a tree falls in the forest and no one's there to hear it, did it make a sound?"

"Um . . . yeah?" I said.

"Well, I always wonder if something happens in Kirsten's life and she doesn't post it on Instagram, did it really happen?"

I should've said something. That would've been the right thing to do. But I guess I was shocked into silence by Ben talking about his wife like that. Was I supposed to call him out for being a jerk? Or was this weird marital dynamic none of my business?

Kirsten was smiling a little as she said to Ben, "Oh, *honey*," in a way that seemed, well, *flirtatious*.

Oh my God, I thought. *Maybe it's kink. Maybe tonight, after Gregor and I are gone and their kids are asleep, they'll continue the performance just for each other? Ben will shred that gauzy dress off Kirsten's body and force her to her knees?*

"Well, I think it's great," Gregor said. "What Kirsten's doing with her brand. Getting visible on social media isn't easy, I know that from personal experience." He smiled at her. She smiled back.

I didn't understand any of it. Not Kirsten's submission to Ben, nor what, exactly, I had witnessed between Kirsten and my own husband and the baby.

All I knew was that I was spinning with queasiness and that the kitchen was way, *way* too small.

"Excuse me," I said. I edged past Ben and walked out the kitchen door, down the porch steps, and into the tall grass.

"Babe?"

Gregor had followed me outside. But I didn't turn to him. I waded into the grass. It crunched under my flip-flops and scratched my hands.

"Babe," Gregor called after me. Then, more urgently, "Low!"

I kept going. I was already feeling better with some distance between myself and the house. And there, up ahead, there was the path from Kirsten's Instagram photo. The path she'd said led to a beautiful, magical forest.

Into the woods we go, to lose our minds and find our souls.

Screw that, I thought. *I just want to be alone.*

The trees loomed up. The egg yolk sun was melting over their pointy tops. I saw the path, a dirt-packed strip.

I slowed. It didn't look very inviting. It made me think of sharp-toothed animals and broken bones and insect bites. I wondered how deep it went, and if it was possible to get lost.

Glancing over my shoulder, I saw Gregor plowing toward me through the grass, his fists balled as he swung his arms, his mouth grim.

It wasn't that I was *scared* of him. Not really. But something primal in me whispered, *Go.*

19

I went into the forest. The trunks of hundreds of trees rose up around me, as straight as telephone poles.

My flip-flops were all wrong for the terrain. The undergrowth raked against my bare ankles.

"Low," Gregor called behind me again.

"Give me some space," I shouted without turning around. I walked a little faster.

"You hate the forest."

"People change."

"The sun is setting."

"I'm fine!"

"You're going to get lost."

"Not if I stay on the path."

"There's more than one path out here. Low! Seriously. *Stop.*"

I kept going.

I walked for a long time. Five, ten minutes, maybe. I couldn't be sure. The trail meandered gradually uphill. I grew winded and worked up a little sweat.

It was surprisingly dark under the trees, considering how bright the evening sky was overhead. The moss was so very green, and the tree trunks looked purple. I felt like I was watching a CGI movie of my life.

It's dissociation, I told myself, remembering something I'd learned in an undergrad psychology course. *You're traumatized from seeing your husband cuddling another woman's baby. Your brain is trying to buffer the pain.*

Except, the problem wasn't only what I'd seen. It was also that Gregor and Kirsten seemed to know each other far better than he'd led me to believe.

I heard the snap of a stick, and I wheeled around.

Motion down the path.

Fear zinged through me.

Then I saw it was Gregor. He must've been following me the whole time.

"Hey," he called.

"I don't want to talk to you right now," I called back.

"Fine. Let's just, you know, walk together. I won't say a word."

I turned and kept going. The path here was almost swallowed up by a patch of knee-high plants on straight stalks.

"Oh shit," Gregor called. "Low! Not there! That's—"

I stopped, conscious of how the plants were brushing my flip-flopped feet and bare ankles. Two seconds later, I felt a feverish, crawling, numb-yet-not-numb stinging where the plants had touched me.

"What is this?" I called to Gregor with a whimper.

"Nettles," he called back. "Get out of there!"

I waded forward on the path, my ankles and feet getting another thorough licking. My skin screamed.

Gregor reached my side. He was out of breath. "Low. Babe. I love you, but you're killing me."

"Oh my God," I said, bending and rubbing my ankles. "What should I do? It feels like I have a million tiny hooks in my skin, but I don't see—"

"There's nothing to see. It's going to take hours for it to stop."

"Hours?"

"Why are you wearing flip-flops?"

"I'm sorry, but I wasn't planning on a wilderness trek. Let's—wait. What are you doing?"

Gregor was ripping at some plants. He waved a handful of leaves at me. "These'll help."

"Ferns?"

"Yeah. See the little yellow bumps on the underside of the leaves? If you rub those on the places you got nettled, it takes the edge off. Okay?"

I thought this sounded crazy, but I was also feeling desperate, so I said okay.

He crouched beside me. The feel of his hot, steadying hand on my waist was oddly unfamiliar, and I stiffened.

"Where'd you learn this?" I asked as he rubbed. The ferns felt scratchy.

"Here on the island. When I was a kid."

As I stood there, Gregor rubbing the ferns all over my feet and ankles, I noticed how close we were to the edge of a ravine.

It was abrupt and deep—at least as deep as a two-story house, I guessed—filled with rampant undergrowth and mossy fallen branches and shadow. And the edge was only about a foot away from where I was standing.

"Why does the path just *stop* here?" I asked Gregor.

"What?"

"The path. It goes through these nettles, and then it just stops."

"Maybe it's a lookout point?"

"For what?"

"How would I know?" He sounded exasperated. "Bird-watching?"

I shifted my weight. I lost my balance and stumbled. I felt the soft earth slump under me. I snatched at some bushes, and thorns bit into my palms.

Gregor grabbed me around my knees to steady me. This only made me fall sideways. My hip smashed into a fallen log with a crack. White-bright pain burst up my side—and then I was rolling downhill.

"Low!" Gregor shouted above me.

Whipping branches. My body tossing like a rag doll in a washing machine. The reversal of up and down and down and up and a thousand points of brilliant pain. My glasses got knocked off. Something hard and sharp slashed my skull. I kept tumbling down—down—down—

I slammed to a stop.

Whimpering, I floundered to my feet. My head throbbed, and something warm trickled into my eye.

I opened my mouth, to cry out or to call for Gregor, but the impulse shriveled in my throat because I'd noticed the thing on the ground.

A head.

A *human* head.

It was blurry because I'd lost my glasses, and the light wasn't great down there. But I *saw* it.

Cheek down. I could make out the profile. The black pit of an eye socket. Long hair straggling over grayish scalp and collapsed cheek. An ear—small, rounded, a *girl's* ear—clogged with dirt—

No, I thought. *I'm not seeing this. How could I be seeing this?*

—and a hacked stump of a neck. A jagged rim of leathery flesh. A slice of yellow-gray vertebrae—

—and the smell. *Oh my God—*

My stomach lurched.

—sweet-sour. Rotten meat and wet mulch.

Then Gregor was beside me. When he spoke, it was hard to hear him through the waterfall surging in my ears.

"Oh shit," he was saying. "Low. Are you okay?"

At last, I was able to tear my eyes away from the head. I looked at Gregor. He, too, was a blur. I swallowed against my dry throat and whispered, "It's a . . . I think it's a head?"

"Low. You're bleeding. This isn't . . ."

"Where's the rest of her?" My voice sounded far away. "Gregor, where's the rest of her?"

His fingers were clamping around my upper arm, turning me. "We have to get out of here. Now."

"But where's the rest of her?"

"Low. You're bleeding. We need to get out of here."

I reached up to touch my head, where the pain was concentrated and from which the wet warmth was trickling, and Gregor shouted, "No!"

"What? Why?"

"You don't want it to get infected. Here—" He stripped off his T-shirt so he was bare chested. His skin seemed to glow in the half-light. He balled up the shirt and pressed it against the crown of my head. "Hold it there. Take my hand."

I took his hand. I couldn't remember why I'd been so desperate to get away from him before. Something about that girl. Kirsten. Something stupid. Something that didn't matter.

We worked our way slowly up the side of the ravine. We didn't go straight up but took a zigzag path, picking our way over fallen branches, pushing through clumps of ferns. I clung to Gregor's hand so hard that I was surprised he didn't complain.

"You're lucky you didn't break your neck," he said as he helped me navigate a rotting log, "falling like that. Jesus."

I may not have broken my neck, but I was battered and bruised and, by the time we reached the top, completely freaked out.

Because *that head*—it had been real. Hadn't it?

If it *had* been real, why wasn't Gregor talking about it?

We stopped, and Gregor wrapped his arms around me and held me tight, and I tried not to cry.

"Did you see it?" I mumbled against his hot, bare chest. "That . . . that *thing*?"

"Don't try to talk, Low. Let's just concentrate on getting back."

"But I saw a—"

"It's okay," he whispered, holding me even tighter. "You didn't see anything, okay?"

20

When Gregor and I emerged from the woods at the Blakeley homestead, it was dusk. The windows of the little house glowed, and I smelled woodsmoke.

Kirsten met us on the kitchen porch. "Oh my gosh, what *happened*, you guys?"

I thought her gaze raked over Gregor's bare chest before she looked at me. But maybe I only imagined that. It wasn't like I could see clearly without my glasses.

"Harlow," she gasped. She'd seen the blood then.

"I'm okay," I said. "We just need to get home." I adjusted my grip on the balled-up T-shirt I was pressing to my head. "We need to call the police."

"The *police*? But what happened?"

"She fell," Gregor said. "She must've cut her head on a rock or a branch or something."

"There's . . . something out there," I said. A smeary image, rot-gray and bone-yellow, flashed in my mind's eye. "It might be a . . . a dead person. Or their head."

"A head?" Kirsten frowned, looking between Gregor and me.

"Yeah," I said.

"Are you sure?"

"Hold on—I didn't see anything like that," Gregor said, interrupting me. "A *head*? Like, a *human head*? Babe. You're kind of shook up right now. I don't think you're remembering things right."

I frowned at him, confused. I couldn't see his face well enough to read his expression.

"I think I have an explanation," Kirsten said. "Harlow? There's something I need to tell you. Um . . . you know that tea I served you earlier?"

I thought of the bitter, dirt-colored brew I'd forced myself to drink. "Yes."

"Well, I thought it was my pennyroyal fertility blend, but when I was cleaning up the kitchen just now, I realized that I mixed it up with . . . a different tea. It was . . . well, to be honest, it was mushroom tea."

"Mushroom tea," I repeated.

"Yeah. Psilocybin?" Her voice quavered on the last syllable.

Was she trying not to *laugh*?

"It's totally pure," she said. "I foraged it myself."

"Magic mushroom tea," I said flatly.

"Oh boy," Gregor said on a chuckle.

"It's not funny," I said. "I'm trying to conceive. I'm—" I'd been about to say, *I'm in the two-week wait*, but that was none of Kirsten's business. I turned to her. "Why would you give me that?"

"It was an accident," she said. "I'm *so* sorry, Harlow. If it's any consolation, I actually think it boosts fertility because I used it before I conceived all of my children. But"—she tipped her head—"it *is* strong enough to sort of help you see alternate versions of reality? Like, you know . . . dead things that aren't really there?"

Kirsten waited—holding her breath, it seemed—for me to respond. I felt cornered.

"I really need to go home," I said to Gregor.

"I'll go and grab Sam," Kirsten said. She left Gregor and me alone on the porch.

"I *saw* something," I whispered to Gregor. "I'm pretty sure. We need to call the police and—"

"If you drank mushroom tea, then I hate to say it, but you're high." Gregor was smiling. "Lean into it, babe. Enjoy."

"Enjoy?" I gave my head a shake and then winced as pain exploded across my scalp. I squeezed my eyes shut. "Gregor. It was awful, like a . . . a Halloween mask or a—"

"You lost your glasses. You—"

"I saw something. Why didn't *you* see anything?"

"Uh, because it wasn't there?"

Confusion rocked through me. Now I wasn't sure of anything. Maybe it had only been a rock, or a piece of wood. I *was* feeling kind of woozy.

"Even if there wasn't a head," I whispered, "how can Kirsten be so sure about it? How could she—"

"Stop," Gregor said loudly.

My breath caught. He'd never raised his voice at me before.

More quietly he said, "Stop it, okay? I know what's going on here."

"Really? Because I sure as heck don't."

"You have a problem with Kirsten—"

"Excuse me?"

"—and I get it."

"You do?"

"But you need to be a grown-up, Low. You can't let your feelings make you see a different person from who she really is. Because she's really just, I don't know, *sweet*."

I stared at him, lit harshly from above by the porch light. His eye sockets were sunk in shadow, and that, combined with my blurred vision and his bare and blood-smeared chest, made him look like a wild man, a man from another time and place.

It made him look exactly how he had that first night by the swimming pool.

But then he lifted his hand and tenderly stroked my jaw, and all that was swept away. It was just Gregor. My husband.

The one I loved.

Inside the house, voices and footsteps grew closer, and then Kirsten appeared with Sam.

"Take care, you guys," Kirsten said, waving as Gregor, Sam, and I set off on foot for home. "Be safe!"

"Have a great night!" Gregor called to her over his shoulder. Then he laced his hand in mine and said to me, "I actually think the two of you could be really good friends. Maybe when you're a mother, too."

In that instant, I realized that I didn't like Kirsten Blakeley very much. No, I take that back; I *hated* her.

21

A blade of sunlight pried my eyes open.

I scrunched them shut again. I longed to go back to sleep, but nausea slopped over me. I pushed off the duvet, careened to the bathroom, and threw up.

As I hunched over the toilet, retching, dream-memories flitted through my mind, too quick for me to pin down. Images like emotions, and emotions I could almost see.

And there was something else, too, lurking within the folds of my memory—what was it? Something unspeakable.

Something I didn't *want* to remember—

I retched some more.

When I was finally empty, I sank to the cold tile floor.

I was sweating and feeble, and God, why did my head hurt so much? It was like I'd gone on a bender the previous night. But of course, I hadn't drunk any alcohol. All I'd ingested was the dinner Emilia had made, roasted chicken and vegetables, brought to me on a tray by Gregor.

"You need to rest, babe," he'd said as he pushed me gently back against the bed pillows. "When I saw you falling, when you landed at the bottom of that slope and you didn't move for a second, I thought . . ." His voice thickened.

He'd tucked the duvet over me and inspected my cleaned-up scalp wound. Though bloody, it turned out to be minor, no stitches required.

"I can't lose you, Low," he'd murmured. "I need you more than you can possibly understand."

I cupped his face in my hand and gazed up at him, and as our eyes met, and then our lips, I thought of Kirsten.

She was like the splinter of glass I'd once stepped on by accident. At first, it had been invisible. But then infection had set in.

So, no, I hadn't drunk any alcohol last night. What was wrong with me, then? Why did my brain refuse to sit still? Why were my hands shaking?

Wait. Was it . . . could it be early pregnancy?

I felt a swing of hope. The vomiting. The general ickiness. Those could be early pregnancy symptoms.

Another surge of nausea launched me back over the toilet bowl.

And then, I remembered.

The head.

Cheek down, matted hair, stump of neck, a slice of yellowed vertebrae—

Footsteps behind me.

"Oh, babe . . ." someone murmured.

It was Gregor, crouching beside me. His hand found the back of my neck. I flinched—then leaned into him.

"Oh my God," I whispered. "Gregor—there was a *head.*"

"No." He curled his arm around me and kissed my tangled hair. "You just had a really bad trip."

"You don't understand. I saw it. I *saw* it. It was real."

"You hit your head. You lost your glasses. You were—"

"But I remember it. The *smell*, Gregor. The *hair*—" My voice broke. "We have to call the police. What if someone's really down there? What if—"

"Shhh." He held me tighter. "I *did* call the police. Just to be safe. Right after I got you cleaned up and tucked in last night."

"You did?"

"They sent someone out this morning to check the ravine. They didn't find anything. Only some rotting animal remains."

"Were they sure it wasn't—"

"It was a deer. Guaranteed not human. They took pictures. Want to see?"

"Ugh. *No.*" I closed my eyes, going limp. I wanted to sink into his calm certainty.

"I took Sam to school," he added, rubbing slow circles on my back. "You were sleeping so deeply. I didn't want to wake you."

I nodded against his shoulder. "What time is it?"

"Almost noon."

"Seriously?"

"You needed the sleep."

I swallowed. My mouth tasted of bile. "So I . . . I was actually high? Kirsten wasn't lying?"

Gregor huffed a soft laugh. "I'm *so* sorry, babe. And I can't say I'm totally surprised she screwed up like that in that weird little hobbit kitchen of hers. Does anything in there even have a label? But hey—congrats on your first trip. You did it in style."

"It seemed so *real*," I whispered.

"Well, it wasn't. And it's over now. Everything's okay. You're safe."

Gregor had to leave for rehearsal at the Blakeleys'. But I wanted to cling to him, to be held, to be reassured. I didn't want to be alone with my thoughts.

He said it could take a full day for the last traces of the psilocybin to work through my system. "You might have a few wacky moments," he said as he kissed me goodbye, "but I promise they'll pass."

I showered, washing my hair carefully. The wound in my scalp stung like crazy, but it didn't start bleeding again.

After I got out of the shower, I parted my hair on the side to cover the wound. There wasn't any good way to bandage it, but I figured it would heal faster uncovered, anyway.

I put on SPF moisturizer, tinted lip balm, and mascara. I pushed on my backup pair of glasses—the other pair was still out there in the ravine somewhere. I dressed in leggings and a T-shirt.

Downstairs, the house was silent and immaculate. Emilia had come and gone. The emptiness ballooned around me.

It's just the mushroom hangover, I told myself. *It's warping my perception.*

Coffee—that's what I needed. Industrial-strength, mind-clearing coffee.

The ticking of the grandfather clock in the entry hall seemed to grow louder and faster.

I needed to get out of there.

I put on sneakers and a lightweight puffer jacket. I grabbed my bag and the Mercedes keys and headed out.

At the coffee shop, I ordered a twelve-ounce triple-shot almond-milk latte. The pregnant barista with the tattoos wasn't there. For some reason that was a relief.

I took my coffee and settled into a table in a dark corner.

I texted Audrey and waited a few minutes, but she didn't text back. Which made sense. In Iowa it was school pickup time. For the next few hours, she'd be driving her Toyota Highlander all over town, to athletic fields and the dance studio and the Hy-Vee supermarket.

I texted Phoebe, and then Owen, too, but I knew it would be hours before I heard back from them, and then it would only be something quick and witty. I was already starting to feel very far away from New York and my life there.

Anyway, I wasn't sure if I *wanted* to tell any of them about Kirsten and Gregor and the mushroom tea and the horrible thing I hallucinated. When I imagined describing it, I sounded unhinged.

I connected my phone to the coffee shop's Wi-Fi. I popped in my earbuds and tapped open my Instagram app.

I typed *IntoTheWoodsWeGo*.

22

The latest on IntoTheWoodsWeGo: a serene Kirsten holding a wooden tray with a steaming mug of coffee, a milk pitcher, and a folded linen napkin. The caption read

> **Coffee just the way my husband likes it—hot and fresh. The world tries to tell me it's wrong to serve my husband, but I believe it is only in service that we can understand the true meaning of Love. To bring offerings, to make sacrifices—these are their own love language, one that is ancient, powerful, and deep. Patriarchy is a "bad word" these days but it means "the rule of the father" and what is so wrong about a family having a leader? When I look around me, I can see all the evidence I need that my offerings and sacrifices to the father of MY family are paying dividends. #traditionalfamily #foreverlove #blessed**

I'd already spent hours scrolling through Kirsten's account. Her posts told a story, about loveliness and simplicity and family. It said that the past was better. Purer. More whole. That women could re-create that lost world by pickling wax beans and letting their kids run wild in the misty trees. I'd come away from those scrolling sessions with a wistful craving.

Today, though, it all looked different.

Wasn't there actually something sinister about her photo filter, which seemed to be hiding something behind its bleached-out glare?

Wasn't there something aggressive in the way she spoke to the camera as she mixed batter with a wooden spoon, with a caption that read **WAY too busy to be a feminist LOL #madefromscratch #happyfamily #tradwife #blessed.**

I felt like I was missing something just below the surface, or past the margins, or in the negative space. Something slippery. Something threatening.

Or—was this just jealousy I was feeling? Sour, paranoid, raw?

I dropped down into the comments. It was mostly exclamation points and hearts and comments to the tune of **You're so amazing and I wish I could be more like you.**

Sure, if you looked hard you could find the odd troll: eye-roll emojis and **Ew do you even KNOW what's in raw milk?** and **You're not a true Christian you're a witch—find God and repent** and **Wait are you a nazi? they were nature worshipper blond baby farmers too ya know.**

But Kirsten didn't engage with any of it, which honestly seemed pretty classy. Aside from what she wrote in her captions, she didn't comment at all. In fact, even though she had a bajillion followers, she wasn't following any other accounts.

This isn't healthy, I thought. I closed Instagram.

The second I did, the image of the head—clinging hair, a dirty ear—reared up in my mind's eye, so sudden that I gasped.

The two older ladies at the next table glanced over at me.

My palms were starting to sweat, and my lungs felt too small.

Seriously. How could I have hallucinated something so grisly? So graphic? It was messed up.

I opened the web browser on my phone and googled *how long do psilocybin mushrooms take to work?*

I scoured the hits. It sounded like mushrooms would typically start kicking in around thirty to sixty minutes after ingestion. The effects would peak in two to four hours, and the trip would last a total of about six hours.

Okay, that tracks, I thought. *I was in that ravine maybe an hour after I'd drunk the tea.*

I hadn't *felt* high, but then, I'd never had mushrooms before, or any drugs except for a couple puffs of a joint one time in college.

I drummed my fingers against the paper coffee cup. My heart was banging in my throat.

I'm not doing it, I told myself. *I'm not going to be that person—the one getting lost in internet mazes.*

Gregor said the police checked the ravine. There was nothing there but a dead deer.

Still, my thumb hovered over the search bar.

Just once, I told myself. *Just to rule it out. Then I'll let it go.*

Feeling reckless and a little bit ashamed, I thumbed in the name of the island and *missing persons.*

Even that felt weird. I was pretty sure I'd never written *missing persons* in my life.

The little blue line crept across the screen—the coffee shop's Wi-Fi sucked.

I sipped my coffee, forcing the lukewarm liquid down even though it made my stomach clench.

Search results:

- King County Missing Persons Database.
- Washington State Patrol—Missing Persons List.
- Community Forum: Lost Pets.
- Last year's viral case of the Seattle college student who went missing—found safe in Oregon two days later.

I clicked through the database and the list. Nothing about anyone gone missing on the island.

A shaky breath rattled out of me.

Okay. Good. This is good.

Except—

Except it wasn't a definitive answer, was it? Bodies could be moved. Dumped. Especially on an island with endless trails and coves and forgotten hollows.

I sat back, pressing the heels of my hands against my eyes.

The police checked. They didn't find a body. Gregor said so.

"You okay, hon?" someone said.

I looked up.

One of the ladies at the next table was watching me, a gentle crease between her eyebrows.

I pasted on a smile.

"Yeah," I said. "Just . . . a long night."

She nodded in sympathy and went back to conversation with her friend.

I curled my hands around my coffee cup, trying to absorb the last of its warmth.

Get a grip, I told myself. Yes, people disappear every day. Horrible yet true. But the odds that I really saw a chopped-off head in the woods—while also tripping on shrooms?

Slim to none.

I rolled into the KinderWild parking lot a little before three o'clock and joined the moms walking into the shade of the forest.

The air was thick with the smell of crushed fir needles and sun-warmed dirt.

I was relieved that I didn't see Kirsten anywhere. It felt like my unhealthy little obsession with her Instagram must be written all over my face.

Sam was sitting alone on a log in the Gathering Place, slumped under the bulk of his backpack. His hair was messy, his cheeks flushed.

"Hey," I said, crouching beside him. "How are you doing, sweetie?"

He shrugged.

"Are you ready to go?"

He nodded, not meeting my eyes.

I peeled his backpack straps from his shoulders. "I'll carry this," I said.

He got to his feet, and we started back toward the parking lot, following a straggling line of women and kids.

The trail twisted under the towering firs. A little boy up ahead jabbed at the packed dirt with a stick like a blind man feeling his way. Two girls, maybe six or seven years old, walked behind him, chattering in high, lilting kid voices that sliced the air.

"New Gilda's better," one of them said.

"Nuh-*uh*," the other replied. "Old Gilda was the best one. She let us paint the pine cones with blackberry paint—"

"No, she didn't. That was New Gilda! And we made acorn necklaces."

"New Gilda doesn't even know all the songs."

"Does too."

"Does not."

"My mama says Old Gilda ran away 'cause she's bad," the first girl said, singsong, almost taunting. "My mama said she ruined everything."

"*No.* They can't run away. And they *have* to be good."

They skipped ahead.

I frowned, glancing down at Sam, who was plodding beside me, eyes on the ground.

New Gilda? Old Gilda?

Gilda was the pale, sad-eyed teaching intern who always seemed to be hovering at the edges of things. Kirsten had also mentioned that Gilda helped with her Instagram photography.

But maybe . . . maybe there had been another Gilda before this one?

If so, it was a strange coincidence. It wasn't exactly a common name.

When we reached the car, I helped Sam buckle into his booster. I tossed his backpack onto the passenger-side floor and got behind the wheel.

"Hey Sam?" I said as I started the ignition.

"Yeah?" He was staring out the window, thumb hovering near his mouth.

"At school . . . is there more than one Gilda?"

He gave me a confused look. "No. Just one."

I didn't push it. But as I drove back toward Himmel Cottage, unease chewed at the edges of my mind.

Gilda went away.

They have to be good.

It was probably nothing. Just little kids' babble.

About half an hour later, when Sam and I were back at Himmel Cottage and playing catch with a softball and mitts on the lawn, my phone buzzed. I pulled it out of my jacket pocket to see a new text message from an unfamiliar number:

Hey, it's Kirsten—got your number from Gregor. I didn't have a chance to ask you if you and Sam would like to come over after school tomorrow, or maybe Monday?

Is she out of her mind? I thought. *She serves me psychotropic tea and thinks I'd want to go back for a refill? Even if it* was *an accident.*

I didn't reply to the text.

23

Autumn dusk had wrapped itself around Himmel Cottage in misty gray layers.

Inside, the kitchen was warm and golden under the hanging pendant lights. Take-out pizza boxes were stacked neatly on the counter, plastic salad tubs balanced on top.

Sam had had his fill of plain cheese slices, and now he was curled up in the den with *PAW Patrol* blaring, and Gregor and I moved around the kitchen, loading the dishwasher in comfortable, tired rhythm.

Gregor hummed snatches of a song under his breath, the same one he'd been humming off and on since we'd sat down to eat. It had that yearning, bittersweet feel he did so well.

At one point, he broke into actual words, singing softly into my ear as he bumped my hip with his.

"You're in a good mood," I said, smiling in spite of myself.

He kissed my temple. "It was a good day. Magic in the barn. I think this album's going to be something really special." He rinsed a plate and slid it into the dishwasher. "Oh, and I booked you a spa day for tomorrow," he added. "While Sam's at KinderWild. Full package—massage, facial, pedicure—the whole deal. Mother says this place is amazing."

I blinked. "It's on the island?"

"Yeah. On the west side."

"Honey, you didn't have to—"

He shrugged, grinning. "You deserve it. After everything."

Warmth flooded my chest. He was smoothing down the edges of me. Wrapping me up in soft, safe things.

He glanced over at me. "You're feeling better, right? Coming down off your wild ride?"

"Yeah." My voice was bright. "Totally fine."

I added inwardly, *Aside from the fact that I see a rotten decapitated human head behind my eyelids every time I blink, I'm amazing.*

But none of that was Gregor's fault. It wouldn't be fair to take it out on him.

We worked for a minute in silence, the clink of plates and the whoosh of the faucet the only sounds between us.

Finally, when Sam let out a whoop at something happening on-screen, I said, keeping my voice casual, "Hey . . . I overheard something weird when I was picking up Sam."

Gregor loaded another plate. "Yeah?"

"Some of the kids were talking about 'Old Gilda' and 'New Gilda.' Like there used to be another one? It was strange. They said—" I hesitated. "They said the old one 'ran away because she was bad.' And then another kid said, 'No, they *have* to be good.' Isn't that kind of—"

"Low." Gregor laughed, wiping his hands on a dish towel. "You can't take what preschoolers say seriously. You know that, right?"

"Of course, but—"

"Seriously. They're little kids. Do you think I believed it when Sam went through his monsters-under-the-bed phase last year?"

I pressed my lips together. It wasn't the same. Was it? Gilda was an actual person, not some figment of a child's imagination.

"And anyway," Gregor went on, slinging an arm around me, "you're not going to have to think about any of that tomorrow. Nothing but massages, seaweed wraps, and bliss. Oh, and that tacky spa music they always pipe into those places." He squeezed my shoulders. "You deserve a break. It's been a hectic month."

I wanted to melt for him. I wanted to forget, to move on. But the words kept itching at the back of my throat.

"I just feel like there might be—"

He kissed my forehead. "Let it go."

Maybe he was right. Maybe I *was* reading too much into what the kids had said.

"Okay," I said. "Thank you. For the spa day. That's so thoughtful of you."

I grabbed the clean, empty salad bowl to put away and went to the walk-in pantry.

The old door creaked when I pulled it open. Inside, the shelves were spotless. Rows of glass jars, canned goods, boxes of crackers and cereal, extra paper towels.

I scanned for a place to stick the salad bowl.

Tea. Flour. Pasta. Extra dishes. Serving ware. Ah—there was a good spot for the bowl. I stood on tiptoe—

And something caught my eye.

A scrap of wallpaper, curling up at the edge, where the built-in upper cabinets met the wall.

I placed the bowl on the shelf and stepped closer to the wall.

There—barely peeking out from the flap of faded floral—was a word in pencil:

Mama.

My heart gave a little lurch.

I hooked a fingertip under the peeling paper and gently pulled it back, feeling like I was picking off a scab.

Underneath, on the old plaster, someone had scrawled a message. The pencil lines were faded and smudged, but I could still make out:

I miss Mama. They say I'm crazy. Crazy Bessie. Nobody believes me, and so I'm all alone here in—

The sentence vanished where the cabinet had been bolted over it, like someone had deliberately sealed it away.

I stood there for a long moment, trying to picture who had written this, and when. A woman, or a girl. *Crazy Bessie.* It had been a long time ago, I assumed, since the wallpaper was yellowed with age and the penciled sentence vanished under the antique cabinetry.

Nobody believes me. I'm all alone.

"Yeah," I murmured, pressing the curl of wallpaper firmly back over the words. "You and me both, Bessie."

I'm not saying my spa day wasn't relaxing.

I mean, I *tried* to relax, anyway.

Gregor had been so sweet to book it. And when I pulled up to the modern building of stone and glass tucked between firs and the gray curve of the coastline, I wanted to give myself over to it. I really did.

Especially after the way I woke up. Still gasping, a scream ringing in my ears.

A girl's head, half-sunk into the earth. Snarled hair. Collapsed cheek. Severed neck a mass of rot and bone—

Gregor had held me and stroked my hair until my breathing slowed. He reminded me I was still coming down from the shrooms. That bad dreams were part of it.

That none of it was real.

At the spa, they gave me a waffle-weave robe, rubber slides, and an earthenware cup of herbal tea. No phones allowed. No clocks. No sense of anything but the languid passage of fog and water and gulls outside the huge windows.

I drifted between the sauna and the soaking pools, between massages and facials, between muted conversations about collagen supplements and juice fasts. The other patrons barely spoke at all. They floated from treatment to treatment like sleepwalkers, wrapped in the ritual of it.

It should've been bliss.

But somewhere between the sea-salt scrub and the massage, I started to feel kind of . . . caged, I guess.

It wasn't just the no-phone rule, although that bugged me.

It wasn't just the pitying smiles on the staff's faces when I kept asking for the time.

It was that I wanted to be *out there*. Doing something. Not trapped in this cocoon of cedar oil and hot stones, my hands metaphorically tied behind my back.

This is good for me, I kept telling myself. *Quite obviously, I need this.*

24

I arrived six minutes late to KinderWild, makeup-free and with dripping wet hair from a hasty shower.

I found Sam standing at the edge of the Gathering Place. The other children were romping, their mothers chatting. The intern, Gilda, was loading what seemed to be stick sculptures into a wooden crate. I saw Teacher Terra talking earnestly with a woman named Gwen, who was the mom of twin boys. The twins were running around them in circles, shouting, but Gwen and Terra were serene.

When I said hi to Sam, I realized he looked like he'd been crying.

"What's wrong?" I asked, crouching so we were eye to eye.

"I hate this place."

"I know, sweetie. I know. Did . . . did something happen today?"

Sam's lower lip quivered. "They said I'm not one of God's children." He rubbed at his eye with a grubby fist.

"*What?* Who said that?"

"The other kids."

"Of . . . of *course* you're one of God's children," I said. I wondered if Gregor would approve of me saying that. He wasn't religious, but he didn't really have a philosophical stance about it. I wasn't religious, either, but I'd grown up in a place where God and grace and sin were part of everyday conversation. "But Sam," I said, "what does that even mean? Why did they say that to you? Is it because of . . ." I didn't finish, but anxiety was balling in my belly. *Is it because of your brown skin?* "Did you tell a teacher?"

"No."

I took his small hand in mine. "The teachers need to know about stuff like this," I said. "Saying that to you was wrong."

Now Terra was the only teacher in sight. Gilda had vanished. So even though Terra was still talking to Gwen, I led Sam over.

"Are you okay?" Gwen asked me, her eyes widening. She had a long, angular face and she wore a flowing green dress. The dress was smudged and speckled with a rainbow of paint, so I assumed she was an artist.

"What? Yes. Of course. Why wouldn't I be?" I must've sounded bitchy, because Gwen and Terra exchanged a glance.

"I'm going to let you deal with this, Terra," Gwen whispered. She wafted away, calling for her twins as she went.

I turned to Terra. "Sam tells me some of the other kids were making unkind remarks today."

"Oh no," she said, frowning with concern.

"He said they told him he isn't one of God's children—"

"I'm going to stop you right there, Harlow," Terra said gently. "Here at KinderWild, we encourage children to be their own advocates."

I blinked. "What's that supposed to mean?"

"I'd like to hear these allegations directly from Sam."

Allegations? I thought. *What is this, a courtroom?*

Terra looked down at Sam. "Can you tell me what happened?"

Sam looked up at her with huge eyes, sucking his thumb.

"There's nothing I can do if he isn't going to talk," Terra said to me. Her tone remained placid. "I'm really sorry."

"He told me that some of the other kids said he isn't one of God's children," I repeated.

"If Sam doesn't say it to me in his own words, I can't do anything about it."

"How is that a thing?" I was starting to lose my temper.

"It's one of the core beliefs we hold here at KinderWild. Advocating for ourselves. Keeping our promises to ourselves. So maybe you should work on keeping the promises *you've* made, Harlow. For example, dropping off and picking up Sam on time? If he sees the adults around him keeping their promises, he's going to keep promises to himself, and that's the basis for self-esteem, right?"

"This isn't a self-esteem issue," I said. "It sounds like he's being bullied, so I—"

"Bullying *is* a self-esteem issue," Terra said softly. "And here you are speaking for Sam and fighting Sam's battles, so how is he going to build up that grit inside himself?"

"He's a little kid. The adults around him are responsible for his well-being."

"Okay, but doesn't that responsibility mean teaching him to stick up for himself?" Terra folded her arms, and I noticed how her fingernails were edged with dirt, and she had a dime-size, weeping red blister on the webbing between her thumb and forefinger.

Gross, I thought. I mean, she *did* work outside. But a Band-Aid would've been a good idea.

"We're going," I said. "But this isn't over, because it's unacceptable for the other kids to verbally bully Sam. Okay?"

Terra gave me a sad smile.

I squeezed Sam's hand and turned to go. But then I stopped and faced Terra again.

"One more thing," I said. "I overheard some of the kids talking about 'Old Gilda' and 'New Gilda.' It seems like a strange coincidence that both of your interns have the same name."

Terra was still smiling. "It's not a coincidence," she said. "That's what we call our interns here at KinderWild. We've found that the interns aren't the most reliable—young girls, you know—so after a little too much turnover, we decided to call them all Gilda."

"What?" I said. "Why?"

"For the children. So they don't get confused. So they have a sense of continuity and stability." Terra tipped her head. "Does that set your mind at ease, Harlow?"

No, actually, it didn't. I thought it sounded creepy as hell.

And I was also wondering, *What happened to the last Gilda? Could she have somehow wound up on the forest floor with her head severed from her body?*

But I wasn't willing to pursue any of that with Sam present. "Yeah," I said. "That makes sense."

"Good," Terra said. "Anything else?"

I wished I could've told Terra to take her bizarre New Age POV and stuff it.

I'll tell Gregor about this, I decided as we walked to the car. *He won't want Sam in such a toxic environment. We'll find another preschool. One with four walls and a roof. And Band-Aids.*

There were only two cars left in the misty parking lot: mine and a mud-streaked silver Prius. Gilda, in a long skirt and a sweater, was stacking crates into the Prius's trunk. From this distance, she looked insubstantial, almost ghostly.

I buckled Sam into the back seat of the Mercedes, brushing a smudge of dirt from his cheek. "Just a sec, sweetie," I said. "I need to ask someone a quick question."

He nodded, eyelids heavy. Poor little guy.

"Hey there," I called to Gilda as I approached.

She started and half turned, one hand still resting on a crate.

Drawing closer, I realized how young she was—maybe still a teenager. Her skin was pale and dewy, her brown hair pulled back in a thick braid. She was pretty in a wide-eyed, innocent way, and in spite of my spa day, I felt ancient.

Her startled expression melted into a smile. "How can I help you?" she said. Her voice was girlish.

"I, um . . ." I glanced toward the path. Terra hadn't emerged yet, but she probably would any second now. "I know all the interns here are called Gilda, but I was just wondering—what's your real name?"

Her brown eyes didn't blink. "I've rejected my old name," she said calmly. "It didn't serve me well."

"Oh. Okay. And . . . did you happen to know the last Gilda?"

Her smile didn't budge. "She was gone before I got here."

"When was that?"

"About three weeks ago."

"You've only been here three weeks?"

"Yeah. But it's—" She smiled even bigger and gazed up at the treetops. "It's *so* amazing. Don't you think?"

There was a flash of movement across the parking lot—Terra, emerging from the thicket, walking quickly toward us.

I looked back to Gilda. "Do you live here on the island?"

"Of course."

"Did you grow up here?"

A shadow across her face. A too-long hesitation. "No. But my life is here now."

Then it hit me: There were only two cars left in the parking lot, which meant Gilda and Terra were both going to leave in the Prius. "Do you live with Teacher Terra?" I asked.

"No. But she gives me a ride sometimes. I live at the Blakeley homestead."

"Wait—what? You live with the Blakeleys?"

"Yeah. Why?"

So that *had* been Gilda darting behind the outbuilding that day.

Then Terra was there, her shadow slicing between us like a knife.

"Gilda, do you need a hand?" she asked brightly, not looking at me.

"No, thank you," Gilda said.

"Okay." Terra smiled. "Have a blessed night, Harlow."

I nodded stiffly. "You, too."

25

Something wasn't right with the Two Gildas thing. And if there was even the slightest chance that it was linked to the head I may have seen in that ravine . . . well, I couldn't just do *nothing*.

I promised myself I was only ruling things out.

I texted Kirsten before Sam and I even left the KinderWild parking lot: Hey, sorry I forgot to reply to your last text, about getting the kiddos together again. Sam and I would love to! Maybe this afternoon if it's not too last-minute?

She responded when we were halfway home: Sounds great! Come on over.

I wondered if Terra had told her about our conversation. I wondered if Gilda would tell her anything.

◆ ◆ ◆

"I don't want to see Magni!" Sam shouted from the back seat, after I told him we were going to pay another visit to Kirsten and her kids.

I glanced at him in the rearview. His fists were clenched. His face was stormy.

"It's just for a little bit," I said.

"No!"

"Just a short visit, okay? Then we'll come straight home."

His lip trembled.

I swallowed. "Is . . . is Magni the one who said that thing to you?" I lowered my voice. "That you're not one of God's children?"

Sam shook his head, still scowling. "No. It was the girl with the two braids."

Relief hit me—and then the guilt followed right behind. What was I doing, dragging him to the Blakeleys' after the day he'd had?

"Listen," I said. "You don't have to talk to Magni. You can . . . you can pet the cat, remember the big black-and-white one? What was his name?"

Sam's expression shifted. "Loki."

"And there are the chickens," I added. "They're pretty fun."

Sam looked out the window for what felt like an eternity. Then, grudgingly: "I guess it's okay."

I felt like the worst person in the world.

When Sam and I got out of the car at the Blakeleys', I could hear the band in the barn. Gregor's voice threaded through a muffled drumbeat and twanging strings.

I felt a stab of guilt.

I'd promised Gregor I'd relax, decompress. And yet here I was, poking into something he clearly wanted me to leave alone.

So much for my spa day.

Kirsten answered the door with baby Barri on her hip. "Come in, come in!" she sang. "It's getting so foggy out there."

The house was cozy inside, lit by beeswax candles and a couple of low amber lamps. In the living room, Alder and Magni were clattering wooden animals across the floor. Sam paused in the doorway to watch them.

"All good?" I whispered to him.

He nodded.

In the kitchen, a pot of something fragrant bubbled on the stove. Something herbal—bay leaves, maybe?—but also meaty and greasy. It made my stomach turn.

Kirsten offered me tea.

Over my dead body, I thought.

"Sure!" I said. "Sounds perfect."

"Mama!" Magni said, bursting in from the living room. "Sam wants to see the chickens."

Kirsten laughed. "Go for it, my love. Oh, you can take them the carrot scraps."

Magni got a bowl of carrot tops and peelings from beside the sink, and he and Sam went outside. Then Kirsten and I sat at the rustic table with music leaking in through the closed windows, muffled and lonely.

"So," she said brightly, pouring hot water into mismatched ceramic mugs, "feeling better after your little adventure the other night?"

I forced a laugh. "Oh God. Don't remind me."

"I felt *so* bad that I mixed up the jars. You're not mad, are you?"

"Of course not." I shook my head. "It was . . . intense, though. And embarrassing."

"Well, you seem great now."

Do I? I thought. I felt like I was about to jump out of my skin.

"Uh-oh," Kirsten said. "I think I need to go and change Barri's diaper—back in a second." She carried her baby away, leaving me alone in the kitchen.

The first thing I did was dump my tea down the drain. It had the same dirt-and-twigs smell as the last time.

Then Alder padded in to grab something off the kitchen floor. He wore thick wool socks and a red turtleneck, his pale hair curling at the back of his neck.

I glanced at the doorway. No sign of Kirsten. I was pretty sure she'd gone upstairs. "Hey Alder," I whispered, feeling guilty, feeling like a weirdo. "Do you know where Gilda sleeps?"

He didn't look up. "She sleeps with the goats."

I blinked. "What?"

"In the goat house," he said matter-of-factly, and carried away his prize—a chunky green beeswax crayon.

The goat house? I thought in disbelief.

By the time Kirsten reappeared with Barri, I had a plan.

"More tea?" she asked.

"Please." I held out my empty cup.

I waited maybe four minutes before making my move. I needed to act natural, but I was also aware that Gilda could be pulling up any second in Terra's Prius.

"I think I left my water bottle in the car," I said to Kirsten. "It's my electrolyte drink. Be right back."

Outside, the mist was thicker now, creeping from the corners of the clearing. The barn loomed dark, music still filtering through its planks. Beyond it, tucked low along the edge of the clearing next to the deer-fenced garden and the chicken coop, was a shed.

That had to be it. The only other outbuilding seemed too small to hold more than gardening equipment.

It was the shed Gilda had disappeared behind the other day.

I heard a childish shout, and then laughter. I could see the shadowy forms of Sam and Magni over by the chicken enclosure.

I crossed the yard quickly, sneakers squishing on damp grass.

The shed had a plank door fastened with a catch. I opened it and slipped inside.

It was dim, and rank with the sour tang of animals. Three goats blinked at me from a rough-hewn pen, their breath steaming faintly in the damp air. Straw covered the floor. A cracked bucket held vegetable scraps. A broom leaned in one corner.

But . . . the far stall was empty of livestock.

I crept closer.

Instead, there was a narrow wooden bunk, built crudely into the wall. A sad mattress sagged in the middle, covered by a wool blanket and a lumpy pillow. An unlit solar-powered lantern hung from a nail. A metal basin held a battered bar of soap. Folded clothes were stacked neatly at the foot of the bed.

I stepped closer, my shoes crunching faintly on the straw. I picked up the top garment—a pale-blue T-shirt—and turned it toward the dim window.

There, on the label, written in thick black Sharpie: L. Reed.

My pulse spiked. *Gilda's real name.* Well, part of her name. It *had* to be.

Hinges creaked behind me.

I spun around.

Kirsten stood in the open doorway of the shed, her hair frizzing slightly in the mist. Her silhouette was backlit by the yellow glow from the house.

"Hey," I said quickly. "I . . . I was just looking for Sam. I thought maybe he wandered in here?"

"Nope," she said. "He's back in the kitchen." Kirsten smiled, but it didn't reach her eyes.

26

The rest of that night passed in a blur.

I wanted to keep digging—comb through social media accounts, cross-reference every L. Reed who'd ever set foot in the Pacific Northwest. I wanted to know who New Gilda really was, because maybe that could lead me to Old Gilda.

And if I knew who Old Gilda was, I could confirm that she definitely wasn't dead and I definitely hadn't seen her severed head.

You know. Normal wife-and-stepmom stuff.

But Gregor was home and wanting together time. He opened fancy mineral water and lit candles and insisted on making dinner, and I couldn't exactly say, "Hey, mind if I disappear into a rabbit hole about the goat-shed-dwelling intern?"

So I smiled. I ate. Pretended I wasn't vibrating with the need to *do something*.

Once Sam was asleep, I brought up the bullying thing with Gregor. We were curled together under a plushy throw in the den, with a wood fire dying down to glowing orange and Ramblin' Jack Elliott on the sound system.

"Something happened today at KinderWild," I began carefully. I didn't want to smother the relaxed warmth between us. "Sam said some of the other kids were saying stuff to him. Saying he isn't one of God's—"

"I know what they said." Gregor pulled me a little more firmly into the crook of his arm. "Terra called, and we came up with a game plan for dealing with it."

I blinked at him in surprise. "You did?"

"Yeah." He leaned in close and tenderly kissed my mouth. "All dealt with. Now will you *please* stop finding things to stress about?"

Later, when Gregor was asleep, I crept into our en suite with my phone and typed into the search bar *L Reed Washington.*

The results were a mess.

Luke Reeds. Lauren Reeds. Leahs, Lindseys, Linuses. An eleven-year-old runaway boy in Bellingham. A Facebooking grandma in Tacoma. A male dentist in Spokane who posted homemade bread content under the handle @bread.by.reed.

Nothing useful.

What had felt like a golden clue in the dim goat shed now felt absurd. Pointless. Gilda's real name could be Lily Reed. Lena. Lucia. Or for all I knew, that T-shirt had been purchased at a thrift store with the Sharpie writing already on the tag.

I closed my phone, got back in bed, and lay on my side, staring at nothing.

Gregor breathed softly beside me.

Why would someone live in a goat shed if they had any other choice?

Why would the Blakeleys let her?

In the middle of the night, I woke up screaming. Heart racing, throat raw.

Gregor shot upright, grabbing my shoulder. "Low—hey—what is it?"

I couldn't speak. Couldn't breathe.

Because I'd seen it again.

The head.

Mired in mud. Lips shriveled like dead leaves. Neck stump crawling with movement—

I struggled upright in bed, then doubled over, trying desperately to pull in enough oxygen.

"It was just a bad dream," Gregor whispered, rocking me. "It's not real."

◆ ◆ ◆

Then it was Saturday night, the night of the party we were hosting for Gregor's bandmates and their significant others. Even though Emilia had spent the entire afternoon making platters of appetizers and setting up a bar on the kitchen island and putting wine to chill in the Sub-Zero, Gregor told me it wasn't a *party* party.

"It's more like a hang, I guess?" he said, pulling on a worn thermal Henley.

"A *hang*?" I looked dubiously down at the short black cocktail dress I'd wriggled into.

"Babe, this isn't New York. You aren't going to need to wear anything like that on this island, ever. I'm not saying it isn't sexy, but . . ."

I went over to Gregor and lifted my hair so he could unzip me. The fabric swished to the floor around my ankles.

"I'll change into jeans and a blouse," I said.

"Okay," he breathed against my spine, "but maybe not right this second?"

I shivered.

27

Gregor and I met one week after I'd decided to take a break from dating. People say that's how love happens: It sneaks up on you. I'd always thought this made love sound like a monster, but now I get what they mean.

In undergrad and in my doctorate program, I dated my fair share of fellow students, usually guys as serious about studying and grades as I was. I wasn't really in love with any of them, though, and my handful of relationships sort of fizzled out.

Once I finished grad school and landed my job at Memorial Sloan Kettering, I spent a few years not dating at all. I kept my head down and worked eighty-hour weeks so I'd be promoted.

I let up on the gas a tiny bit after my promotion to senior research associate—enough for me to notice I was turning thirty so if I wanted a family, I'd better get cracking.

I joined all the classier dating apps, the ones that promised relationships rather than hookups. I was relentless about swiping left on any and all shirtless photos, or photos with fancy cars, and even, after some trial and error, photos with dogs. While cute on the surface, I learned that guys with dog profile pics were manipulative. Sometimes it wasn't even their dog.

Even after all my careful screening, for years I was trapped in a cycle of seemingly nice guys ghosting or ditching me after only a handful of dates. I was getting desperate to fall in love, get married, have a family.

But everyone knows that even the faintest whiff of desperation makes men run.

I just want to have fun, one of the guys I'd made it to four dates with told me, *and this just isn't fun anymore.*

I'm not ready for the whole picket-fence-and-baby-stroller lifestyle. (Two dates.)

Can't we try taking it really slow and see where things end up? (Three dates.)

So, at the age of thirty-three, I was still single.

I decided on a six-month break from men. I was going to work on becoming more cunning. I was going to learn how to pretend I didn't give a damn. I was going to change from *needy* to *fun and sexy.*

I deleted all my dating apps.

Exactly one week later, I met Gregor.

I almost hadn't gone to the bar that night, a live music place in Brooklyn, but at the last minute I joined some work friends for a Friday evening out. *This band is amazing,* they told me. *Like if the Lumineers had never sold out—or maybe more like the Strumbellas? Or Noah Kahan? Super poetic and soulful, but catchy, too.*

Even though I don't believe in love at first sight, seeing Gregor for the first time was . . . *something* at first sight. He was onstage with Journey's End, singing and playing the guitar. The spotlight blazed down on him like sunshine, his eyes shadowed by the brim of a black fedora.

Later on, he told me the fedora was to keep the lights from blinding him, but that night I just thought it made him seem mysterious.

Music poured from his throat, deep and rough and plaintive. He was singing about swaying prairie grasses and lost love, and longing built inside my ribs with every syllable. I know it sounds crazy, but I truly felt like the song was about *me.*

When it ended and the crowd hooted and clapped, he looked out across the ocean of faces and met my eyes.

Time thickened.

Why me? I remember thinking. Out of all the beautiful, glamorous, captivating women in this place, why *me*?

When the band was on their break between sets, I was at the bar trying unsuccessfully to get a bartender's attention, and someone beside me said, "Hey."

I turned to see the man from the stage. "Oh," I said, confused. "Hey?" I had the comical urge to look over my shoulder to make sure he wasn't addressing someone else.

"I'm Gregor," he said. "I was just—" He made a vague gesture toward the empty stage.

"Yeah," I said. "I know."

He smiled, and it was so beautiful it literally made me dizzy. "On the off chance you don't have a significant other, could I buy you a drink?"

"What?" I was sure I'd misheard him.

"Sorry," he said, shaking his head. "You're taken. Of course you are."

"No," I said, too loudly. I swallowed, and said in a quieter voice, "No. I'm . . . I'd love a drink. That would be great."

How is this happening? I frantically wondered. *Look at him. He's gorgeous. He's cool. He's the preposterously talented lead singer in a band. And he wants to talk to* me*?*

None of it added up.

On our first date, I was so nervous that I knocked over not one but two glasses of water. After our second date, I went back home and cried because I knew I was falling in love, and I was sure it was hopeless. So on our third date—an afternoon walk through Central Park with the autumn trees starting to turn pink and gold—I said to Gregor that there was something I needed to tell him.

We stopped, and he studied my upturned face, inch by inch. "There's something I need to tell you, too," he said.

Here it is, I thought. *Here's the catch. He's going to say he's married. Or that he wants to "just have fun."*

"You go first," I said.

He shook his head, lips twitching. "That's not fair. You brought it up."

I took a deep breath, let it out. I peered past his shoulder, studying the progress of a pigeon on the ground. "Okay, well, I wanted to get something out there now, before we go on any more dates, because I've . . . in the past, I've been hurt. By men."

"I'm sorry," he said gently.

"Men get scared off by the fact that I want to get married and have a family. Not, like, right this second, but in the not-too-distant future. I think you're amazing, Gregor, which is actually why I'm putting this out there now. This is what I value: Family. Commitment. I know I'm just a cheesy Midwestern girl, and maybe it comes off as too—"

"Hey. I'm not those other guys, Harlow. I'm me. And, I mean, obviously we're still getting to know each other, but I want those things, too. A wife. A family. Stability."

Finally, I met his eyes again. They radiated kindness. "You do?"

"Yeah. I do."

"You don't think I sound, you know . . . desperate?"

"I think you're perfect."

"But you're in a band." I tried to say it jokingly.

"Yeah, I know, a lot of musicians are players. I probably used to be, too. But I'm . . . well, this ties into what I wanted to tell you. Harlow, I have a child."

I blinked. I hadn't been expecting that. "Oh. Okay. Are you . . . ?"

"His mom—my wife—died. Josephine. She . . . it was a skiing accident. I've been raising him alone. His name is Sam. He's almost four."

I was nodding, trying to process. I imagined a small boy who looked exactly like Gregor, with blond hair and blue eyes, and my heart swelled. Then, against my will, I imagined babies of my own who also looked like Gregor, golden and beautiful, and my heart felt like it would explode.

"Is it a problem?" Gregor asked, sounding a little bleak. "That I'm already a father?"

"No," I said. "No. I . . . I love kids."

He drew me close. "How did I get so lucky?"

That made no sense to me, because *I* was the lucky one.

28

There were four musicians involved in the album, and they were calling themselves the Settlers, like Gregor had dreamed up the other day. Gregor was on guitar and lead vocals, Ben Blakeley was on drums, Ruby Watts was on the fiddle and backup vocals, and Seth Bruzek was on banjo and keyboard.

At seven o'clock, Gregor turned up Johnny Cash on the speaker system, opened himself a beer, and fixed me a sparkling water with lime. Sam had been invited to hang out, too, but he'd chosen to stay in the den and binge cartoons.

Ruby arrived first, a glamorously made-up redhead in high-waisted black jeans and a black top. She'd brought her girlfriend, Anna, a thin young woman with a face like a *Game of Thrones* princess and a buzz cut.

"Hey," Ruby said, giving me a hug. "Harlow. It's *so* nice to finally meet you." She gave me a red-lipsticked grin. "Wow." She looked me up and down. "You are *not* what I was expecting."

"Ruby," Anna muttered.

"No, it's not—it's fine. You're lovely. It's just that when I toured with Gregor in the Sail Aways, he had this thing for girls with brown skin and—"

"You are *not* making it better," Anna interrupted. She gave me a sympathetic expression. "Sorry."

"No, it's okay," I said, feeling my face go hot. *Gregor likes girls with brown skin?* I thought. *Besides his first wife?* He'd never mentioned that. But then, why would he?

"Oh my God this *house*," Ruby said, lifting her arms and twirling across the entry hall. "We hung out here when we were rehearsing for that Sail Aways tour. We had *so* much fun. I mean, I *assume* we did because I can barely remember a thing." She gave a throaty laugh. "It's all so lumber-baron gothic I can barely stand it." She looked up at the ornate face of the grandfather clock. "Exactly how many sleeping pills do you have to take to fall asleep with *this* thing ticktocking away all night, Harlow?"

"Oh, I think I've gotten used to it," I said. "Hey, would you guys like a drink? Wine? A cocktail?" I led them toward the kitchen.

"Is there still that creepy painting of Gregor's great-grandpa hanging over his mom's bed? I swear to God, one time when I was doing mushrooms with my ex in this house, that dude stepped out of the painting and tried to *get with* us. And that, boys and girls, is why you're always supposed to do mushrooms in nature. You don't want the interior decor to start humping you."

"No one wants to hear about your exes, my love," Anna said tersely. She sent me an eye roll. "Musicians," she muttered. "Aren't they *such* a joy? You're a cancer researcher, right?"

"Yeah," I said.

"Very cool. I work at Amazon. Web design."

"Wow," I said. "That's so interesting."

"You don't need to lie. My job is boring as hell, but hey, it has benefits. I'll just have some of that vodka on the rocks." Anna was inspecting the several bottles of wine, liquor, bitters, and the dishes of lemons and olives that Emilia had set out. "Rubes? Want vodka?"

"Are you shitting me? *No.* Bourbon, please."

Seth Bruzek was the next to arrive, with his girlfriend Molly. Seth was an affable, husky guy wearing a *Star Wars* T-shirt under his denim trucker jacket. Molly was a pretty girl with sooty kohl, a push-up bra, and glassy, stoned eyes. I tried to make her feel comfortable until she pulled out her phone and started scrolling.

And then, the moment I'd been dreading: Kirsten and Ben arrived.

I got the door because Gregor was already deep in conversation with Seth. When I swung the door open, I barely caught Ben saying in a low voice "—go running your mouth again, sweetheart, so just—" at the same time Kirsten was snarling "—the police, you'd be *completely* up shit creek without a—"

They both fell silent when they saw me.

"Hey," I said brightly. But I was thinking, *Well, well, well. Do I detect a glitch in the tradwife matrix? And also: the* police*?*

"Hi." Kirsten switched on a smile.

Ben gave me a nod.

Anger crackled between them.

"Come in," I said with a smile as fake as Kirsten's.

Apparently, we were both going to pretend the whole goat shed thing never happened. Fine by me.

"It's *so* great you could make it." I opened the door wider and stepped aside. "Drink?" I led them to the kitchen.

"Whiskey," Ben said.

"Oh, none for me," Kirsten said, running her palm over her flat belly.

She's pregnant? I thought confusedly, furiously, as I went to the bar. *Again? How is that even fair?*

"Hey!" I heard Gregor say. "Buddy!"

I kept my back turned, pouring Ben's whiskey slowly and then meticulously wiping a droplet off the side with a napkin.

I didn't want to see when Gregor hugged Kirsten as he'd hugged each of the new arrivals. It wouldn't *mean* anything. But I still remembered what he'd looked like, gazing down at baby Barri in his arms. *She even has your dimple, Mama,* he'd said.

I knew it would still hurt.

◆ ◆ ◆

For the next hour or two, I made small talk with all the guests except Kirsten. I hoped she couldn't tell I was avoiding her.

I studiously refilled glasses and offered snacks and chatted and nodded, pretending to get it when people talked about chord progressions and cadences. I leaned into Gregor when he put his arm around me, and I laughed at Ruby's hilarious jokes and Seth's not-so-hilarious ones.

But then somehow, despite all my efforts, I found myself alone with Kirsten in the kitchen. I turned away from the refrigerator, from which I'd grabbed a fresh bottle of pinot grigio, and there she was, rearranging flowers in the crystal vase on the counter.

"Oh," I said, struggling to collect myself. "Hi. Are you . . . can I get you anything?" Against my will, my eyes snapped to her belly and back again. "Sparkling water?"

"I'm good, thanks," she said.

"I was half expecting you to bring your kids tonight," I said.

"Honestly? I almost did. It's *so* hard for me to be away from my nurslings. But Ben said I need some time away from being a mama. Gilda is babysitting."

Our eyes met.

"The boys *adore* her," Kirsten said. "And she's so eager to help."

I was the first to look away. "And . . . you're expecting again?" Damn. I hadn't meant to say that.

"Yeah. A *total* surprise—we weren't even trying."

"Must be nice," I said before I could stop myself.

"I'm sorry. I shouldn't have . . . I mean, I know it's been hard for you. I actually—"

"Hey, you know what?" I cut in. "I need to go and check on Sam."

29

The nerve of Kirsten, I fumed to myself as I went to the den. *Commenting on my fertility struggles? She has no idea what she's even talking about.*

In the den, cartoons were flickering, and Sam was asleep on the sectional. I turned off the TV, draped a throw blanket over him, and tiptoed out.

I went upstairs to use the bathroom, to check my makeup, and to make sure the scabby wound on my scalp was still disguised by my hairstyle. By the time I arrived downstairs again, everyone had gone outside.

The long covered porch was softly lit by string lights. A cold breeze rustled up off the harbor.

Kirsten sat in one of the rattan armchairs, wrapped in a blanket. Gregor on one side of her, Ben and Seth on the other. She was saying something in her lilting, girlish voice, gesturing with her hands, and Gregor and Seth had their faces turned toward her, rapt. Ben was glowering out over the dark water, sipping his drink.

If Gregor noticed my return, he gave no sign of it.

Ruby, Anna, and Molly were way down at the other end of the porch. Ruby was on her knees in front of the chiminea, trying to get it lighted.

I went over to the women. No way in hell was I joining the Kirsten fan club.

I settled into a chair near the chiminea, which was belching smoke. "Everyone good on drinks?" I asked.

Molly didn't look up from her phone.

"We're *wonderful*," Anna said. She lifted the bottle of bourbon balanced on the porch railing and gave it a sloshing shake.

"Yes," Ruby said. "Assuming we manage not to burn down your ancestral mansion." She was slurring slightly. "I used lighter fluid. Is that bad?"

"No idea," I said.

"Jesus Christ," Molly said in her low, rough voice.

Anna, Ruby, and I looked at her, astonished. She'd said so little all evening.

She was glaring at Kirsten and the men. "Seth is such an asshole." Without moving her gaze, she stuck a cigarette between her lips.

Seth was leaning into Kirsten, laughing as he said, "Stop torturing us like that!" and Kirsten placed her hand on his arm.

"Oh," Ruby said. "Yeah. Our lovely local crypto-fascist tradwife. Men can't tell what she is. Too pretty, I guess, although personally for me, the Viking braids are kind of a giveaway."

"What?" Molly said, startled for once out of her flat expression. "Fascist?"

"Don't tell me you haven't seen her Instagram," Ruby said.

"Yeah, I saw it," Molly said. She finally lit her cigarette. "She's, like, one of those mom influencers."

"Well, yeah, but with a twist. She's basically on a mission to populate the world with as many blond babies as humanly possible—it's weird that her kids don't look anything like Ben, isn't it?—while telling other women that they're not actually *real women* at all if they do anything but mind the damn homestead all day."

"How is that fascist?" Molly asked.

"Um, well, aside from her obsession with quote-unquote 'hereditarily important families' and ancient European religions and an awful lot of talk about blood and soil—that was a favorite Nazi trope, you know—she quotes Julius Evola all the time."

"Who's that?"

"Only the favorite philosopher of neofascists around the world? He was this weird combination of antisemitic-slash-white-master-race shit combined with occultism."

"It's not *that* weird of a combination," Anna said. She was flicking her thumb on a mini Bic lighter, trying to get a joint lit. "I mean, the Nazis were deep into the occult. Dude, haven't you seen *Indiana Jones*?" The joint caught fire and she took a crackling drag. "The occult, and drugs," she said on a choked, smoky exhale. "Lots of drugs."

"But you guys," Ruby said. "We can't sit here talking about Kirsten all night. That would be very messed up. Let's go upstairs and look at that creepy painting." She gave me a mischievous smile. "Is it still there?"

"I'm not sure which painting you mean," I said.

"The one over Pauline's bed. I *have* to see it." She laughed. "I want to know if he still has feelings for me. Not that it would be personal—I mean, can you *imagine* how horny those guys would get out in those olden-days logging camps without any women around? If they didn't go for boys, I mean."

She was even drunker than I thought.

"It's still up there?" Ruby said. "The painting of the famous lumber-baron ancestor?"

"You mean Jakob Himmel?" I said.

She pointed at me. "That's the guy, yeah. Jakob."

"Honestly, I haven't ever been in Pauline's room," I said. "And I think it's locked."

I knew for a fact it was locked because I'd ventured up to the third floor and tried the knob the other day, just for kicks.

"Okay, well, where's the key?" Ruby said, glugging bourbon into her glass.

"I'm not really—"

"I bet the housekeeper has a key. There's still a housekeeper, right?"

"Hold on."

I went inside to the utility closet by the cellar door. I'd noticed Emilia's keys in there when I'd gone looking for dishwasher detergent. And there they were, hanging on a hook. A steel ring bristling with keys.

I felt triumphant as I brought the keys back to the porch. I jingled them in the air.

"Nice!" Ruby said.

"I guess we're really doing this," Anna said with a sigh, stubbing out her joint on the bottom of her boot. "You coming, Molly?"

"No, I'm good," Molly said. Her eyes were still glued on Seth and Kirsten.

◆ ◆ ◆

I led Ruby and Anna up the main staircase, along the upstairs hall, and then up to the third floor.

The air was cool and stale. I could hear only the faintest threads of music from down below.

We stopped at the door to Pauline's bedroom. I tried the doorknob, just in case, but it was still locked.

I sifted through the keys. Most of them had those little colored plastic caps with handwritten labels: mudroom, cellar, pool house. But a few of them didn't. I tried the first key without a label. It didn't fit. Neither did the second or third.

The fourth unlabeled key, however, slid neatly into the lock.

"Sweet," Ruby said.

I turned the doorknob and the three of us pushed into the room.

It was pitch dark and stifling with the punch of Chanel No. 5. I groped around until I felt a light switch and flipped it.

The room bloomed in dim light. Wallpaper with pink roses. Closed curtains. A four-poster bed. A seagrass rug. Chairs and chests of drawers and a writing desk.

I didn't, however, see any artwork.

“Where’s the painting you were talking about?” I asked Ruby, who was walking across the carpet, her bourbon glass held high.

“Over here. Right over the bed so Gregor’s mom can look up at it when she’s doing the missionary position with her leathery old Microsoft boyfriend.”

To my horror, Ruby was climbing onto Pauline’s hotel-perfect duvet and standing on the bed. In her high heels.

“Um,” I said, “I’m not sure if you should—”

“Voilà,” Ruby said. She’d yanked aside a curtain hanging over the head of the bed, revealing a large oil painting in a gilt frame. She tossed me a grin. “What do you think?”

I stared at the portrait. “Oh my *God*,” I whispered.

30

"Looks just like Gregor, right?" Ruby said. "If he was sixty and had a beard?"

The man in the portrait—Jakob Himmel—sat, legs crossed, one hand draped carelessly over the arm of his chair and his other hand resting on his knee. He wore a dark three-piece suit and a tie. The hand on his knee sported a large gold signet ring. His thick hair, swept back from his temples, was lint gray, and so was his bushy beard, and his forehead and under-eyes were creased with age.

Yet his resemblance to Gregor was uncanny. The hooded eyes, the wide mouth, the firm jaw. His nose—high bridged, with that distinctive curve to the nostrils—was what Pauline had called *the Himmel nose*.

But Jakob's blue gaze was so haughty and cold. Cruel, even. Gregor never looked like that.

"Why was it behind that curtain?" I asked.

"To protect it from UV damage maybe?" Anna said.

"No, it's weirder than that," Ruby said. "Someone told me the housekeeper won't come in here to clean unless it's covered up."

"Why?"

"Because it creeps her out, I guess."

My eyes locked with Jakob's. I could've sworn he blinked.

"I'm sorry," Anna said, "but am I the only one who thinks it's weird that Pauline has this painting over her *bed*? I mean first of all, he's her grandfather, and also, he looks exactly like her *son*. Isn't that just—"

"*So* nasty," Ruby said. "Agree. But God, so *The Fall of the House of Usher*? These old money people sort of worship their own families, you know? Like they're—"

"Ruby," Anna said in a scolding undertone. "This is Harlow's family you're talking about." She sent me a wince. "Sorry."

"It's fine," I said. "I'm still trying to figure the whole thing out myself." I stopped beside the bed, arms wrapped around my torso, peering up at the painting.

An axe leaned against Jakob's chair. And now I noticed the open window behind him, showing layers of shadowy green hills. A full moon hung over the hills in a dusky sky. A small table stood beside Jakob, on it a dish of mushrooms. The mushrooms had skinny white stems and wavy, caramel-colored caps.

What is it with the Himmels and fungi? I thought.

"The axe is a weirdly sinister touch," Anna said.

"Well, he was a logger, right?" Ruby said. "Before he made his fortune?"

"Yeah," I said. "According to Pauline, he brought an axe all the way from Germany. But . . . why the mushrooms? And the moon?" In my mind's eye I saw Emilia dragging the dining room curtains shut. I heard Pauline say, *She told me once that the light of the full moon can curdle milk, or something like that. Just a superstition she brought from her homeland.*

"No idea," Ruby said. "Maybe he was a Freemason or something. Don't they use all kinds of obscure symbols?"

My gaze returned to the moon in the painted sky. The artist must've used iridescent pigment, because it truly seemed to glow.

Suddenly, I needed to get the heck out of there.

I started toward the door. "I think we should go, you guys," I said.

Our guests started leaving soon after that. Kirsten and Ben first, then Seth and a silently fuming Molly, followed a minute later by Ruby and Anna.

Ruby gave me a big, drunken hug at the front door. "It was so great to meet you, Harlow, and it's amazing to play with Gregor again. I haven't seen him since, like, the June before last? Way too long."

"Oh," I said. "Were you in New York then?"

"What? No. He was here on the island."

"Okay," I said, my mind spinning.

The June before last? I thought. *Gregor was here, on this island, the June before last? This is the first* I'm *hearing about it.*

Anna tugged Ruby away.

I shut the door and found myself alone. Gregor had gone upstairs to get Sam into bed. I went through the downstairs rooms—dirty glasses and empty bottles and crumpled napkins everywhere—switching off lights and locking doors and turning off the sound system.

Then I went upstairs to our bedroom and sat down by the unlit fireplace. I pulled out my phone and opened the calendar app to the June before last.

Gregor and I had gotten married the August before last. That June, we'd been dealing with the wedding planner and bridesmaids and groomsmen and our honeymoon plans. We'd still been working, too, me at the lab and Gregor with Journey's End. He'd been away with the band every weekend that June and July.

I remembered how achingly I'd missed him. I remembered how I'd fall asleep with my phone connected to his while he was away in Maine or upstate New York or Maryland or wherever. In the morning, he'd still be there on the other end of the line with the call duration—seven hours, eight hours—ticking up and up and up.

But I didn't remember him traveling to Washington state. And there was no note of it in my calendar.

I was sure I'd remember it, because the band would've had to fly, not drive. They'd almost always driven because most of their gigs had been in the Northeast. Flying was a big hassle because of transporting all their instruments and sound equipment.

Why hadn't Gregor told me he'd been here on the island? Did he want to hide that he'd been visiting his mother? From the start, mutual dislike had taken root between Pauline and me. Not that we'd spent much time together. We were just very different women.

Or did Gregor want to hide that he'd been visiting someone else on the island? Someone like—

"Babe?"

I started, almost dropping my phone.

"Gregor," I breathed, looking up at him. "You scared me." I turned my phone face down on my lap. "Hey. Is Sam asleep?"

"Out cold." He sat down in the other armchair. "What're you looking at?" he said, gesturing to my phone.

"Oh. Nothing. Checking my email." I couldn't face asking him about the summer we got married and his travels. Not yet.

"Thanks for hostessing tonight," he said.

"Of course. We're a team."

"Did you have an okay time?"

"I had a great time, honey. It was great to get to know everyone, and everyone was super nice."

"Everyone?" He was watching me closely.

I smiled, cupping my elbows in my hands as I nodded. "Of course."

"Even Kirsten?"

"Yeah. I . . . I really like her." I swallowed. "But I mean . . . who even *is* she?"

Gregor frowned. "Who *is* she?"

I took a shuddery breath, let it out. Then I asked the question—or one of the questions, anyway—that was gnawing at my mind. "Who is she to *you*?"

Gregor sighed. "Listen, I wish my life began the minute I met you, but it didn't, so—"

"How long have you known her?"

"I met her at their wedding. Ben's and hers. That was, well, I guess about five years ago. No, I guess closer to six. But you're really . . . this isn't a good look for you."

"What isn't?" I asked in an icy voice.

"The whole jealousy thing. It's . . . ugly."

I drew back, scalded by his words. "I'm just . . . I'm only trying to understand—"

"Well, how about you *don't* try to understand? Jesus. Give it a rest. We came here for *you*, so you could try to de-stress, and here you go fabricating a whole new drama with the wife of my bandmate."

God, how I felt triggered by that word. *Drama.* I knew I was acting just like Mom, but I couldn't stop. It was like I was high on the destruction. Was that how Mom had felt when she was henpecking poor Dad to pieces?

"We came here for *me*?" I said. "I never wanted to come here. I'm doing it because you were so adamant about making this album, and about Sam needing more nature in his life. This isn't for me. I gave up my *career*."

Gregor leaned forward over his knees and laced his fingers behind his neck. "Fine, Low. Whatever. You're always the one who's sacrificing everything in this marriage. Got it."

"Something isn't right," I said, struggling to sound level. "That's all. Something's not right with Kirsten and the KinderWild interns, and I—"

"Do you realize what you sound like?" Gregor looked up. The whites of his eyes flashed. "Listen. Whatever you think is *off* about Kirsten, I guarantee that you are one hundred percent projecting. She's really not that complicated. She's just a young mother trying to raise her kids, and there is nothing more to her than that."

"How can you say that, when she's making a living with a heavily curated and aesthetically pleasing representation of her life—and her kids' lives—on Instagram? You can't believe that's all *real*."

"I do, actually. I do. And you sound crazy, Low. You sound *obsessed*." He got to his feet. "I'm really tired. I'm going to get ready for bed."

He went into the bathroom, shutting the door a little too hard behind him.

31

The house was hushed on Sunday morning, washed in watery light trickling in past the curtains. I padded downstairs in my robe, made coffee, and warmed milk on the stove for Sam's hot chocolate. He appeared in the kitchen like a sleepy little elf, thumb in mouth, hair standing up on one side.

"Hey, sweetie," I said.

He only made a little grunt in response. But then, he'd never been a morning person.

We climbed onto the den sectional and watched cartoons with the volume low. He clutched his mug in both hands, sipping loudly. I cradled my coffee, trying not to think too hard.

Last night had been *way* too much.

The party. The portrait. The argument with Gregor.

He thinks I'm fabricating drama out of thin air. That I'm paranoid. Jealous.

Maybe he's right.

I glanced over at Sam, cross-legged on the couch, entranced by animated monsters on the screen. What would it feel like if I just . . . let it all go? The head. The Gilda stuff.

I mean, if Gilda was fine with living in a goat shed, who was I to judge?

I took a sip of coffee. It had gone cold.

I sighed. *Time to clean.*

The entire downstairs was a wreck from the party. I spent the next hour ferrying wine and cocktail glasses, greasy paper napkins, dirty plates, empty bottles, and the sweating remnants of charcuterie to the kitchen. I filled the dishwasher, scrubbed the counters, and took out the trash. When I went to replace the kitchen trash bag, I couldn't find any extras under the sink.

I went to the utility closet. The door groaned on its hinges.

I clicked on the light.

Mops. Buckets. Jugs of white vinegar. Bottles of bleach. Spray bottles of Windex and countertop cleaner. And there, at the very back of a lower shelf, a battered cardboard box of Glad bags.

I grabbed it—then froze.

One of the wallpaper panels above the baseboard had sloughed off, revealing the plaster beneath. A shadow of old adhesive stained the wall, but cutting across it, in faint pencil lines, was another message.

I squinted, crouching to see it better.

They tell you it's forever love
They show you the mark

My stomach flip-flopped. *Crazy Bessie strikes again,* I thought.

The rest of the words were badly smudged, but I could pick out some of them:

too late
this house

And below the words, with a precision that told me it was no mistake, the conjoined double X symbol.

The exact same one I'd seen tattooed on Teacher Terra's arm, and that pregnant barista's arm.

A chill slithered through me, despite the warm air from the floor vent.

Whatever that double X symbol meant, this suggested it had been here on the island long before KinderWild. Before Kirsten. Before Terra and the barista. It was *old*.

Behind me, a floorboard creaked.

I straightened abruptly, heart hammering, right as Gregor padded into the hallway in sweatpants, shirtless, blinking.

"Hey," he said, rubbing the back of his neck. His voice was rough with sleep. "You been up long?"

I backed out of the utility closet and flipped off the light. "A while."

"About last night," he said. "I was a jerk. I'm sorry. I didn't mean to make you feel like I wasn't listening." His eyes were soft. "Forgive me?"

My throat tightened so much, I didn't trust myself to speak. *It's okay*, I thought. *We're going to make it.*

I nodded, allowing him to wrap me in his arms. He smelled like sleep and woodsmoke and *home*.

"I love you," I mumbled against his chest.

"I love you, too," he whispered.

And then a third voice chimed in: Crazy Bessie's scribbled words inside my head.

They tell you it's forever love
this house
too late

◆ ◆ ◆

I made a point of keeping Monday low key.

It wasn't that I was trying to keep myself out of trouble. Not exactly. But every time my mind drifted in the direction of the ravine, or the goat shed, or Gilda's maybe-not-thrift-store T-shirt, I tugged it back like a naughty puppy on a leash.

I did a yoga video called *Radical Nervous System Repair* and tried not to roll my eyes. I got a manicure in a color called Shell Beige and told the tech I wanted to feel "put together." I finally got Phoebe on the phone during her lunch break and told her how great everything was going. At the pharmacy, I browsed forever before buying an overpriced shampoo that promised unbeatable shine and bounce.

By the time it was KinderWild-pickup-o'clock, I felt almost smug.

Look at me, being chill. Being the kind of woman no husband would call crazy.

◆ ◆ ◆

I took Sam home and fixed him his favorite snack, a peanut butter, honey, and banana sandwich.

Emilia was prepping dinner in the kitchen, head bent, focused on her work. Discomfort seemed to radiate off her.

Actually, I'd been getting the distinct feeling she didn't like me, but I told myself that was silly. I mean, she barely even knew me. On the other hand, she spent her days scrubbing blobs of toothpaste from our sinks, emptying the dishwasher, Vitamixing endless green smoothies.

Laundering our bloody clothing.

Why would she like me?

Sam and I went to the den and turned on *PAW Patrol*, waiting for Gregor to come home. Sam stared glassily at the cartoon dogs, slowly chewing small bites of sandwich.

Four thirty rolled around, then five, then five thirty and six. Emilia had popped her head in to say she was leaving and that the dinner was keeping warm in the oven.

Gregor still hadn't texted.

I prided myself on the fact that I wasn't one of *those* wives. You know what I mean: the kind who micromanage their husband's comings and goings, who bitch about ignored texts, who make paranoid accusations.

But I was starting to feel annoyed. Because I mean, *six o'clock*? That was a little ridiculous.

Yes, I was fully aware that Gregor was an artist, that he didn't have the kind of job where you clock in and clock out, but still. He had a wife. He had a kid. He couldn't text?

"I'm hungry," Sam said as the credits started rolling on an episode.

"Me too," I said, clicking off the TV. "Let's go get Daddy."

Sam and I pulled on shoes and jackets and went out into the evening. The sun was setting over the harbor. Shadows pooled thick under the driveway trees.

The orchard, though, was flooded with an unearthly yellow light that left me blinking. And why were the trees still so green? It was October.

The apples in the boughs and on the ground seemed too red. The air was perfumed by all the decaying, fermenting fruit. I thought I heard, but couldn't see, humming wasps.

I saw Kirsten first, her pale sheaf of hair flipping in the breeze. She was walking with a man. With Gregor.

32

There was Kirsten. There was Gregor. Walking together in the orchard. And here came her two little boys, Magni and Alder, scampering underneath the apple trees, shouting and laughing.

I felt an upsurge of jealousy, so sour and potent I reeled.

Take a good, long look, Harlow, said an icy little voice inside my skull. *It's the picture-perfect family.*

Sam drew close to my side. He took my hand and corked a thumb in his mouth.

We kept walking. The others were walking toward us, but they hadn't seen us yet because they were so focused on each other.

Kirsten's dress kicked up around her shins as she went, flashing glimpses of ankle boots, petticoat, bare tan legs. Barri was bound to her front in a fabric carrier. Gregor said something with a big silly grin that I hadn't seen in a while, and Kirsten tipped back her head and laughed.

Something was building inside my throat, a gummy wad that I realized was a scream. *What the hell?* I wanted to cry. *What the HELL?*

I didn't let it out, though. Nobody likes a crazy lady.

Kirsten noticed Sam and me first. Her smile slipped.

Gregor followed her gaze. When he saw me, his face went wary.

We all came to a stop with a few yards between us.

This does not feel okay, I thought.

"Harlow," Gregor said. "What are you doing out here?" He looked at Sam, who was still clutching my hand and sucking his thumb. "Hey, buddy. What's with the thumb-sucking? I thought you were done with that."

"We were coming to get you," I said with a forced smile. "We were getting hungry, and we thought maybe you'd lost track of time?"

"Yeah," Gregor said, running a hand through his hair like he used to when we first met. *Nervous.* "We came up with some really good material this afternoon. A ballad."

"It's *amazing*," Kirsten said to me. "You're going to love it."

All I did was nod.

"Well, good night," Gregor said to Kirsten.

Their eyes met. Something I didn't understand passed between them.

"Have a great night, you guys," Kirsten said. "Boys," she called to Magni and Alder, who were trying to climb a nearby tree. "Let's go."

The boys ignored her, so she went over to the tree. "You guys need to come when I call you," she said. "And besides, it's chicken stew and dumplings for dinner, your favorite."

"Stew and dumplings!" Magni yelled.

"Stew and dumplings!" Alder echoed.

"Stop copying!" Magni shouted. He kicked Alder in the shin, and Alder burst out crying.

Kirsten shook her head, laughing. "These little guys," she said to Gregor and me over Alder's wailing. "Teaching empathy is *such* a challenge." She took her little boys' hands. "Good night. For real this time."

◆ ◆ ◆

Walking back to Himmel Cottage, Gregor held Sam's hand. I trailed behind, trying to slow my breathing, trying not to say anything I'd regret.

The scene in the orchard kept replaying in my head like a cruel home movie. The perfect family, blond and laughing and bathed in harvest light—and very much *not mine.*

My family was something cobbled together. Disjointed. And, I'd learned since we arrived on this island, way more fragile than I realized.

Gregor was waiting for me to say something. I could see it in the hitch of his shoulders, his sidelong glances.

He was waiting for me to explode.

Well, I wasn't going to. I kept my mouth shut tight. For Sam's sake—but also because I knew exactly what Gregor would say. I was *fabricating drama*. I was *just jealous*.

He thought Kirsten was a simple young mom. Sweet as sugar. And so damn pure.

Really? Then why the hell had she hissed at Ben about *the police* when they showed up at our door the other night? Why was Gilda living in her *shed*?

No. There was something wrong with her.

Dinner was the salad and butternut squash lasagna Emilia had left. Gregor scarfed down two steaming helpings while Sam picked out bits of spinach. I listened to my pulse in my eardrums and struggled to swallow even a few morsels. Every time I caught Gregor glancing at me, I smiled. *Everything's fine!*

But I was obsessing about the goat shed. The lumpy mattress. The folded T-shirt. L. Reed.

Halfway through the meal, it hit me: *I'd been googling the wrong thing.* I'd been so locked in, so laser focused on trying to figure out who New Gilda was.

But maybe I should've been trying to figure out who *Old* Gilda was.

After dinner, Gregor and Sam went upstairs to build a LEGO dinosaur. I said I was going to clean up, but instead I went into the pantry, shut the door quietly, and pulled out my phone.

I typed: *L. Reed missing person Washington state.*

A few hits popped up. Most were irrelevant. But then—

Lizbeth Reed. Age eighteen. Last seen in Kennewick, Washington, four months ago, right after her high school graduation.

Oh my God.

I clicked on the regional news link and read faster, heart pulsating.

Her parents had reported her missing. She'd left behind everything—phone, clothes, even her car. The day after she disappeared, she'd left a voicemail for her parents: *I'm fine. I need to follow my convictions. I love you, Mama and Daddy.*

The police hadn't pursued it. She wasn't a minor. There was no sign of foul play.

But her parents said it made no sense, that she'd never even spent a night away from home without telling them first. They said she'd graduated from high school and had plans to apply to culinary school. They asked that if anyone knew anything to please contact them.

I stared at the photo at the bottom of the article. It looked like a yearbook headshot. Lizbeth Reed was young. Cute. Long dirty-blond hair. Rosy cheeks, big blue eyes.

She wasn't the current Gilda.

But she could've been the *other* Gilda. The one before.

I took a screenshot of her picture.

My mind flashed with the image of the head in the ravine, the stringy hair, the gray skin—

It definitely could be her.

But I needed to know for sure.

33

I was wearing jeans and a sweater at breakfast and for Sam's KinderWild drop-off the next day. But as soon as I got back home, I changed into black leggings, a sports bra, a T-shirt, a black hoodie, and running shoes. I tied my hair in a low ponytail and then put on a baseball cap to protect my still-healing scalp.

After double-checking that my phone was fully charged, I set off on foot down the driveway. The landscapers were there, clipping hedges and raking leaves.

Which would be a perfect excuse, should I need one: *The landscapers were around, so I decided to take a walk off the property until I had the place to myself again.*

It said a lot about the current state of my marriage that I was making up explanations to throw at Gregor.

I went through the gates and crossed the road. Then, instead of entering the Blakeleys' driveway—because that was not an option—I walked along the road, looking for a different way into the woods.

It was more difficult than I'd foreseen. On the other side of the ditch, undergrowth billowed out from beneath the trees. It seemed dangerous, even, where spiny blackberry canes barred the forest like something out of a dark fairy tale.

I was starting to worry that I was going to have to somehow access the ravine via the Blakeley homestead after all when I noticed a gap in the undergrowth.

Was it a gap? Yes. A deer path, maybe.

I jumped across the ditch and ducked into the forest.

I didn't like how it smelled. That was the first thing that registered. My sinuses seemed to fill with mud and minerals and bitter plants and moist rot. Under the trees the air was about fifteen degrees cooler than it was out on the sunny road. It was clammy against my cheeks.

As I followed the deer path, the undergrowth dragged at me. But I was going in the right direction: uphill and away from the road.

Before leaving the house, I'd studied a satellite image of this hillside on Google Maps. It mostly looked like a lot of dense trees, but I'd identified the Blakeleys' rusty metal roofs. And there was a long, dark pleat in the trees not too far from their house. It had to be the ravine I'd fallen down the other day.

I gained elevation for several minutes.

Then I lost the path.

I stopped, breathing hard. I was in a stand of small evergreens. They were growing so densely that their whiplike lower branches were bare and dead.

I thumbed the map on my phone. *No Internet Connection.* Zero bars.

"Are you serious?" I muttered, stuffing my phone back into my hoodie pocket. I looked around. No path.

Then I noticed a vague gap in the interwoven branches. Murky light shone through.

I stepped closer to peer through the gap.

Yes! A path. A *real* path this time, a human path, packed dirt about ten inches wide.

I pushed through the opening and continued uphill.

I'd been walking about a minute when I heard a loud *crack*.

I stopped, stumbling on my own feet.

Fear shot into my fingertips.

That had been a stick snapping. Somewhere deeper in the trees? As though someone or something had stepped on it?

The base of my skull felt buzzy.

I should go back, I thought. *Straight back.*

But then the smeary image of the head flashed in my mind's eye, followed by a cold swell of fear. I needed to know if that image had been real or not. It felt like my entire future was hinging on it.

I forced myself onward.

After a few more minutes of walking, I spotted the stinging nettle patch. I could just make out the shadowy line where Gregor and I had trampled the plants before. Then something caught my eye, and I stopped.

A small, black, plastic thing was mounted about seven feet up on a tree trunk.

It was a security camera, with its own tiny solar panel. It appeared to be aimed right at me.

Why? I thought. *Why is there a security camera out here? Or does it have some other nonsecurity purpose? Counting woodpeckers? Tracking raccoons? People do stuff like that.*

I heard another crack.

I froze.

It had been closer than the first one, but quieter, too. I was pretty sure it had come from the other side of the ravine.

I peered across the way, but all I saw was a wall of trees.

It's only an animal, I told myself. *Forests are full of animals. No need to freak out.*

I went through the nettles. This time, I was wearing leggings, socks, and sneakers so I didn't get stung. And it was easy to find the place where I'd fallen down the ravine. I could see raw dirt where the edge had given way.

I couldn't tell if there was a head down there, but I could see exactly where it *would* be, behind a clump of ferns at the bottom.

Here goes, I thought. *Please God, let there be no head, because I'm not sure I can handle it.*

I started picking my way down to the steep slope. Along the way, I looked around for my lost glasses. Nope.

I arrived exactly where I'd landed in my fall the other day. And—no head.

I breathed a sigh of relief. I didn't want there to be a head. I wanted to be wrong about all of this.

I prodded clusters of plants with my sneaker, just to be sure.

Nothing.

And yet, this was the place. The trail of debris and crushed plants I'd made on the way down the other day was unmistakable.

Hold on, though—what was this?

The ground where the head had been in my memory looked . . . wrong. A shallow divot, the dirt slightly darker, looser. Crushed dead leaves pressed in around the edges.

I reached down and brushed aside a few damp twigs.

The earth was disturbed, as though someone had been digging.

Then, just uphill: the resounding *crack* of another snapping stick.

I gasped. I tripped and fell to my knees, and then hard onto my palms. Pain skewered up my arms.

I struggled to my feet, hyperaware that there was something—or someone—up the slope. Hidden. Watching.

I felt exposed.

I felt like a target.

34

Instinct propelled me for a few long strides, and then I threw myself behind a big, mossy rock. I huddled down, my own quick breaths sounding primal in my ears.

Every cell in my body told me I needed to move. *Now.*

Then I became aware of something strange.

There wasn't just the one divot where I'd thought the head had been. The entire floor of the ravine was dotted with low mounds of freshly overturned earth and shallow holes.

Dead leaves had been swept aside, soil had been displaced. A dozen holes. Maybe two dozen. Various sizes, none more than four or five inches deep. The largest might've held a big suitcase. The smaller ones could've held a shoebox.

I didn't know what it meant, exactly. Only that someone had been here in the past few days. Digging things up, or maybe burying them.

A *lot* of things.

Like . . . what? Evidence? *Treasure?*

I fumbled out my phone and opened the camera. I aimed it at the nearest hole in the ground, trying to get it to focus, but I couldn't stop shaking. I took one out-of-focus picture, then another.

There was a hard *pop*, and then a *thunk* on a tree trunk nearby, and as my startled body convulsed, the original pop reverberated again and again and again into the forest all around me.

A gunshot.

I'd never been near actual gunfire, but I'd seen enough TV and movies to get that *someone had just shot at me.*

With a *gun.*

What was I supposed to do? Run? Hide?

Think, Harlow. Think!

I had to make a run for it. What else? If I stayed still, I was a sitting duck. Whoever it was could walk right up to me and shoot me point blank.

That thought launched me to my feet.

I shoved my phone into my hoodie pocket. I scrambled and stumbled and clawed my way up the side of the ravine, darting behind tree trunks whenever I could, practically incandescent with adrenaline.

I felt eyes on my back the whole way up. Right between the shoulder blades.

I broke into a run at the top and found the path, the one I was on before.

I ran all the way down the slope until I reached the edge of the Blakeleys' homestead.

I would've liked to take the shortest route and go right through their yard, but I couldn't be seen. Not by the Blakeleys, and sure as heck not by Gregor.

I needed time to calm down, time to think.

I sneaked through the trees around the homestead and waded through the underbrush alongside the driveway. Muffled music leaked from the barn, and then a shout of laughter.

I crossed the main road, tapped the entry code to open the driveway gate to Himmel Cottage, and then I was safe.

Or that's what I told myself, anyway, as I speedwalked down the driveway.

It was only when I was inside the mudroom with the door shut that the full horror hit. I could've been seriously injured. I could've been *killed.* And all those holes in the ground. What *were* they?

The fact that the shooter had seen me but I hadn't been able to see them, that was the really freaky thing. Did they know who I was? Even if they didn't, they'd gotten a good look at me. They'd figure it out soon enough.

Why were they even out there—and with a loaded gun—at all?

I counted on my inhales, held them, let them out slowly, fighting to keep calm.

Someone was hiding something in those woods. Something horrible.

I had to go to the police.

About fifteen minutes later, I was sitting across a desk from a King County sheriff's deputy at the station in town.

"Okay," she said. "Tell me what happened. Start at the beginning." The name tag pinned to her dark-blue uniform said SGT. MARCUS. She was a delicate, pretty fortysomething woman with a reddish braid and freckles on her forearms.

The goal was to keep it simple—and to sound like a levelheaded, nondramatic woman.

I explained that I'd been walking in the woods near my house, that I'd gotten disoriented and ended up in the bottom of a ravine. That I'd noticed a lot of disturbed areas in the soil—freshly dug holes, like someone had been searching for something. And that immediately after I took a photo, someone fired a gun in my direction.

I hadn't really been lost, but that was irrelevant.

The whole time I was telling my story, Sergeant Marcus was leaning forward on her elbows. Her green eyes were bright, but I couldn't read her expression. Her face was made of stone.

"I have pictures," I said to finish. "Of one of the holes." I pulled out my phone and opened the better photo of the two. I slid the phone across the desk.

Sergeant Marcus stared down at the phone without picking it up. "What exactly am I looking at here?"

Sure, the photo was blurry and the lighting wasn't great. But if you knew you were looking at a hole in the ground, it was unmistakable. Wasn't it?

I leaned forward and tapped the phone's screen. "See? There. You can see the fresh shovel mark?"

"I'm sorry, ma'am, but digging holes in the ground isn't a crime." She pushed the phone back to me.

How can she be so dismissive? I raged inwardly.

"What about the gunshot?" I said.

"What were you wearing out there in the woods?"

"Ex*cuse* me?"

She gestured to my black hoodie. "Were you wearing that?"

"What does that have to do with anything?"

"Are you aware that it's deer hunting season?"

"No, but—"

"It's a bad idea, going out in the woods during hunting season wearing all black. You might get mistaken for prey."

"Oh. Okay." The bluster was draining out of me fast.

"I'm just glad you're not hurt. And a little friendly advice? Folks have every right to hunt on private property in October, so I'd suggest you keep your walks to the county-maintained roads until the season's over. And get yourself a high-vis safety vest. They've got them at the hardware store."

I took a deep breath. I needed to try one more time to make her understand that this was serious. "You guys checked out that same ravine last week," I said, trying to keep my tone even. "My husband reported it. They sent someone. Don't you think those holes could be related to the, um, the thing I thought I saw?"

Sergeant Marcus seemed puzzled. "Ma'am, we didn't get any calls about a ravine last week."

"Wait." I frowned. "Are you sure? My husband called. He said the police searched—"

"I was on shift all last week," she said. "No one called in anything like that. I'd remember."

I stared at her. "But he said—"

Then I shut my mouth.

My skin went cold.

Gregor hadn't called. There hadn't been a search.

He'd lied to me.

And not just lied—he'd gaslit me. With Kirsten. That entire performance—the soothing voice, the slow back rubs, the way he shushed me and told me I was safe, that it was all over, that it had only been a bad trip—it was all fiction.

And what probably *wasn't* fiction?

The head.

"What's your husband's name?" Sergeant Marcus asked.

"Gregor Sullivan."

Something flickered across her face. Understanding, and then . . . was it *alarm*?

She was reaching for the landline phone on her desk. "Look. I'll call your husband, all right? Just to make sure we're all on the same page. Make sure you get home safe? You're looking a little shaky."

"You don't need to call my husband." I got to my feet. I felt like I might throw up.

Why, Gregor? I thought. *Why?*

"It's no problem at all." Sergeant Marcus tucked the beige phone receiver between her ear and shoulder. She had to turn her head a little to do so, and I saw dark marks behind her ear.

A tattoo. Two vertically interlocked X's.

The same tattoo Teacher Terra had. The same tattoo the pregnant barista refused to talk about. The same symbol Crazy Bessie had penciled on the wall of the utility closet at Himmel Cottage all those years ago.

Sergeant Marcus met my eye. I glanced away.

"It's real nice to meet you, Mrs. Sullivan," she called after me as I left.

35

I was driving too fast.

Because, of course, I was late for KinderWild pickup. Again.

The two-lane road curled through the woods like a furtive snake, and I could feel the car's weight shift with every bend. Dark trees rushed past on both sides, firs and cedars rising from blackberry-choked ditches. The fields were bleached and silent.

Gregor would still be at rehearsal right now, which meant I'd get his voicemail. Fine.

I jabbed the call button on the dash.

His voicemail greeting was still the same one he'd recorded the week we moved. *Hey, you've reached Gregor. Leave a message and I'll get back to you as soon as I can. Unless you're Harlow—then I just want to say, I love you.*

Pain bloomed behind my ribs. *Why, Gregor?* I thought for the thousandth time. *Why did you lie to me about calling the police?*

The beep sounded, and I said, "We need to talk."

Then I hung up.

◆ ◆ ◆

When I reached the Gathering Place, the forest opened out into its usual fairy-tale scene: children laughing, running in circles, tugging on their mothers' skirts. The mothers, in their drapey knits and muddy boots, stood in little knots, murmuring over mason jars of bone broth and tea.

The second I stepped out of the shadows, eyes slid in my direction. Voices faltered and then dropped into a lower register. It was all so subtle, I could've convinced myself I saw nothing.

But I *felt* it.

I scanned the clearing, searching for Sam.

No sign of him.

I went quickly around the logs. My stomach tightened as I peered into the encircling shadows. I pictured the fresh-dug holes I'd seen at the bottom of the ravine only about an hour ago.

"Sam?" I called, hating the shrill edge in my voice. *"Sam?"*

A little girl in overalls looked up from her pile of rocks.

"Sweetheart," I said, crouching. "Have you seen Sam?"

She nodded. "He went to the pond. He likes the frogs."

"Where's the pond?"

"That way." She pointed to a narrow trail disappearing into gloom.

I stood and started walking fast, then faster, my sneakers thudding on packed dirt and exposed roots. The trail curved left, then down a slight slope. The air smelled dank. My pulse ticked up.

"Sam?" I called again.

No answer.

I rounded another bend in the trail—

And nearly collided with someone.

I let out a yelp, stumbling on my own feet. *"Oh my God!"*

It was Gilda.

"You scared me," I said, panting, hand to my chest.

Gilda's skirt was smeared with dirt, her braid coming loose. No Mona Lisa smile. No glassy eyes. Instead, her gaze slid nervously left and right.

"Are you okay?" I asked. For the moment, my worry about Sam went on the back burner.

"Yeah. I'm just . . . I'm glad I ran into you, Mrs. Sullivan, because I have a question for you. Because you seem . . . different than the other mamas."

"Okay," I said slowly.

"Sometimes people come to this island for one reason . . . and then something changes. They stay for a different reason."

"Okay," I said again. She was speaking in riddles.

She glanced past me.

"So I'm just trying to figure out . . . well, if someone wanted to leave—*really* leave—do you think it's bad to want that?"

I heard the little kids' voices in my head:

My mama says Old Gilda ran away 'cause she's bad.

No. They can't run away. And they have *to be good.*

"No," I said to Gilda. "I don't think that's bad. You should leave whenever you want to."

She nodded like she was convincing herself.

"Gilda!" someone said sharply behind me.

I turned to see Teacher Terra striding toward us. Her smile looked like a mask. "Can I borrow you for a moment?"

Gilda cast her eyes down. "Yes, Teacher."

"Well, come on, then." Terra beckoned Gilda with an impatient hand.

Her hand was bandaged—a square of gauze taped over the webbing next to her thumb. I had a flash of how it had looked the other day. That large, weeping red blister.

Kind of like what you'd get from digging with a shovel, actually.

As they both walked away, I called, "I live next door, Gilda. The shingle house by the water? If you ever need anything."

Neither she nor Terra looked back.

"Harlow?" a little voice said.

"Sam!" I bent to wrap him in a hug. "Oh, Sam, I'm so happy to see you."

He pulled back from my embrace, looking up at me curiously. "Why?"

"Well, because I didn't know where you were. And because I love you."

Sam nodded solemnly, as though he was thinking this through. "Okay," he said. "I love you, too."

My heart squeezed. He'd never said that to me before.

I took his cold little hand in mine.

"You have to hear me out."

That was the first thing Gregor said to me, with a grim set to his face, hands in jacket pockets, hunched shoulders. He'd come over from rehearsal at the Blakeley barn. He'd found me on the beach, where I huddled on a driftwood log, shivering even though it wasn't that cold out.

"Fine," I said. It hurt to look at him.

He walked across rocks and broken shells until he was standing over me. "Can I sit?"

"Sure."

"Where's Sam?"

"Inside with Emilia. Eating peanut butter crackers."

Gregor sat carefully beside me, not quite touching. "Sergeant Marcus called," he said. "She said you told her someone shot at you in the woods? And that you'd seen dug-up holes in the ground? That you thought it meant someone had been looking for something?"

I stayed quiet.

"She was concerned about your mental health," Gregor said. "And I guess I am, too—"

"Why are you avoiding the real issue here?" I interrupted.

"Which is what?"

"Are you kidding me?"

He sighed. "Okay. I should've told you. I didn't call the police last week because I didn't want to get you in trouble. Mushrooms are illegal in Washington. I figured if the police came sniffing around, it might blow back on you. That's the only reason that—"

"That you *lied* to me?"

"To protect you, Low."

I turned toward him. I studied his wide, pleading eyes, the flush across his cheekbones. He looked so earnest. Like the stakes for me believing him were incredibly high.

He really does love me, I thought. *Why else would he care so much?*

"Look," he went on, "it's not like I wasn't taking you seriously. I went back up there myself. That night. With a flashlight. There was nothing. Well, just the rotting deer." He glanced at me. "And when Ben went up there, he didn't see anything, either."

"Wait—Ben?"

"Yeah. He actually went up there again this afternoon to deal with the deer. He didn't want his wife or kids stumbling upon it."

"Ben was up at the ravine *this afternoon*?" I said. "What time?"

"I don't know—like one thirty? Maybe two? Why?"

"That's when someone *shot* at me, Gregor." I could so easily picture Ben scowling through a rifle's scope, aiming at my back. My skin crawled.

"Babe. No. No way. Ben's not a hunter. He . . . why would he shoot at you?"

"Maybe he saw me on the security footage—I saw a camera up there. Maybe he thought I was going to find something I shouldn't."

"Low, the likelihood that someone actually shot at you is slim, and the likelihood that it was *Ben* is zero. This is my buddy we're talking about. I've known him forever." Gregor was shaking his head. "You've got to stop spinning every little thing into a conspiracy."

"Something's not right, Gregor. With Ben. And Kirsten. Why can't you see that?"

"See *what*, exactly?"

"You don't think it's strange that the teaching intern lives in their goat shed? That she looks like she's afraid to speak? What if—"

"Jesus," Gregor said loudly. "Would you give it a rest?"

I drew back, stunned.

Gregor's face softened. "I'm sorry. Babe. It's just . . . You know what? Screw the Blakeleys. Just the idea of you not trusting *me*, babe, it kills me." He tipped his head toward me until our foreheads touched.

The chilled softness of his skin was a shock. The scent of him muddled my thoughts.

"I trust you," I whispered thickly, my eyes falling shut.

I tried to mean it so, *so* hard.

I felt confused about a lot of things—the head, the double X tattoos, the gunfire, the two Gildas, and why Gregor hadn't told me about his visit to the island the June before last.

I was only certain about three things.

One, I still loved my husband. Blindly, hungrily, in exactly the way all the self-help books say you shouldn't. I *needed* him.

Two, he was hiding something.

Three, whatever he was hiding, it involved Kirsten and Ben.

My gut told me it was all connected. Another part of me, though, was afraid I was becoming one of those whackos with their corkboards and red string.

But I owed it to Gilda and Liz—and myself—to at least *try* to figure this out.

"Honey," I said to Gregor, "you have to understand that you've become my entire world, so when I realized you'd lied to me . . . it was like the world ended."

"No," he whispered, taking both of my hands in his. "Our world is just getting started. You'll see."

36

While I was heating up the casserole Emilia had left for dinner, Gregor and Sam were engrossed in another LEGO session upstairs. I had the kitchen to myself.

I opened a new tab on my phone.

If I was going to figure out what Kirsten and Ben were hiding—and whether Gregor was part of it—I needed to start connecting the dots.

Well, *here* were some dots: the double X symbol that kept showing up everywhere. Behind the sheriff deputy's ear. On the arms of Teacher Terra and the pregnant barista. Etched into the wall of this house by a madwoman decades ago.

Maybe it was random. Or maybe it was the thing that tied everything together.

I googled *XX symbol.*

As I'd expected, the hits included quite a few porn sites, plus pages about Roman numerals, a Wikipedia entry on "NATO Joint Military Symbology," and scientific information about chromosomes.

Then I found a page about Freemasonry symbolism, and I felt a little ping of connection. Hadn't someone—Ruby? Or had it been Anna?—said that the full moon, axe, and plate of mushrooms in Jakob Himmel's portrait might be Freemasonry symbols?

I opened the article. It said that XX signified a pair of gloves, which had something to do with purification.

That wasn't quite right, though. The symbol Crazy Bessie had drawn on the wall, the symbol that I'd seen tattooed on the pregnant barista's arm, Teacher Terra's arm, and behind the ear of Sergeant Marcus, depicted the two X's stacked one on top of the other, forming a diamond in the center. That wasn't the same as the Freemason gloves symbol.

I thought back to when I'd first noticed the barista's tattoo. Taken with her other ink—the spotted mushroom, the flowering vines—I'd gotten a New Age vibe. I remembered thinking that the double X might be some kind of rune.

In the search field I deleted *XX symbol* and typed *XX rune.*

And *bam*. There it was. The two stacked X's joined to form a diamond.

I skimmed the hits.

Norse runes translator.

Inguz rune meaning.

Using rune stones for divination.

The Old Norse runes alphabet.

I tapped one of the entries about the "Inguz rune."

> Inguz literally means "seed" or "the god Ing." It is the rune of family and integration, transformation and gestation, male fertility and sexuality, agriculture, male mysteries, stored-up energy that is released in energetic bursts of self-sacrifice designed to bring into being a new form—the true meaning of sacrifice.
> The very ancient Germanic fertility god Ing, Inguz, or Ingwaz was the original name of the Old Norse god Freyr, the god of prosperity, virility, and the phallus.

Whoa, I thought. *I had it totally wrong.*

All that religious talk on Kirsten's Instagram posts? It wasn't Christian.

It was *pagan*.

◆ ◆ ◆

Now that I knew what the XX symbol meant—now that I knew we weren't dealing with crunchy Christians but something else entirely—I had to examine everything again.

Including @IntoTheWoodsWeGo.

I strained my ears. Hearing a shout of laughter from Sam upstairs, I decided I still had time.

I opened Instagram.

Kirsten's post that day was a photo of her holding Barri on her lap. They were both wearing white dresses, and diffused sunlight irradiated their near-white hair. Kirsten smiled down at the baby, and the baby beamed up at her.

The filtered loveliness of the two of them, mother and child, was too much to bear. It was an ache behind my eyeballs, a twist in my belly. I hoped Gregor wouldn't see the picture.

Or had he already?

The caption read

> **Girls these days are expected to be intimate with men before marriage, no questions asked. But I'm here to tell you that not only is it OK to wait, but you should wait. Yes, I said it: SHOULD. If you want a quality husband, keep yourself pure. There is a magic to virginity, a special forcefield. A sacredness. Your purity is your POWER girls. Use it wisely. #traditionalfamily #foreverlove #blessed**

I scrolled down into the comments. The first few dozen were enthusiastic praise for Kirsten, her baby, her beauty, and her message, including one that said **Thank you for showing everyone what a REAL family looks like.**

Whatever *that* meant.

Then I had an idea. What about Liz Reed? Could she be in any of Kirsten's photos from over the summer?

Liz had disappeared from her hometown on June 24, so I scrolled down, down, down, watching Kirsten move in reverse through the summer—suntan fading, braids unbraiding and rebraiding, Barri getting balder, kale harvests replaced with peas.

Finally, I reached late June.

Kirsten had posted a close-up of fresh-baked bread on June 25. I scrolled up slowly, making the timeline move forward again. A "forest foraging" selfie on the twenty-seventh. A photo of Magni and Alder throwing rocks into the Sound on the twenty-eighth. I tapped each image open, scanning the backgrounds like I was working for the FBI.

Then, on July 2, a shot of the goats. They were nosing at a blackberry thicket next to their shed, the caption reading **How do you keep your naughty goats busy? Let them loose in the blackberries! #homesteadinglife #goatmama**

And there, in the doorway of the goat shed, a blurry figure.

I zoomed in.

A girl, or a young woman. Long blond hair. Pale skin. A shapeless dress. Her face was turned away, revealing her profile—

In my mind, I saw a lumpen head on the ravine floor, hair straggling, the outer tip of an eyebrow, an ear canal clogged with dirt—

Gasping, I pushed the vision away.

I forced myself to think instead of Liz Reed's photo in the newspaper.

Sure, it could've been Liz in Kirsten's goat post. The background was too low res to say for sure. I took a screenshot anyway.

Just then, Sam's voice ricocheted down the staircase. Gregor's voice, too—low and warm, so homelike it hurt.

Dinnertime.

I slid my phone into my hoodie pocket.

◆ ◆ ◆

That night, after Sam was asleep and we were getting ready for bed, Gregor said he had a gift for me.

"I've been going back and forth about whether or not I should give it to you," he said. He went to the dresser, opened the top drawer, and pulled out a brown paper-wrapped package. He passed it to me. "When I saw it, I immediately pictured you in it, but then I realized you might not like it, and since things between us have been kind of tense lately, I wasn't sure . . ."

"What is it?" I said.

How should I be acting? I wondered. *Shy? Flirty? Can he tell I'm not "giving it a rest" like he told me to?*

"Just open it," he said.

He watched as I sat down and undid the knotted twine and rustling paper.

Inside was a white folded garment. I saw a frill of delicate lace and tiny, lustrous mother-of-pearl buttons.

I started to feel sick.

"Do you like it?" he asked.

I held up the garment, and the gauzy cotton length of it tumbled down into my lap. It was a nightgown. An old-fashioned nightgown with long sleeves, a pintucked bodice, and a high collar. It reminded me of the nightgown Kirsten had worn in that Instagram selfie. **Full moon's out! Anybody else having a hard time getting their beauty rest? #foreverlove**

37

“Where did you get this?” I asked Gregor, holding the nightgown with trembling hands.

“At the antiques place in town,” he said. “I stopped in on a whim the other day.”

“It’s . . . beautiful.” A total lie.

“I know it’s not your usual style, but I saw it and thought you’d look *amazing* in it. Oh, and braid your hair, okay? Like the sexy prairie girl you are.” He grinned.

The nightgown was straight out of a Victorian nightmare. But the last thing we needed right then was more conflict.

When I came out of the bathroom a little later, Gregor was lying naked on the bed looking at his phone. He glanced up.

“Babe,” he said on a rough exhale. He tossed his phone aside and propped himself on an elbow. “Oh my God, you look so hot.”

I didn’t feel hot. I didn’t even feel like myself. The nightgown was constricting, and I never wore my hair braided. I felt like a bargain-bin Kirsten Blakeley.

But I went to the bed and lay down next to Gregor. He leaned over me and we started to kiss.

After a few minutes of kissing, I felt the overwhelming need to take off the nightgown. I wanted to feel like myself again. I didn’t want to be thinking about Kirsten while in bed with my husband.

Even if *he* might be thinking about *her*.

I reached up to the collar and picked at the top button.

"No," Gregor said with a grunt, pushing my hands away. "Keep it on." He bundled the long skirt around my waist, and then he swiftly pushed himself inside me.

I gazed up into his flushed face as he thrusted rhythmically, his eyes squeezed shut. The nightgown's lace collar chafed my throat. I felt numb between my legs.

As he groaned and shuddered and spilled himself into me, an image flashed in my mind's eye: Kirsten and Gregor, heads bent together over a perfect little baby, with two little boys romping behind them in an orchard heavy with rotting fruit.

◆ ◆ ◆

Gregor fell asleep quickly. I stripped off the nightgown, and then I lay in the dark listening to him breathe.

I was wide awake. Wired, but not clear. My thoughts spiraled and folded upon themselves with ever-increasing speed. A sick little hunch was growing like a tumor in my mind.

I plumped up my pillow. I tried box-breathing exercises. I visualized a peaceful waterfall. None of it helped.

When 2:00 a.m. rolled around and I was still wide eyed, I got up.

I belted on my robe, pushed on my glasses, and, using my phone as a flashlight, went silently downstairs to the library and rolled the pocket doors shut.

I didn't dare turn on a light. The glow might find its way up to our bedroom and wake Gregor.

It took me a few moments to find what I was looking for, slowly scanning the bookshelves with the cold light of my phone.

I'd only been half listening when Gregor told me he'd been white blond as a little boy. Now, that throwaway tidbit seemed like the most important fact in the world.

Okay. I steadied the flashlight beam on the bookcase. There they were—I knew they'd be in there somewhere. Family photo albums, a matching set of four in green leather with gold embossed spines that read HIMMEL and numbered I, II, III, IV.

I pulled out volume I, knelt beside the bookshelf, and spread it open on the floor.

These were old photographs. Really old. Blurry black and whites, some of which must've dated to more than a century ago, sealed under protective film.

The very first photo in the album was a portrait of a middle-aged man in a suit with dark eyebrows, pale hair, and a pale beard. He was, without a doubt, the same man in the oil painting up in Pauline's bedroom: the fabled Jakob Himmel. German immigrant, self-made man, founder of the family fortune, and the builder of this house. He was very, very handsome. Well, of course he was; he was a dead ringer for Gregor, only older.

I flipped through the album.

There were antique wedding portraits and pictures of this very house being built. There was a grainy photo of a bunch of young men in suspenders leaning on the most massive fallen tree I'd ever seen. Loggers, judging by their huge double-handled saws.

I picked out Jakob Himmel in the back row, very young in this image, without a beard, and with his hair pulled back from his face. He couldn't have been more than twenty-two.

These old photographs, though, weren't what I'd come to see.

I slid the first album back onto the shelf and pulled out volume IV. I set it on the floor, opened it to the middle, and aimed my flashlight.

My breath caught. The page I'd chosen at random held four color snapshots of a boy, around three years old. In lobster-print swimming trunks on a beach. On a swing with chubby legs dangling. Hugging a golden retriever. Grinning gummily with what looked like ketchup on his cheeks.

The light shuddered, and then I realized it was because my hand, holding the phone, was shaking.

The boy in the photos was the spitting image of Kirsten's younger son, Alder. Same pale, wispy blond hair and impish smile. Same shape to the eyes. Same nose.

I knew who the boy in the photographs was, because who else *could* it be? Gregor didn't have any siblings. He'd never mentioned any cousins, nor had any attended our wedding.

But a little voice in my head was begging for there to be some kind of mistake. So I peeled back the protective film and pried up the photo of the boy with the golden retriever. I turned it over.

Someone had written on the back *Gregor, April 1995*.

I stared at the blue ink. It went smeary, and I realized my eyes were filling with tears.

I slapped the photograph back on the page. I smoothed the plastic film over the top, shut the album, and slid it back on the shelf with the others.

I got unsteadily to my feet.

Was this why Gregor never told me he'd traveled here, to the island, the June before last, around the time six-month-old Barri was conceived? Was this the real reason he'd been so eager to come to this island? Not to make music but to be with Kirsten? To be with his children, Magni, Alder, and Barri?

But if that were the case, why bring *me* along? Why not just cut me loose and move on?

And how exactly did Ben factor into all this?

I was a biologist. I worked with data. With genes. It was obvious what I needed to do: Check Gregor's DNA against the DNA of Kirsten's kids.

38

I sat down on the edge of the library sofa. I browsed the DNA paternity test options online.

My stomach sank as the reality set in. I was going to have to steal stuff to do this. From Gregor, and from one of Kirsten's kids. It was an ethical and legal threshold I'd never even dreamed of crossing, yet now it seemed like a bare necessity.

The good news was the test websites confirmed they could extract DNA not only from fingernails, bloodstains, semen stains, cheek swabs, and hair roots but also from eating utensils, drinking straws, and cigarette butts.

I don't have to be a massive creep to do this, I told myself. *I don't even need to touch anyone. All it is, really, is a science experiment. Testing a hypothesis. No biggie. And it's the right thing to do. I have to know the truth about my husband and Kirsten and those children. In fact, don't I have an obligation to find out, for the sake of my own theoretical future children?*

I felt—or perhaps only imagined—a twinge in my lower belly.

Tapping my phone's screen, I selected one of the more reputable-sounding companies. I put a paternity test kit in the shopping cart and chose express shipping. I checked out using my private PayPal account, because heaven forbid Gregor saw Paternitrust.com on the credit card statement.

According to the website, in about three days the kit would arrive in the mail in "discreet packaging."

Until then, there was nothing to do but wait.

◆ ◆ ◆

It was pouring rain later that morning, and I felt like hell.

I hadn't slept. Not after the nightgown. Not after the photo album. Not after placing a secret paternity test order like the kind of woman who ends up on *Dr. Phil.*

My eyes were gritty, my head throbbed, and my stomach felt like it had been scrubbed out with steel wool.

Rain slapped the windshield as I pulled into the Shell station on the edge of town. I needed to fill the tank and clear my head before heading home. I'd just dropped Sam at KinderWild—all suited up in rain pants, boots, and jacket, poor little guy. No Gilda sighting, but that didn't necessarily mean she wasn't there.

I jammed the pump nozzle into the tank. Rainwater dribbled down the back of my neck. Everything was gray—the sky, the pavement, my thoughts.

"Hey!" someone called. "Harlow!"

I turned.

Anna—Ruby's girlfriend from the party the other night—stood on the other side of the pump. She was hunched under the oversize hood of a technical raincoat, and she was clutching one of those huge metal Yeti mugs. Her brown eyes were bright and curious.

"You okay?" she asked. "You look kind of like you've been hit by a truck."

"I *feel* like I've been hit by a truck."

"Want to join me? I'm about to grab a muffin from the mini-mart, and I could use the moral support. It's an existential crisis in there."

"Sure."

She finished filling her Honda, I finished with my own car, and we headed toward the mini-mart.

"Actually," I said, following her through the door, "there's something I need to ask you."

"Oh yeah?"

Inside, everything looked too bright and somehow dusty at the same time. Garish bags of chips rustled faintly under the HVAC. The smell of scorched coffee and old hot dogs hung in the air.

Anna beelined for the pastry rack and chose a cellophane-wrapped muffin that had no business calling itself *blueberry*. It was the size of a softball and an upsetting shade of grayish purple.

"This is probably made of the same materials as a yoga mat," she said, holding it up like a specimen. "But Ruby has banned carbs from our house, so I'm craving junk."

I followed her to the counter, where a young man in a SeeYouSpaceCowboy T-shirt slouched behind the register. He looked half asleep.

Anna set down the muffin and her travel mug and added a Powerball ticket to the order. "If I win, I'm buying a remote compound and an excessive number of rescue Chihuahuas," she said, tapping her credit card on the reader.

"Sounds wonderful." I smiled for the first time in what felt like ages.

As we walked toward the exit, she said, "So. What did you want to ask me?"

"This might sound a little strange," I said, holding the door for her, "but have you noticed anything weird about the women at KinderWild?"

"I don't have kids," she said, ripping the wrapper off her muffin. We stopped outside the door, mostly sheltered from the rain by an awning. "So I haven't met any of them besides Kirsten. But I mean, I can only *assume* they're weird? Aren't they the type who have COVID parties and eat their own placentas and shit?"

"I'm worried about the teaching intern," I said. "Gilda. Did Ruby ever mention her?"

"Why would she?" Anna took a bite of muffin.

"Because she's living in the Blakeleys' goat shed."

Anna stopped mid-chew. "That's . . . wait, seriously?"

"Right next to the hay and manure. There's a mattress in one of the stalls. A blanket. A few clothes."

"Shit," Anna muttered, tossing her muffin wrapper into a trash can. "Is it some kind of brainwashing situation?"

"That's what I'm worried about." God, it felt so good to hear someone else taking this seriously. "Do you think Ben is . . . I don't know. A good guy?"

"Ben? I mean, I *think* so? Ruby never said anything bad about him. But she doesn't really talk about him, either. It's like they all fall into this vortex. Nothing matters but the music."

I thought I saw a flicker in Anna's eyes—something unsure.

"Will you ask Ruby?" I said. "About Ben? And Gilda?"

"Yeah. I will."

"Thanks. And one other thing—there's this symbol I keep seeing around the island. Two stacked X's, like a diamond? Apparently, it's a Norse rune—Inguz or Ingwaz, some predecessor of Freyr."

"I've heard of him. One of those penisy gods."

"Right. Well, the head teacher at KinderWild has it tattooed on her arm, and I've seen a few other people with that same tattoo, and then I saw it drawn on the wall of my utility closet—"

"Wait—what? Like, the KinderWild women broke in and—"

"No." I shook my head. "It's even weirder than that. I think it was drawn on the wall a long time ago. Maybe decades ago."

"*Decades* ago? I don't get it."

"Me neither. But maybe it's some, like, island history thing? Because the KinderWild women are tradwives, and tradwives love . . . the past?"

"Okay, well, I was supposed to spend today fixing a bug in a layout widget," Anna said, "but this sounds way more interesting. If that rune's really some part of the island's history, there might be something buried in the historical society archives."

"You think that—"

"Meet you there," Anna said, flipping up her hood and heading for her car. "It's on Bank Road, in that old house next to the fire station."

39

The door hinges groaned as we entered the Island Historical Society. Inside a damp-smelling entry hall, steep stairs climbed into shadow. They were blocked by a velvet rope and a sign that said Do Not Enter.

To our left, a doorway opened into a large room filled with little kids. They were all inspecting a taxidermized coyote crouched mid-snarl on a pedestal.

One boy said, "It's stuffed with real guts."

"No it's not, stupid," his friend said.

"Is too! My mom said."

"Kids," their teacher said wearily.

Another doorway opened to a large room on our right. This one was wallpapered oppressively in sepia florals. Framed pictures lined the walls.

At a desk inside the room, a plump old man in a sweater looked up from an ancient Dell computer.

"Welcome," he said. His thick glasses sat crooked on his face, and when he smiled, his dentures were a startling white. The name tag clipped to his sweater said Edgar.

"Good morning," I said.

"Heckuva day out there," Edgar said.

"It really is," I said.

Anna elbowed me.

I cleared my throat. "I have a question," I said to Edgar. "If you're familiar with the island's history, and with the archives?"

"Well, of course I am." He looked annoyed, like I'd just insulted him.

"I keep encountering a particular symbol here on the island—"

"Where are you from?"

"Oh. Um, New York."

"Ah." He nodded like that explained a lot.

"The symbol is two X's stacked on top of each other to form a diamond."

Edgar's smile didn't falter, but something might've flickered in his eyes. "I've never seen that."

"I think it's an Old Norse rune? Pagan, maybe?"

His expression hardened. "This island was settled by devout Protestants."

"But maybe some of them brought the symbol from Europe when they immigrated," Anna said.

The man gave her a cold glare. "Are *you* from New York, too?"

"Nope. I live here."

"Oh. I see."

Edgar and Anna locked eyes.

"I'm Harlow Sullivan," I said brightly. "My husband's Gregor Sullivan. Pauline's son?"

That did it. Edgar's expression softened again. "Oh, wonderful, wonderful. Have you seen our Himmel room?"

"Uh, no?"

Without another word, Edgar got up and led us to a back room that stank faintly of mildew. Cases displayed rusty saw blades, logging hooks, a faded bowler hat. Newspaper clippings were pinned in warped frames, and black-and-white photos cluttered the perimeter.

He stopped in front of a glass case holding a small, battered book. "Jakob Himmel's Bible," he said. "In German. He came from Württemberg—but of course, you must know this already. Pauline likes to say that family history is written in the blood."

"I married in," I said.

"Ah, but blood isn't that simple, is it? Your children will have Himmel blood running through their veins—"

"Who was this Jakob guy, exactly?" Anna interrupted. She sent me a bug-eyed look: *What a crackpot.*

I hid a smile.

"Jakob Himmel arrived in the United States in 1880," Edgar said, his voice taking on a rehearsed drone. He told us the now-familiar rags to riches story about Jakob's opportunity with the shingle mill. "And from there"—Edgar gave a reverential smile—*"empire."*

Anna raised her eyebrows. "Where'd he get the money to buy that first mill?" She gestured to a photo of grimy young loggers. "I bet they got paid peanuts."

"Jakob Himmel was shrewd," Edgar said. "Frugal. A persuasive man, by all accounts, so he found backers. And, of course, he believed in hard work—and sacrifice. Lessons we'd all do well to learn."

"Edgar?" someone said behind us.

We turned.

Another member of the museum staff—a woman in Bogs boots and a bun—was in the doorway, asking Edgar to help wrangle the school group.

He sighed. "If you have questions," he said to Anna and me as he left, "I'll be just in the other room."

"This shit gives me the creeps," Anna said to me in an undertone. "These dudes stole the land from the people who already lived here, razed the forests to the ground, and then we're supposed to think they were some kind of saints?"

"Let's go," I said. "The rune thing's a dead end."

"If you're interested in the *real* story," someone said in a creaky voice, "I could tell you."

I swung around.

"Jesus," Anna gasped.

A papery, stooped old woman had appeared beside us, in orthopedic shoes and a platinum wig. Her red lipstick was uneven. Her eyes were watery and rimmed in blue. Her name tag said SHIRLEY.

"What's *the real story*?" I asked.

The woman—Shirley—leaned in. "My mother took care of old Mr. Himmel when he was dying. She was a nurse, you see. This would've been the late fifties, when he was nearly a hundred. Bone cancer, I believe." Her expression darkened. "His wife died before him. I'll bet Edgar didn't tell you that. *Suicide.* People said he was so cruel to her she couldn't take it anymore. Mother said *he* was on morphine in his last days, screaming about Hell. He said it was opening to swallow him whole. Mother tried to calm him, but he kept crying, saying he'd done unspeakable things to earn his wealth when he was young." Shirley smiled, showing brown teeth. "*That* part isn't in the exhibit. Pauline wouldn't allow it."

I pictured the portrait of Jakob that hung over Pauline's bed. His expression so haughty, so cold.

Chills crawled down my back.

"So, what were these unspeakable things he did?" Anna asked.

Shirley shook her head. "I don't know."

"Stealing?" Anna said. "Murder? Or . . . I'll bet he blackmailed the mill owner into selling the mill for cheap."

"No one knows," Shirley said. "But old Jakob was convinced his soul was damned."

I asked Shirley about the double X rune, but she was just as puzzled by the question as Edgar had been.

Then, as Anna and I were about to leave, something caught my eye: a framed photograph on the wall behind the Bible display.

It was a large black and white of Himmel Cottage. Several people in uniforms posed, unsmiling, on the porch steps. Judging from the women's bobbed hairstyles, I guessed that it dated to the 1920s.

Shirley followed my gaze. "The domestic staff of Himmel Cottage in 1922. A cook, three maids, two gardeners, and a chauffeur. Old Jakob Himmel had a Rolls-Royce, shipped all the way from England."

In the back row stood a middle-aged woman with fair—or maybe gray—hair. She wore a dark dress with a white apron. But her *face* . . . it was badly scarred on one side, caved in, puckered from her cheekbone to her jaw.

"The woman in the back," I said to Shirley, pointing. "Do you know what happened to her face?"

Shirley squinted. "Oh, yes. Bessie."

My breath caught. *Bessie?*

"Poor dear," Shirley went on. "It was a logging accident when she was young—she arrived in the camps when she was eighteen years old. People say it was an axe that got her. She's lucky she didn't get killed. Although, truth be told, she was never quite right in the head."

"She was the cook at Himmel Cottage?"

"Yes. Folks called her Crazy Bessie."

Oh my God, I thought. *It's her. The woman who wrote those strange things on the walls of the house.*

I turned again to Crazy Bessie's image. Her eyes weren't looking at the camera, but beyond. At something only she could see.

40

Anna and I parted ways in the parking lot, exchanging phone numbers and with her promising to pump Ruby for information about Ben and Gilda.

After that, I decided to head back to Himmel Cottage. Gray clouds churned, and raindrops splattered the windshield as I drove. Wind tore yellow leaves from the trees, sending them fluttering across the road.

At the driveway gate, I leaned out the car window to type the code into the security panel.

With a jolt I noticed a little circular gleam, like a watching eye.

It was a camera lens inside the hedge behind the security panel. I'd never noticed *that* before.

I glanced nervously around. Almost instantly I spotted a second camera inside the hedge on the passenger side.

They'd been here all this time.

Who was watching on the other end of the transmission? Nobody, probably. Just a computer database.

I tapped in the security code. The gate swung open, and I drove forward.

My heart was pumping with anxiety, but I told myself that Himmel Cottage, cute name aside, was the estate of a wealthy family, and of course they—no, *we*—had a security system in place.

◆ ◆ ◆

Back at the house, I paced the kitchen, still in my damp jacket, replaying that last part of the museum visit—Crazy Bessie, disfigured as a girl in the logging camps, working as the cook at Himmel Cottage in the 1920s.

What had she seen in this house? What had she survived? Jakob Himmel—visionary, empire builder, guilty of something unspeakable—had been her boss?

Or something worse?

I went to the pantry.

The air in there was stuffy and floury. I lifted the loose paper on the wall beside the cabinet, revealing Bessie's penciled scrawl:

I miss Mama. They say I'm crazy. Crazy Bessie. Nobody believes me, and so I'm all alone here in—

The writing disappeared behind the heavy wall-hung cabinet.

Next, I went to the utility closet. I crouched to read Bessie's writing down by the baseboard:

They tell you it's forever love
They show you the mark
too late
this house

The conjoined XX rune.

My heart stuttered. Hold on—

forever love.

Where had I seen that before?

I sank to the closet floor, pulled my phone from my jacket pocket, and punched open Instagram.

I *knew* it. Kirsten's post from just yesterday: **Your purity is your POWER girls. Use it wisely. #traditionalfamily #foreverlove #blessed**

Those words—*forever love*—and the rune . . . somehow, they connected Bessie from a century ago to Kirsten's Instagram posts.

What were you trying to say, Bessie? I thought. *Who were you trying to say it to?*

◆ ◆ ◆

I asked Gregor about the driveway security cameras that evening, over beef bourguignon that Emilia had left in the warming oven.

"Cameras by the driveway gate?" he said.

He *sounded* puzzled. He *looked* relaxed. But even though I loved him desperately, I couldn't help wondering if he was lying to me again.

"You don't know about them?" I said.

"Well, I mean, I'm not surprised." Gregor forked a chunk of meat into his mouth. "I think a few years back Mother had some kind of security system installed, but I don't know the details. Are you sure they're cameras?"

"Um, yes," I said. "What else would they be?"

"How do the cameras take the pictures?" Sam asked. "Don't you need a person to hold the camera?"

"No," Gregor said. "They're like robots. They can take pictures by themselves."

"That's weird," Sam said, spooning up macaroni and cheese. "I don't like it."

"You used to think robots were cool," Gregor said.

"Teacher Terra says robots are bad. She says they steal things from people."

"Was she talking about AI, buddy? That's not quite the same thing as robots." Gregor looked at me. "Since when are you interested in security systems?"

"I'm not saying I'm *interested*. It's just that I happened to notice the cameras for the first time today, and I guess they surprised me. That's all. Not a big deal."

◆ ◆ ◆

Kirsten's Instagram post the next day was a still life–style photo of several items shot from above: a burning taper candle, a blown glass goblet of what looked like white wine, a loaf of bread wrapped in a linen cloth, a shiny red apple, and a saucer holding five tiny golden rectangles. All artfully arranged on a ticking stripe tablecloth.

The caption said simply **Treasure for treasure. Gold in gratitude. #mamaknows #blessed**

Weird, I thought. *What's she promoting here?*

I magnified the picture and inspected the golden rectangles. They were about as long as a quarter, and they looked like actual gold. They also had something stamped on them. Letters, or numbers, or maybe both.

I blew up the picture as much as possible. I was pretty sure I could make out one word: *Valcambi.*

What the heck was Valcambi?

I googled it.

The top hit was for Valcambi.com. The second hit was a Wikipedia entry. I opened it.

> Valcambi is a precious metals refining company located in Balerna, Switzerland. Founded in 1961, Valcambi refines gold, silver, platinum, and palladium into various forms, including cast and minted bars.

So those were actual gold bars in Kirsten's picture. Probably one gram each, so—I googled some more—valued at around $66 each, or $330 total. Not that impressive as far as *treasure* went.

What was Kirsten doing with this post? It made no sense to me. And when I scrolled through the comments, I only saw things like **LOVE the tablecloth, mind sharing where you got it?** and **You are a beautiful soul Kirsten, please never stop sharing your amazing light with the world.**

It was so gross. She could do no wrong.

The next afternoon, I'd just buckled an exhausted, muddy Sam into his booster seat when I spotted Gilda.

My shoulders loosened in relief. After I hadn't seen her yesterday or this morning, I'd been starting to seriously worry.

But there she was, across the drizzly parking lot, thumping a crate into the back of Teacher Terra's Prius.

I needed to make sure she was okay.

"Hey," I said to Sam. "I'm just going to—"

Angry shouting erupted.

I saw a black pickup truck brake in the middle of the parking area. Exhaust mushroomed, and the windshield wipers thumped.

A man was leaning out the driver's window on his elbow. "—isn't mine! I figured it out, Hildy! I figured it out!" He was addressing one of the moms, who was clinging to the child in her arms and saying something I couldn't hear. She looked frightened and angry.

The other moms, watching from afar, looked wary.

"No! Fuck you," the man shouted at Hildy. "I should've thrown you out way before that little shit came along. I swear to God, I'll kill you if you try to squeeze even one more penny out of me!"

I jerked open my car door and scrabbled in my bag for my phone. "Sit tight, Sam," I said to him around the headrest. "Don't get out of the car."

My heart was in my throat. I was scared, but I needed to be documenting this. If the man saw me recording him, it might work as a deterrent. And if it didn't, I'd capture whatever he did next.

I opened my camera app, tapped "Video," and started to record.

"—whore!" the man screamed. "Why am I paying child support for some other guy's kid? I'm gonna sue you and your whole psycho bitch group!"

He jerkily turned the pickup around, engine roaring and mud spraying, women and children stumbling back, and then he was bouncing away.

I got a clear shot of his license plate before he disappeared around the bend.

41

I stopped recording. My heart pumped painfully. But the angry dad was gone, and no one had gotten hurt.

"You okay?" I asked Sam, who was still snug in his booster.

"Yeah," he said. "Who was that?"

"I'm not sure. But he's gone now. Will you be okay if I go and talk to Gilda for a second? I'll be right there." I pointed.

"Okay."

I approached Gilda. She'd resumed her task, stacking crates into the Prius.

"Hey," I said softly, stopping beside her.

She spun around, blinking. Her pupils were so dilated, they eclipsed the blue of her irises.

Wait, I thought. *Is she on drugs?*

She smiled. "Oh. Hey, Mrs. Sullivan."

"I didn't see you yesterday," I said, keeping my voice low. "I was worried."

Gilda tilted her head, still smiling. "Worried?"

"Have you thought any more about what you mentioned?" I asked. "About leaving the island? I could help."

Her brow creased. "Leave the island? Why would I leave? This is my home."

My stomach dropped.

"Gilda," I said gently. "The other day, you said—"

"I need to be good," she said. "It's very important for me to be good."

She turned back to the Prius, humming under her breath, reaching out to smooth the edge of a folded blanket in the trunk.

The sleeve of her sweater rode up, and I saw, just above her wrist, four small purple dots.

Bruises. The kind left by rough fingers.

Oh no, I thought.

"Gilda," I said softly. "Is someone hurting you?"

"Please leave me alone."

"But I—"

"Leave!" she screamed.

From all around the parking lot, mothers and children stared.

"You know where to find me," I whispered to Gilda. "Next door."

She was bent over the trunk again, and she didn't reply.

I drove about a mile away from KinderWild before pulling to the side of the road.

Sam was singing to himself in the back, kicking his boots against the seat. I forced my voice into a mom tone. "Hey, bud? I need to make a quick phone call, okay?"

"Can I play games on your phone?"

"Not right now."

I stepped out into the drizzle and closed the door gently behind me, trying to breathe around the pressure in my chest.

Gilda's voice was still ringing in my ears. *I need to be good.*

I scrolled to Anna's name and hit call.

She picked up on the first ring. "Hey."

"Hey. Did you—?" I swallowed. "Did you have a chance to talk to Ruby?"

A beat of silence. "Yeah. I did. I was planning on calling you this afternoon. It . . . didn't go great."

My stomach twisted. "What happened?"

"She got defensive. Said I was always looking for something to criticize, always trying to tear people down. That I hate everyone she likes."

"Jesus."

"Yeah. Oh, and she accused me of being jealous of Ben."

"Are you?"

Anna laughed. "Of *Ben*? No. But that just made me dig harder, obviously."

"What did she say?"

"She claims she's never even talked to Gilda. She says Gilda's always gone at KinderWild during the day, and by the time she gets back to the homestead, the band is finishing up. Which, honestly, tracks."

I felt a flicker of relief. This was true of Gregor, too.

"But Ruby did admit that Ben's not exactly a saint," Anna said slowly.

"*How* not-saint?"

"Well, she said she's heard things. From other women in the Seattle music scene. That Ben's the kind of guy who gets a little too handsy, corners women backstage, makes them feel like saying no would be bad for their careers or whatever. Just your classic predatory douche."

"Any legal charges?"

"That's a good question. We should check. But listen—here's the kicker." Anna lowered her voice. "Apparently, the woman he was dating before Kirsten? She disappeared."

I smeared rain off my forehead. "What do you mean 'disappeared'?"

"She was a bartender. Her name was Lucy Nowak. This was . . . I don't know, five or six years ago? Ruby didn't know her personally. But she said Ben was seeing her for a few months and then—boom. One day she didn't show up for work. Never turned up again. Officially a missing person."

I was starting to feel queasy. "What are we dealing with here? Serial killers?"

"That's not even funny."

"I'm not sure it was supposed to be."

I hadn't told Anna about the head I might've seen when I'd fallen down the ravine. Or all the fresh-dug holes I'd discovered when I'd returned. That was going to have to wait for another time.

"Lucy's disappearance," I said. "The cops just . . . dropped it?"

"Basically. No suspects. No evidence. She was young, worked nights, didn't have a big support system. You know how it goes."

My throat had gone dry. "Okay. And how did Ben and Kirsten meet?"

"I asked. Ruby wasn't sure. Probably at a gig? That's how these guys always meet women."

That's how I met Gregor, I thought. Suddenly it seemed not romantic but a little bit sleazy.

I swiveled to look at Sam inside the car. He was drawing on the fogged window with one finger. Our eyes met. He grinned. My heart cramped with love.

Whatever happens with Gregor, I thought, *I need to make sure this kid is always a part of my life.*

"Listen," I said to Anna. "I was just at KinderWild, and I spoke to Gilda—or tried to, anyway. She looked . . . kind of drugged."

"Shit."

"Yeah. And she had bruises on her wrist."

"*Jesus Christ.* Really?"

"I feel like I should do something, but—" I let out a frustrated breath. "If a grown adult tells you to leave them alone, what are you supposed to do? *Force* them to accept your help?"

On the other end of the line, Anna sighed. "Yeah. I get it."

A beat.

"I could run a background check on Ben," she said. "My friend in HR swears by this site—super legit. You technically need his consent, but . . . who's going to know the difference? If Ben has a documented criminal history, maybe *that* would convince Gilda to get out of there."

"Would you?" I said.

"I'm already pulling up the website," Anna replied. "I'll let you know as soon as I have the results."

◆ ◆ ◆

Another missing woman tied to Ben and Kirsten Blakeley.

What rattled me the most was how unsurprising it felt. Like I'd been bracing for it. I mean, let's be honest—a pattern was emerging.

Maybe *serial killers* was too dramatic. There were only two missing girls, Liz and now Lucy. Who knew if either of them was even dead. So far, I hadn't even been able to confirm that Liz ever came to the island.

But there had been *so many* holes down there at the bottom of the ravine. And that chopped-off head I may or may not have seen?

It still looked real in my memory.

So now, I was trapped in a purgatory of waiting.

I was waiting for my period to start—or not.

Waiting for the DNA kit to show up.

Waiting for Anna to find out what else Ben might be hiding.

Saying I *felt anxious* is an understatement. I was electric. My body was stuck in a fight-or-flight loop, waiting for a blow that never came. Every sound made me flinch. Every silence felt like a warning.

Acting normal was my new Olympic sport.

42

I was wearing the old-fashioned nightgown again, late on Friday night, because Gregor had asked me to.

It was bunched and twisted around my waist as I lay underneath him. But apparently even the nightgown and my braid weren't enough, because he abruptly pulled out of me, cursing under his breath, and got off the bed.

He stalked naked to the windows. The dim light from outside illuminated his flat belly, his limp penis. Frustration radiated from him.

"I'm sorry," I whispered.

He didn't answer for a second. He was looking out the window, although it was so dark he couldn't have seen much. Then he said, without turning, "Are you going to be one of those women who's only interested in sex if it can get her pregnant?"

"What?" I said. *"No."*

"You were lying there like a corpse. I assume it's because you aren't fertile right now so why bother?"

"Well, I'm sorry," I said, "but this nightgown isn't exactly conducive to gymnastics."

"It's just a lot of pressure, okay?" he said. "For me."

"Pressure?" I repeated.

"How is that a surprise, Harlow? We've been trying to conceive for a solid year with nothing to show for it. How could I *not* feel pressure? I mean, *Jesus*." He raked a hand over his head.

"But it's not . . . it's not *you*, honey. It's me. My body. You're great—your sperm is great. The doctor said so—"

"Jesus," Gregor muttered.

My heart sank. I'd gone too far. Again.

"Little asshole," Gregor said, hunching to peer through the window.

He wasn't talking about me, I realized first with relief and then swift alarm. He was talking about someone outside.

"I've had it with this bullshit," he said, and he turned and strode out of the bedroom. I heard him going down the hallway, and then the stairs.

What was *happening*?

I bolted out of bed, yanking down the nightgown as I followed him. Was there an intruder? Someone he'd seen sneaking around on the grounds?

When I reached the bottom of the staircase, I saw Gregor's silhouette crossing the hall from the library into the dining room.

"Gregor?" I whispered, following. "Honey, what's wrong?"

I stopped in the dining room doorway. Gregor, still naked, was pulling open one of the French doors leading to the porch. As he stepped outside, a blast of cold air swirled around me and stuck the nightgown to my shins.

Then I saw what he was carrying. Something long and slim.

A rifle.

I thought of the ravine. The pop of gunfire.

"Gregor?" I whispered again, louder now. I was quaking from the cold, or adrenaline, or both.

Out on the porch I heard him half snarl, half whisper, "Quiet, you fool, you'll scare him away." I was pretty sure this time he *was* talking to me.

But it didn't occur to me to run. My only thought was to go to him, coax him, talk him down.

I went to the open doors. Gregor was standing at the porch railing with the gun braced against his bare shoulder and aimed at something on the lawn.

Against the glow of the harbor, I saw the silhouette of a buck walking sedately through the night. I made out its pronged antlers and the flick of its tail.

Gregor made a sound, something between a snort and an inhale.

"Don't," I whispered as he squeezed the trigger.

A boom rebounded across the harbor. I jumped. With a high-pitched bawl, the buck crumpled to the ground.

"Gotcha," Gregor muttered.

"Honey, why?" I said, half sobbing, and it was far away because of the ringing in my ears.

He turned to me, lowering the gun.

He was smiling. Even in the poor light I could see the flash of his teeth.

"They're parasites, babe. Getting rid of that buck will prevent God knows how many more deer from being born. Way more efficient than killing the does and fawns."

I opened my mouth. The question forming on my lips was, *Who are you?*

Instead I said, very precisely, not wanting to sound hysterical, "Is that the gun from the library?"

"Yeah. My father's old Winchester."

"But your mom said it was only decorative."

"She did?" Gregor laughed. "No. It's kept in working order."

"Isn't that dangerous?"

"Country living, babe. Gotta be ready for anything."

I glanced over to the dark, dead lump on the grass. "Should we just leave it? What if Sam sees?"

"The landscaping guys will clean it up. And Sam's old enough for a little reality."

Gregor stepped toward me, tossing the gun carelessly on a settee. He wrapped me in his arms and held me too tightly, and I could feel that now, finally, his penis was hard.

◆ ◆ ◆

I lay in the dark after Gregor went back to sleep, my hips ensnared by that horrible nightgown and his seed trickling slowly from between my legs, and I imagined him stalking me through the forest as though I were an animal.

Watching me from behind a blind.

Tracking my progress up the treed slope.

Raising the rifle, pressing it against his shoulder.

Pulling the trigger.

I woke to the sound of a scream.

I bolted upright in bed, squinting in the morning light, heart pumping, tangled in the now-sweaty nightgown. I strained my ears.

Silence.

Memories of last night punched into my consciousness. Gregor with the rifle. The boom and the scent of gunpowder. The crumpled dead buck.

I turned my head. Gregor was still asleep, sprawled on his belly, a faint smile on his lips. How had he slept through that scream? Or . . . maybe I'd only dreamed it?

No—downstairs. Sounds. Not a scream this time, but—could it be?—sobbing.

Climbing out of bed, I slid on my glasses. I grabbed my robe and pulled it on as I walked out of the bedroom and to the top of the stairs.

Definitely sobbing, and low, chanting murmurs. A woman's voice.

Emilia.

I knotted the belt of my robe as I went downstairs.

Emilia was standing by the kitchen sink, hugging herself and rocking as she prayed. She swung her head when she heard me come in, and I saw that her eyes were red, her cheeks wet.

"Mrs. Sullivan," she whispered. "Sorry. I'm sorry. Did I wake you?"

"What's the matter?" I asked, reaching for a roll of paper towels on the counter. I ripped one off and passed it to her. "Are you okay?"

"I am silly," she said, taking the paper towel. She pressed it to one eye and then the other, soaking up her tears. "There is something dead outside. It frightened me."

I glanced out the window. Fog made the morning an empty white glow. I couldn't even see the harbor. But I could see the buck on the grass, a tangle of antlers and legs and fur blotched with blood. Or maybe I only imagined the blood. Surely it was too foggy for me to make out that detail.

"Gregor shot it," I said. "Last night. It's okay. It's only a deer."

"Yes, Mrs. Sullivan. Thank you. I'm sorry I woke you. It will not happen again."

"Did you . . . think it was something else?"

Her eyes went wary. "I don't know what you mean."

"Please," I said. "Tell me."

Her eyes were brimming again. "It isn't time."

"Time for what?"

"For him to come."

43

"For *who* to come?" I whispered urgently to Emilia.

She looked away.

"Please," I said. "I need to know."

She lowered her voice to a murmur. "Sometimes when the moon is full, a man comes."

I remembered what Pauline had said about Emilia: *Silly woman. She hates the full moon.*

"A *man*?" I said. "He comes here? To the house?"

"Not inside the house—I have never seen him inside, but once I saw his footprints on the porch. He walks on the grounds. In the trees. He stands on the lawn and stares up at the house. My cousin, she was here with me once and she saw him on the beach, running. He is always naked. He comes out of the dirt, I think, because when I see him, he is covered with dirt and . . ." Emilia's hand shook as she wrapped it over her mouth.

"And what?" I said. "He's covered with dirt and what?"

"Blood," she whispered into her palm.

"Harlow?" Gregor called. It sounded like he was in the hall.

"He is the grandfather," Emilia whispered. "From the painting upstairs. He crawls out of a hole in the ground that leads to Hell."

Blood. Dirt. Running. Hadn't I seen all that with my own eyes our first night on the island?

But Emilia wasn't magically seeing Jakob Himmel. She was seeing my husband. And she was making it sound like he ran around on this property, high and naked, a *lot*.

"Low?" Gregor called again, closer now.

"How many times have you seen him?" I whispered to Emilia.

She glanced past me. "I should start my work."

"How many times?"

"Harlow?" This was Gregor, in the kitchen now.

Emilia turned to the sink. She flipped on the faucet and water gushed.

"What's going on?" Gregor asked. He was wearing nothing but a pair of boxer briefs, and he was holding his phone.

"Just chatting with Emilia about the grocery shopping," I said lightly.

"That's not what it sounded like."

"Really?"

He was frowning at Emilia's back. "It sounded like someone's upset."

"Oh, well, she *did* see the dead deer out there. I think it surprised her?"

"Emilia." Gregor said her name loudly, commandingly.

Slowly, Emilia turned off the faucet. She looked over her shoulder with wide eyes. "Yes, Mr. Sullivan?"

"Tell the landscapers to come and take away that buck. The sooner the better. Tell them they can keep it for the meat if they want."

"Yes, Mr. Sullivan."

"And brew some coffee. I have a killer headache."

"Yes, Mr. Sullivan."

Gregor sat down on one of the island stools—wasn't he cold with basically nothing on?—and started thumbing through his phone.

◆ ◆ ◆

It was Saturday, so Gregor, Sam, and I had breakfast together, and then the three of us went to the farmers' market in town.

When we returned to the cottage, laden with lettuce and peppers and kale and plums, the dead buck was gone. I could see where it had been, a flattened patch of grass. And Emilia was gone, too. She usually didn't leave until the afternoon, and I could see she hadn't vacuumed or even emptied the dishwasher.

I said something about this to Gregor as I was putting the produce away in the crisper bin.

"Yeah," he said, biting into a plum. "I let her go."

"What?" I shut the refrigerator door and turned. "You fired her?"

"Uh-huh." He took another bite of plum, and yellow juice trickled down his chin.

"Does your mom know?"

"Believe it or not, I'm able to make decisions without my mother's help." He smeared the plum juice away.

"That's not what I . . . I mean, Emilia's technically your mom's employee, so—"

"Then when my mother is living in this house again, she can rehire Emilia, if that's what she wants."

"Did Emilia . . . What did she do? To make you fire her?"

He heard what she said, I thought.

"Well, first of all, you're not working," Gregor said, "so why are we paying some other woman to cook and clean for us when you could be doing those things?"

"I thought you wanted me to be . . . de-stressing." It sounded ridiculous said aloud.

"Why is it that you never learned how to keep a house?"

"*Excuse* me?"

"When we met, I thought you were this wholesome small-town girl, but you can barely put together a peanut butter and jelly sandwich, and I haven't seen you vacuum even once."

"Because we've had housekeepers doing that stuff for us." I was holding my own elbows tight. It felt like if I didn't, I might float away.

"And I was working sixty-hour weeks at the lab long before we met. Since when do you care about any of this, anyway?"

"Ever since you stopped working sixty-hour weeks."

"That was *your* idea."

"Because *you* want a baby."

I drew back. "I was under the impression that you wanted a baby, too."

"I do." Gregor spat the plum pit into the sink. "Look. I just think it would be good for us, for you, for me, and especially for Sam, if we tried for a little more, I don't know, *normalcy* at home. Sam goes to school with kids who have mothers who not only cook three scratch meals a day and clean their own houses but who also grow their own food."

Why don't you just be with her? I wanted to scream. *Why are you trying to make me* into *her?*

"And I see their kids," Gregor went on, "and they're thriving. And I want that for Sam. And I want that for you, too, Low."

"You want me to become a domestic drudge?"

"God, why do you have to put such a negative spin on everything? No. I want you to embrace family life. There's nothing wrong with being traditional."

Hashtag tradwife, I thought. *Hashtag masculinefeminine.*

I took a big breath. "I love you, Gregor, but . . . what is happening to you?"

"To *me*? I think the better question is, What's happening to *you*? It's like the minute you stepped on this island, you became a total train wreck." He was walking away, but he added over his shoulder, "Get yourself together, Low. You're never going to hack it as a mother if you can't even take care of yourself."

I stared after him, mute. I couldn't even process the cruelty—the *unfairness*—of all that he'd just said.

Kirsten's Saturday post showed a ruffly white apron tied around someone's waist. At first, I thought I was only imagining the spatter of fine red droplets across the fabric.

I used my thumb and forefinger to zoom in.

The apron was flecked with something red. *Blood*red.

> I culled one of our hens today. Lucy hadn't laid eggs for a good long while. She was also causing some issues with Magda, our rooster's favorite wife, pecking her and being all-around a jealous troublemaker so it's good riddance plus chicken stew again for dinner LOL. I get a lot of questions about how to humanely cull chickens. THE most humane way possible is by decapitation. Lots of people think neck dislocation is best, but death doesn't occur for 15-20 seconds, but with decapitation it's all over in a moment. Yes, it's messy. So what? I feel like modern civilization is scared of blood. Blood is GOOD. It's beautiful. It's the most precious, sacred thing on this planet. So let's stop being scared of blood and start celebrating it. Things that are natural are good and right. Period. RIP Lucy!!

Lucy? I thought. *She named a hen after her husband's disappeared ex? That is sick. It's deranged.*

I skimmed the comments.

> Good for you doing it humanely!

> Could you share your chicken stew recipe?

> Didn't you slaughter another hen named Lucy like three months ago?

44

All that day, I tried to pretend it wasn't strange how Gregor had fired Emilia, and I tried to pretend he hadn't savaged my feelings when he'd accused me of being a *train wreck*.

An outside observer would've thought we were a happy little family as we spent the evening making dinner together and watching the movie Sam picked out—one of the Minions movies—snuggled under blankets in the den.

Gregor even reached for me in bed that night, and he didn't ask me to put on the nightgown.

◆ ◆ ◆

The next day, Sunday, was the day my period was due. There was no sign of it in the morning. But when I went to the bathroom after lunch, I saw blood on the toilet paper.

I think I died for a second.

I tore off more toilet paper and wiped again, and there was more dark blood. No way I could tell myself it was early pregnancy spotting. This was my period: aggressive, irrefutable, and unwanted.

Over the last days I'd experimented with telling myself that, considering my doubts about Gregor, and knowing that he'd lied to me at the very least about calling the police and at most about his relationship to Kirsten and her kids, maybe I wasn't sure I *wanted* his baby.

But now, as I rummaged around the vanity drawers for a tampon, I knew it didn't matter. My desire for a baby was so powerful, it didn't matter how many lies Gregor might've told me.

A soft rap sounded on the bathroom door. "Low?" It was Gregor. "Babe, are you okay?"

That's when I realized I was weeping aloud, harsh barking sobs, and the reason I couldn't find the stupid tampons was because I was blinded by tears.

"Yeah," I managed. "Just a minute!"

He rattled the doorknob, but I'd locked it. I'd been locking the bathroom door every time lately, it occurred to me.

When exactly did I start doing that?

Here were the tampons, finally, under the box of pregnancy tests. The sight of the tests unleashed a fresh wave of sobs.

"Low!" Gregor called.

"Just a second!" I called back, tearing the wrapper off a tampon.

One minute later, I unlocked the bathroom door and opened it.

"Babe," Gregor murmured when he saw me. "Did . . . ?"

"Yeah," I said, my face crumpling.

"I'm so sorry." Something I didn't understand passed across his face and was gone. "I'm so, so sorry, babe."

I sagged into his arms. He held me close and rocked me, and I told myself that at least I wasn't all alone in my pain.

We lay down on our bed together and I clung to him, weeping, until I fell asleep.

◆ ◆ ◆

It was dusk when I woke. Gregor wasn't there, but I heard kitchen sounds downstairs. Then Gregor's muffled voice, and Sam's.

I lay there for a long time, swamped by misery.

It wasn't getting easier.

No, each month that I failed to conceive only brought more despair. And, more than anything, the panicked sense that time was running out.

Ticktock, bitch.

I saw a sudden flash of the expression on Gregor's face earlier, when I'd told him my period had started. At the time I hadn't understood what it meant, but now I knew.

Relief.

When he learned that, once again, I'd failed to conceive, my husband had been *relieved*.

On Monday morning I couldn't face getting out of bed, so Gregor took Sam to KinderWild.

I lay in bed for hours in the silent house. Its stubborn emptiness seemed to mock the emptiness inside my womb. I tried to remember what, besides having a baby, I even cared about. Everything else seemed flat and stale. Even my love for Gregor seemed like something I was viewing through a pane of glass.

I finally hauled myself out of bed.

Downstairs, the kitchen was a disaster. Dirty dishes were piled up in the sink, the floor needed vacuuming, the sink strainer was clogged with macaroni, and, when I peeked in the fridge to see if anything looked tempting, I was confronted with stinky containers of aging takeout.

I shut the fridge.

Suddenly, all I wanted to do was go for a good, hard, sweaty run.

I knew it was against Dr. Zakarian's recommendations, but I needed to feel like there was more to my life, more to my own body, than just my reproductive capacity.

I put on my running gear, plugged in my earbuds, turned a dance music playlist up as high as I could stand it, and went.

It felt amazing. I hadn't gone running for weeks, since that day at the fertility clinic in New York. As I stood in the shower afterward with the hot water coursing down my tired, relaxed muscles, I felt almost like myself again.

◆ ◆ ◆

The newest from IntoTheWoodsWeGo: a photograph of a belly in a delicate pink dress with a fleecy cardigan over it. The cardigan's lower three buttons are undone because the soft swell of the belly had pushed it open in an almost lewd way.

> **They try to tell you your life ends with motherhood. That is totally wrong. My life BEGAN when I became a mother (at the ripe old age of 20, LOL). Looking back, I can see that before I was blessed with my firstborn, I wasn't a full person yet. I was only half-formed, because I hadn't come into my full inheritance as a woman and as a human being. I feel SO bad for all the women out there who are struggling to conceive, especially the older women who might not ever get their chance. But there is hope. It lies in finding the sacredness, the sacrifice, and the rebirth inside of yourself. #fertility #naturalmotherhood #blessed**

That evil bitch, I thought. *Kirsten knows my period started. Gregor must've told her. And she must've somehow known I'd see this post, because she's taunting me.*

◆ ◆ ◆

Paternitrust.com had sent me a USPS tracking number once they mailed my test kit. I'd been obsessively checking the package's status online, watching it creep from Illinois to Colorado to California to Washington in a route that seemed maddeningly indirect.

At last, on Monday morning, the tracking notice I'd been waiting for appeared in my inbox: Your package has been delivered.

At the mailbox, I was mindful of the security cameras by the gates. I carried the box hidden underneath a stack of catalogs and envelopes.

In the house again, I went upstairs and put the box inside one of the empty suitcases in Gregor's and my closet. Then I locked the suitcase zippers together with the tiny padlock and buried the key in my underwear drawer.

◆ ◆ ◆

That afternoon, I approached Kirsten in the Gathering Place. She was trying to coax her sons from a game of Throw the Mud with some other little boys.

I took a deep breath and locked on a smile. "Kirsten," I said. "Hi."

She turned to me, Barri in her arms. "Harlow. Hey. How *are* you?"

"Great," I said. "Really great." I willed myself not to look down at her belly. "Hey, I was wondering—Sam's still struggling to come out of his shell socially, and I was wondering if maybe you and your kids would be up for an after-school playdate today? I was thinking maybe some one-on-one time with Magni might be a more comfortable way for him to start getting to know some other children. I think he's overwhelmed here at school."

Being such a liar didn't feel great. Neither did using Sam as an excuse.

Kirsten looked right into my eyes. I felt sweat spring up on my palms.

She knows, I thought. *She knows everything.*

But then she smiled, and I told myself I was imagining things. "A playdate would be *so* nice," she said. "Maybe we could use your beach?

This could be the last dry day for a while, at least according to the forecast."

"Oh," I said. "Yeah. Definitely. Would today work?"

"Absolutely," Kirsten said, sounding so genuine that my belly curdled with guilt.

I'm not a monster, I reminded myself. *I just need to know the truth.*

45

Kirsten followed me in her Volvo back to Himmel Cottage.

We parked and then walked with the children down the lawn and out onto the beach. The water was a sparkling, surreal blue. Little waves made the pebbles roll and click together.

"How was your weekend?" I asked Kirsten after we'd settled ourselves side by side on a driftwood log. The three little boys had gone down to the shoreline. "Were you guys able to enjoy the nice weather?"

It was hard not to slide my hand into my jacket pocket to make sure the sandwich-size Ziploc baggie was still there.

"My weekend?" Kirsten said. "It was fine, I guess." She had baby Barri on her lap. Barri was gumming on a wooden teething ring that gleamed with saliva. "Gilda and I took about a million pictures. I think we ended up with some usable shots, but we need one good one for almost every day. It starts to seem like a lot." She sighed. "And things are kind of crazy at our place, ever since the band started working. There's no running water in the barn, so they're always coming into the house to use the bathroom, and then they make a mess in the kitchen when they have lunch, and it seems like every day someone forgets to latch the chicken run or the garden shed door or whatever."

"Oh," I said. "For some reason I had the idea the band was holed up in the barn all day."

"I wish." Kirsten laughed. "Ben says that's not how the creative process works. They'll be, like, lying out in the field smoking weed, or they'll go for super long walks in the woods. One time I came home to find Ruby sleeping in my bed. Can you *believe* her?"

"Wait—*all* of them go for walks in the woods?"

In my mind I saw Gregor stalking me through the underbrush.

Raising the rifle.

"Yeah," Kirsten said. "The woods are *so* inspiring."

For a second our gazes locked in what felt like perfect mutual understanding: She knew I'd been shot at.

She knew I was picturing my own husband pulling the trigger.

But then she looked away, over to her sons playing by the water's edge, and her profile was so young-looking, so tender, that once again I was overcome with the feeling that I'd gotten it all wrong.

Stop falling for her act, I told myself.

"Mama!" Alder shouted. "*Mama!* I found crabs! Take a picture! Take a picture!"

"Could you hold Barri for a minute?" Kirsten was pushing her baby into my arms.

The compact lightness of the baby was a shock. I held her awkwardly as I watched Kirsten walking away.

Then I came to my senses. Kirsten's back was turned. It was time to act.

Barri was still gumming her wooden teething ring. Her fat little fist was locked around it.

I pinched the ring between my thumb and forefinger and gave a tug. This only made Barri grip it more tightly. I tugged a little harder. She held on.

I glanced over at Kirsten. She was bent at the waist, squaring her phone with something on the ground.

"Get the claws, Mama," Alder was saying. "They're real sharp."

I repositioned Barri on my lap so I could use both my hands. I took hold of the slimy teething ring again. With my other hand, I pried away Barri's surprisingly strong little fingers.

She let out a whine.

Kirsten was straightening. Turning.

I slid the teething ring into the Ziploc in my pocket.

Kirsten's eyes met mine just as I pulled my hand from my pocket again.

Barri started crying, stiffening and twisting and turning pink.

"I'm sorry," I murmured to her, jouncing her gently up and down. "I really am."

Kirsten was approaching, frowning at her baby in concern.

She scooped Barri from my arms and pressed her against her shoulder. Instantly, Barri stopped crying.

"Don't worry," Kirsten said to me. "It's not an acquired skill. It's buried in your DNA somewhere."

I looked up at her, my entire body going cold. Had she seen me pocketing the teething ring? "What is?"

"How to comfort babies," she said.

"Oh."

"Even if you're, like, the most unnatural woman in the world, when you become a mama, you figure it out. Primal nature kicks in, I guess." She smiled down at me, but her green eyes looked empty.

"I'm already a mama." I forced myself to match her smile. "I'm Sam's mama."

"Well, *step*mama."

My face went hot. "What's the difference?"

Kirsten sat down beside me and put Barri to her breast. "Mother's milk. Blood."

"So you're saying that bodily fluids are what's standing between me and enlightenment? It's not about love? Care?"

"I had trouble conceiving, too," Kirsten said. "At first."

That surprised me enough that I forgot to be angry for a second. "You did?"

"Yeah. It just wouldn't happen for me, and I wanted a baby so, so badly. Like, I *craved* a baby. To feel it growing inside me. To hold it in my arms, and to smell it? So I could feel like my life was on the right track, or, I don't know, to feel like I had a place in the timeline of humanity? And, I guess also because of the way I grew up, and because of what a disaster my own mom was. She was in and out of rehab for my whole childhood, until she wound up OD'ing on fentanyl last year . . ."

"Oh God," I murmured. "I'm so sorry."

"I just wanted to prove to myself that *I* could do it. That *I* could be a good mom, even if my own mom sucked. You know?"

"So how did you make it work?" I asked. *Here we go,* I thought. *Truth time.* "Getting pregnant, I mean. If that's not too personal a question."

Kirsten gazed dreamily out at the water. A breeze blew hairs like platinum threads across her cheek. "Things weren't great with Ben," she said. "Before we got married there was this other girl—Lucy."

The name went through me like an electric rod.

Lucy. Ben's old girlfriend who disappeared.

"She just couldn't get over Ben," Kirsten went on. "They'd only gone on, like, one date—and it got really awkward. But we figured it out—that was a huge stepping stone."

"You . . . figured it out?" I said.

How? I thought. *By murdering your husband's ex?*

"Once I finally figured out that it's really about sacrifice," Kirsten said, "and faith, and your sense of the sacred, once I recognized that it's all, like, bigger than you are, that's when I finally conceived Magni."

What is she even talking about? I thought wildly.

She kept going. "You can go to doctors, and they'll give you drugs or whatever, but the truth is, science has no way to explain that really, it's all about dirt and sky and water and blood and *love.* I mean, I wasn't getting pregnant because, bottom line, I wasn't in love and I didn't believe in anything. But now . . ." She smiled down at her suckling baby and stroked her cheek with a fingertip. "Now, everything is different. Now I'm in love."

With who? I wanted to rage. *Who are you in love with? Who do you believe in? Is it my husband? Your husband? Your pagan penis god?*

"Got it," I said, getting to my feet. "Interesting theory."

"When your time comes, Harlow, you'll understand."

"Putting a pin in that." I started walking. It felt hard to breathe. "I'm going to check on Sam."

Inwardly, I added, *You absolute freaking psycho.*

46

Sam was drawing in the wet sand with a stick. He was so focused that he didn't seem to notice my approach.

When I was close enough to see what he was drawing, my lungs tightened even more.

It was the rune with the double X's. The one symbolizing the ancient male fertility god Inguz.

Oh my God, they're even brainwashing the preschoolers with their crazy pagan stuff, I thought. *We have to take him out of that school.*

"Hey," I said to signal my approach.

Sam gave a startled little jolt and looked up. His eyes were huge.

"That's an interesting design," I said, crouching beside him. It took all my energy to act casual.

He shrugged.

"Did you learn it at school?"

No answer.

Magni came running up from behind us, dragging a driftwood branch. He stopped beside Sam and me, scowling down at the X's in the sand. Then he dropped the branch, stepped right on top of all the X's in his filthy bare feet, and started kicking.

"Magni," I said. *"No."*

"Stop," Sam said tearfully. "You're wrecking my work."

Magni ignored us. Sand sprayed. In another moment, all the X's had been obliterated, and Magni picked up his branch again.

"That wasn't very nice, Magni," I said, my voice shaking with anger. *Wait,* I thought. *Do I hate a child?* "You ruined Sam's pictures."

"He can't draw those," Magni said. "They're not *for* him."

"Sam can draw whatever he wants," I said, struggling to keep my voice gentle.

Magni shook his head, pale locks brushing his shoulders. "Nuh-uh. It's only for *us*."

"For who?" I asked him. But my eyes were on Sam, whose chin was starting to quiver.

"The children of God," Magni said, and he was on the move again, dragging his piece of driftwood behind him.

I looked back to Sam. His face was crumpled, thumb in his mouth, and he was stabbing viciously at the sand with his stick.

"Who are the children of God?" I asked him.

"Them," Sam said around his thumb. "The rest of the kids. But not me."

"Oh, sweetie. No." I tried to wrap him in a hug, but he shook me off.

"Sam," I said, my voice breaking, "you're just as much a . . . a special person as any other kid. Actually, I think you're *extra* special."

"I don't *care*." He kicked savagely at the sand, sending wet, dark globs flying. "I don't care I don't care I don't *care*."

"Let's go home," I said.

Sam looked at me sharply. His thumb dropped from his mouth. "To New York?"

I felt a pang. "No, baby, I just meant . . . our home here. The cottage."

His shoulders sagged. "Oh."

"Are you ready?"

He nodded. "I told you Magni was mean," he said as he got to his feet.

"Yeah," I said, standing, too. "I believe you."

◆ ◆ ◆

Hand in hand, Sam and I walked back to Kirsten. She was still on the log nursing Barri.

"I think Sam's had enough for the day," I said. "But you guys are free to use the beach as long as you like."

"Hey," someone called behind us, and we both turned to see Gregor crunching through the pebbles. "I saw you guys from the house."

He stopped, pushing his hands into his jacket pockets. Wind fanned his hair against his taut throat. His eyes crinkled up against the light on the water. The sight of him gave me something like a sugar rush.

Frowning, he glanced to Kirsten and then back to me again, as though he couldn't figure out why we were together.

I also saw him look at Sam's hand, still clasped in mine. He seemed more annoyed than confused by that part.

"How was the afternoon session?" Kirsten asked Gregor, as though *she* were his wife. "Did you guys finally figure out a bridge for the turpentine song?"

He smiled at her and Barri with bright, warm eyes, and I wanted to scream.

They led the way, that golden couple, one's unspeakable beauty multiplying the other's into infinity like a hall of mirrors. Through the driftwood, up the seawall, and across the lawn toward the house.

Sam and I straggled behind them. My feet were so heavy. When I glanced over my shoulder, I saw Magni and Alder making their way in our direction. They were somehow wrestling and walking at the same time.

"I'll go out to the driveway gate and open it for you," Gregor said to Kirsten. "It was acting glitchy, and I want to make sure you don't get trapped."

I hadn't noticed the gate acting glitchy. Did Gregor just want an excuse to talk to Kirsten alone?

"Sam's cold, so I'm going to get him inside," I said, but it didn't seem like Gregor had heard.

Kirsten smiled over her shoulder. There was a flash of triumph in her eyes.

The thought of her baby's DNA sample safely inside the Ziploc in my pocket was some consolation.

Sam and I went inside.

◆ ◆ ◆

I watched from the kitchen window as Gregor and Kirsten walked to the parked Volvo.

What were they talking about? The band? Her children? Could they be talking about *me*?

Kirsten got her kids into the car, talking with Gregor the whole time. Then she was pulling something from her cardigan pocket—an envelope—and giving it to him. He stuffed it into his own jacket pocket.

What's that? I wondered with a hot rush of jealousy.

Kirsten got behind the wheel of her Volvo, laughing again. Gregor shut the door for her before striding away toward the gate. She started her car and rolled slowly after him.

I waited for the pain to hit. It didn't come. I'd gone blessedly numb.

I clicked into efficiency mode.

I went upstairs, locked myself in the bathroom, and packed Barri's Ziploc-bagged teething toy in the DNA test kit return box, along with, in a separate baggie, a snipping of the nightgown stiffened with Gregor's semen.

I'd already filled out the enclosed forms and created a profile on Paternitrust.com. The kit had come with a prepaid label, which I stuck to the box, and I sealed it with packing tape and slipped it into my shoulder bag.

"Where are you going?" Gregor asked me as I braked the Mercedes beside him on the driveway. He was walking back from the gate.

"I totally forgot that I need to get something to the post office before they close."

"What?"

"Something for Audrey. I'll be right back."

He was opening his mouth to say something else, but I pressed the gas pedal and left him behind.

The box's prepaid label meant I didn't need to stand in line at the post office. Still, I felt like I might jump right out of my skin when I rolled up to the drive-through mailbox and tipped the box in.

One more week. Then I'd have the results.

47

Back from the post office, I forced myself to ask Gregor about the envelope. Part of me wanted to stay oblivious. I also didn't want another fight.

But I needed to know.

"What did Kirsten give you?" I asked, walking into the kitchen. He was slicing an apple at the island. Sam sat across from him, unscrewing the lid from a jar of peanut butter.

Gregor looked at me blankly. "What?"

"I saw her give you an envelope?"

"Oh, *that*."

"Yeah," I said stiffly. "That."

"Babe." He set down the knife, closed the distance between us in one stride, and then his arms were tight around me. "It's the rent check."

"What?" I pulled away, frowning up at him.

"Didn't I tell you? Ben and Kirsten are our tenants. Their house is on our land."

I was so relieved, I almost burst into tears.

I kind of got into a groove for a few days. I wasn't zen, exactly. But I wasn't going to form any opinions—and not even *think*, if possible, until I got the DNA test results back. So it was Thursday, after I'd dropped off Sam, gone for a run, and made myself a blueberry smoothie, that it finally hit me:

If we were the Blakeleys' landlords and owned their homestead, didn't it follow that we also owned the forest next to the homestead?

And the paths?

And the ravine?

Excitement swelled inside me. If that security camera by the ravine was on our land . . . then *it* belonged to us, too. And if I could gain access to the footage, maybe I could catch a glimpse of whoever had shot at me. Maybe I could see who dug those holes.

Maybe I could even see, once and for all, if there had been a head or not.

My entire body went shivery with anticipation. And dread.

I went to the library.

This was the room with the family photo albums, all pine paneling and green leather chairs. The rifle Gregor had used to shoot the buck was once again hanging over the fireplace. A desk stood by windows overlooking the forest behind the house, and there was a computer on the desk, the kind with a separate monitor. Little blue lights flittered. It was always on. I'd never given it a second thought until now.

I went over and tapped the space bar on the keyboard. The monitor flashed to life.

A field for a password appeared in the middle of the screen.

Of course. Nothing was *that* easy.

I thought about it. Gregor's mom Pauline was in her sixties. Definitely not of the tech generation, plus she'd never worked for a living. I pictured her sitting here with reading glasses on, peering mystified at the screen, tapping at keys with one finger. What kind of password would she choose? Since she didn't to my knowledge have any pets, she'd probably choose something to do with Gregor, her only child.

I typed *Gregor1992*.

Nope.

I tried it with a lowercase *g*.

Nope.

I hesitated. If I tried too many times, I was going to get locked out of the computer entirely. It might even send a notification to Pauline that someone was trying to hack in.

Stop, I thought. *Breathe.*

Impulsively, I pulled open the desk's center drawer. An organizer tray held office supplies. A small dog-eared brown notebook was nestled in a compartment with some paperclips. I picked up the notebook and flipped it open.

Penciled numbers, letters, and symbols filled the pages.

Passwords.

For Amazon. Netflix. Wells Fargo Bank.

Library Computer.

My hands shook as I entered the library computer password. The desktop screen blinked on, cluttered with little blue folder icons.

Bingo.

I sat down then, trying to be calm as I studied the labels on the folders.

Landscaping. Sailboat. Utilities. Domestic Help Payroll. Gardening. Swimming Pool.

Security.

Okay. Here we go. Calm the freak down, Harlow.

I clicked on the Security icon. A window popped open with still more folders. One of them said Cameras.

This was really happening.

I clicked the camera folder, and a new window opened. About a dozen black icons were labeled with things like Driveway Gate I, Driveway Gate II, Boathouse, Pool House, West Lawn, East Lawn, Beach Path.

The next row of camera icons were labeled Orchard, NW trail, Ravine, SW trail.

I clicked Ravine.

A window opened, showing a grainy grayscale image of trees and bushes. At the top, milliseconds sped by on a clock. It was showing a real-time feed of, well . . . trees.

I watched it for a minute. The camera was aimed at what appeared to be a nondescript section of forest. I saw tree trunks, bushes, leaves vibrating in the breeze. A bird arrowed past.

I clicked the cursor on the clock, and this opened a little subwindow filled with a long column of numbers.

No, not just numbers—dates.

I found 10/10, the day I was shot at, and opened yet another window. I quickly figured out that I could use the cursor to move a little slide bar to fast-forward or rewind through the entire twenty-four hours.

The day I'd been shot at, I was pretty sure I'd gone to the ravine sometime around two o'clock. I slid the bar to noon. Then I fast-forwarded through the gap of time, but slowly enough that I would be able to detect motion.

At 1:41 I saw something. I rewound a little and clicked play.

A figure moves into the frame.

Me.

I look jumpy, my head turning from side to side. I stop and look straight up into the camera. Then I pass from view.

I scanned through the next several minutes of footage, but I didn't see anyone else until nine minutes later: me again, now running past the camera in the opposite direction. My eyes are hidden by the baseball cap, but I imagined I could see my mouth gaping in terror.

I scanned the previous and following hours, but I still didn't see anyone else.

I checked the same time period on the two other likely cameras: NW trail, SW trail.

Nothing but trees. Whoever shot at me hadn't passed in front of any of these cameras.

Did that mean they knew where the cameras were positioned?

By this point, I'd opened several windows on the desktop. I was clicking them closed one by one, when a new thought hit me: What if one of those cameras recorded whatever Gregor was doing outside that first night on the island?

There was a pool house camera. At the very least he would've been captured by that one.

I could see him so clearly in my mind's eye. His bare moonlit skin, caked with viscous darkness. Muscles working. Penis semi-erect.

Jealousy knifed my belly.

What were you doing? I thought for the millionth time.

And then I thought, *Wait. Maybe I can find out.*

48

I found 9/29 on the list of dates for the Pool House camera. That had been our first night on the island. I clicked it.

This camera was obviously fixed to the outside of the pool house, and when I fast-forwarded to the nighttime hours, it showed the moonlit surface of the pool. There were the folded umbrellas, the chaises, the hedges.

I didn't see anyone, though. Not even myself.

But then I realized when I'd seen Gregor by the swimming pool, it really had been very early on 9/30.

After clicking on 9/30, I slid the timer bar carefully, not wanting to miss a single thing.

At 1:33, a figure moves into view. It's me in my pajamas, holding my elbows, head on a swivel. I sit down shakily on one of the chaises and hunch forward. After a minute or so, I lift my head.

Moments later, there he is. My husband. High and naked.

Only the back of him is visible because of the camera's position. He walks to the edge of the pool and looks down into the water. I'm watching him from the chaise, and then I open my mouth and say something and his head whips around.

Now you can see his profile. The video quality is poor and so is the lighting, but there's something uncanny about the set of his face. His jaw is thrust forward in an uncharacteristic way.

Then he's turning and breaking into a run, and he's gone. Meanwhile, I'm trying to stand up. I sway and grab hold of the chaise to steady myself. After several seconds, I walk shakily out of the frame. It's 1:35.

All that definitely happened, then. Exactly the way I remembered it.

My next idea was to find out where Gregor went. But then I realized that wasn't really what I wanted to know.

I wanted to know where he was *before* he arrived at the swimming pool.

I opened the West Lawn camera and moved the timer to 1:30.

Gregor lopes into view just after 1:32, a silhouette edged in moonlight. Then he's gone. But he clearly came from the driveway.

I opened the Driveway camera and found him emerging from the shadows of the trees and passing behind the parked Mercedes at 1:31.

I opened one of the Driveway Gate cameras and then the other, but I didn't see him. I opened the Orchard camera to see a dim figure striding between the trees at 1:28. He had emerged from the darkness at the far end.

Where had he been before that?

On an impulse, I clicked open the Ravine camera to the very beginning of 9/30 at 12:01. I slid the cursor forward.

There was motion and lights on the recording a few minutes after midnight.

I clicked play.

Blurry shades of charcoal and black. Floating orbs of light. The orbs come into focus as lanterns that partially illuminate the people carrying them.

One by one, women pass through the camera frame. Naked, hair hanging loose or braided, the lanterns lighting up their bare breasts and pale limbs. One woman, two, three, four, five, six, seven women—

I paused the feed.

The seventh woman looks like the pregnant barista from the coffee shop. The one with the Inguz tattoo. I thought I could just make out black ink on her arms, the bulge of her belly.

I clicked play again.

Two more women pass, then another—

Oh my God. Teacher Terra. Her breasts sway with each step, and her mouth moves rhythmically.

Chanting, I realized.

Or praying?

Then another woman—only she isn't naked like the rest of them.

She is wearing a white nightgown. It seems to glow, long and diaphanous.

She tips her head up to the sky, and—*Am I really seeing this?*—she looks a lot like Sergeant Marcus from the sheriff's station.

And then—

I stopped breathing.

Another figure steps into the frame.

But this one isn't holding a lantern. She is naked, too—but her wrists seem to be bound in front of her. And— *Oh. Oh no.*

A rope is looped around her neck. *She's being led.*

Led by another nude woman with a long, pale braid. Kirsten. I was sure of it, even though I could only see her face in dim, blurred profile.

And the girl Kirsten was leading?

I zoomed in. The picture got darker, grainier.

The girl's head is bowed. Her hair is wet or matted, and her skin looks ghostly. She isn't struggling, but the rope around her throat is unmistakable.

The curved cheeks. The set of her neck.

Could it be?

I fumbled my phone from my pocket and pulled up the screenshot I'd taken of Liz Reed's yearbook photo. Smiling. Hopeful. Painfully young.

I turned back to the footage.

Was it her?

It sure as heck could be. Except . . . something wasn't quite right. I couldn't pinpoint what it was, though. It was just a little itch at the back of my mind.

I hit play again.

Another woman follows, carrying a lantern. Then another—and she holds something, too.

An axe.

My mouth went dry.

She carries it low, right under the double blade, handle pointing down. Lantern light hits its edges.

The feed went still. Nothing remained but dark smudges of tree and shadow.

Thirteen women in all.

Thirteen chanting women. Naked, barefoot, braided. Snaking through a moonlit forest path shortly after midnight on September 30—

With an axe.

And a girl on a leash.

My pulse was a drumbeat in my ears. I didn't want to believe what I was seeing.

I felt dizzy. I felt hot.

I slid the timer forward. 12:30. 1:00. Darkness, darkness, darkness. And then, at 1:17, there he was.

My naked husband, stealing past the camera. Away from the direction the women had gone.

49

Black splotches danced across my vision. It felt like the floor under my chair was tipping.

I was going to pass out.

I shoved the desk chair back and dropped my head between my knees, fighting to breathe through the rush of heat, the lightheadedness, the rising sense that none of this—*none* of this—could be real.

I would've *loved* to pass out, because I didn't want to process what I'd just seen on the security footage.

But after a minute or two, the dizziness passed. I sat upright slowly. And immediately, my mind began doing what it always did: try to get Gregor off the hook.

Maybe Gregor's mushroom trip had only coincidentally taken him out into the woods.

Maybe he'd never even crossed paths with the women.

It was technically possible.

Some pathetic little part of me still wanted my marriage to be something I could save. Still wanted the man I'd built my life around to be salvageable.

But there was no salvaging this.

That chopped-off head had been real. Which meant Gregor had seen it, too.

And he'd let me believe I'd hallucinated the whole thing. No, correction—he had actively lied and misled to *make sure* I thought it was a hallucination.

Gregor was a liar. A gaslighter. And almost certainly a criminal.

I went to the kitchen, poured myself a glass of cold water, and gulped it down. I poured another. The water helped. It cleared the buzzing from my ears, steadied my hands. I felt myself begin to click into place. Like my mind and body were realigning around one unshakable truth:

Sam came first.

Dr. Zakarian's words, back at the fertility clinic in New York, sounded in my head. *Motherhood takes sacrifice.*

He'd meant quitting my job. Cutting back on coffee. Giving up running. But now it took on a new, crystal-clear meaning. To protect Sam, I had to give up my needy delusions. I had to give up the man I thought I loved.

Every instinct told me to go get Sam, get the hell off this island, and figure out the rest later. But although I'd legally adopted Sam, he wasn't my biological child. Children usually stayed with their biological parent in the event of a divorce.

I pulled out my phone and typed into Google: *how to prove a parent unfit for custody.*

A law firm FAQ popped up. *A parent may be deemed unfit if they have a history of violence, mental illness, addiction, neglect, or criminal behavior.*

My hand tightened on the phone.

How about a parent who gets high and then participates in pagan blood sacrifices in the woods?

I needed to copy that security footage and get it into the hands of people who could do something. Not anyone from the local sheriff's office, obviously—not when one of the women in the video looked exactly like Sergeant Marcus.

No. I needed the feds—like the FBI. Or a journalist? And Liz Reed's parents.

But first, I had to figure out how to make a copy of the footage. A flash drive? A screen recording? I had no idea. My tech knowledge topped out at the software I used at the cancer lab.

Anna, I thought. *Of course. She'll know exactly how to copy it.*

◆ ◆ ◆

The dive bar in town, where Anna had suggested we meet, was mostly empty.

It was still early afternoon, so there was only a barfly muttering to the bartender and a pair of TVs tuned to sports highlights. The place smelled like spilled bourbon mopped up with bleach, and the jukebox was playing country music loud enough to make eavesdropping impossible.

Anna was already there, slouched in a sticky vinyl booth in the back corner. Her hoodie was up, and her eyes were hollowed out with exhaustion.

The sight of her hit me in the chest. My one friend on this island. My only ally. I blinked fast, trying to keep it together.

She gave a tired smile. "You look like hell."

"So do you." I slid into the booth. "And, hi."

"Hi." She pushed a shot glass across the table. "Figured you'd want one."

I sat down. "God, thank you."

She waited while I knocked it back.

Tequila. I winced. But I wouldn't mind numbing out a little.

Anna said, "So, I'm guessing this is about the background check?"

I nodded slowly, still uncertain how much to say. It would sound crazy. Plus, once Anna knew we were dealing with murder, she couldn't just opt out. It didn't feel fair to trap her like that.

She leaned in. "Well, it turns out Ben's clean. Not a single criminal charge. Nothing sketchy. I was ready to find a trail of creepshots and unpaid child support and assault charges. Not even a parking ticket."

"Seriously? He's so . . ."

"I know." Anna hesitated. "Kirsten, though? That's a different story."

I sat up straighter. "What?"

"She changed her name. When they got married, she didn't just take Ben's last name—she changed her first name, too. From *Kri*sten to *Kir*sten. Slippery little rebrand. That's why you can't find anything about her outside of her Insta posts."

"Oh my God."

"She grew up in Aberdeen—out on the Olympic Peninsula. Kind of a depressing logging town. Her dad worked at a paper mill until he got hurt and went on disability. Her mom bugged out when Kirsten was little."

"She told me her mom OD'd on fentanyl."

"Nope. Alive and living in Texas and active in a megachurch, according to Facebook. But here's the kicker. Kirsten was a cheerleader in high school—"

I actually laughed. "Shut up."

"No, for real. Wild, right? So one day at cheerleading practice, another girl joked that she'd hooked up with Kirsten's boyfriend, and Kirsten—sorry, *Kristen*—flipped out. Picked up a baseball bat that was lying around and beat the crap out of her. Like, hospitalization level. Facial reconstructive surgery."

"Oh my God."

"That was when she was sixteen. Did over a year in juvie. Got her diploma from a detention program. I guess the state sealed her record, but my friend pulled it up through a back channel."

I stared at her. "So she really is a psycho."

"Yeah." Anna gave me a strange look. "That's why you called me? About the background check?"

I hesitated.

She narrowed her eyes. "What's going on?"

"I don't want to drag you in deeper."

"Deeper?" She gave a bitter laugh. "Ruby's already threatening to dump me. She caught me reading the report and freaked. Said I'm obsessed, that I'm sabotaging the band, that I can't stand seeing her happy."

"I'm so sorry," I said.

Anna looked at me, hard. "What's going on?"

"I need your help copying some security footage off a computer at Himmel Cottage."

"Okay. What kind of footage are we talking about?"

"The kind where a girl with a rope around her neck is led into the woods by a bunch of naked KinderWild moms. Where my husband also shows up on camera, high as a kite and apparently in on the act. The kind of footage that would grant me custody of Sam."

Anna's eyes were huge. "You're kidding."

"God, I wish."

"Is this . . . is it, like, live action role-play? Or like, they were filming a music video, or—"

"It's real."

"How can you be sure?"

I thought of the rotting head in the dirt, and bile surged up my throat.

I'd never told Anna about the head. Before, I wasn't sure if it had been a hallucination or not. It felt foolish to talk about it. But now, she needed to know. So I took a deep breath and backed all the way up to the day I fell down the ravine.

By the time I was finished, her face was pale.

"Holy shit," she whispered. "This is insane. You have to tell the police—"

"I *tried* to. At least one of the local cops is in on this thing. I want to go to the FBI, but they're going to laugh in my face or have me committed unless I can give them concrete proof. That's where you come in. I want to copy that security footage so I can get it to law enforcement. And to Liz Reed's parents."

Anna nodded. "Okay. Yeah. It makes sense. And . . . you're sure that was Liz Reed in the footage?"

"Pretty sure. But . . . well, here's the thing. If that *was* Liz, then she'd only died a few days before I saw the head. But the head I saw was pretty, you know . . . decomposed. It couldn't have been hers."

"Fuck," Anna said. "They're serial killers. For real." She was quiet for a long beat. Then: "Okay. I'll bring what we need tomorrow—I'll have to go over to the mainland in the morning to get it. We'll probably need a portable hard drive, maybe a backup laptop, or at the very least an HDMI recorder."

"You sure?"

"I'm already blowing up my relationship and risking a felony. Might as well commit."

50

Back from the bar, a little buzzed and a lot on edge, I had forty-five minutes before I had to go pick up Sam. I decided to find our passports—just so I knew where they were when it was time to leave.

Hopefully tomorrow.

I started in Gregor's and my bedroom. Desk drawers. Top dresser drawers. Nightstands. Nothing.

I moved faster, pulse kicking up. Downstairs, I tore through the kitchen junk drawer, then opened every drawer in the huge carved sideboard in the dining room. Fondue forks. Cloth napkins. A corkscrew.

I leaned to open one of the smaller doors on the top shelf—

My eyes caught on a faint scrawl of pencil: *bitches*.

Bessie? I thought.

A loose strip of wallpaper was lifting up from the wall beside the sideboard.

I peeled it back carefully, heart pounding.

The words were fragmented, badly faded, but I could make out:

bitches
those witches in the moon
and old man Himmel
say

dances with them
frolics with
they made him rich

I stared at the words until my eyes stung.

This was what that old lady at the historical society—Shirley—must've been talking about. Jakob Himmel's deathbed confession. The "unspeakable things" he was afraid were going to land him in Hell.

Was Bessie saying that old man Himmel danced with witches in the moonlight?

If so, then whatever had happened in those woods two weeks ago—with Gregor, with the women, with the axe—it wasn't new.

It was a family tradition.

There had to be more of Bessie's writing.

I moved through the house, scanning every wall for bubbles, seams, lifted corners. My movements were unsteady. My breath came short. I needed Bessie to tell me more. I wanted to understand the nightmare of a family I'd married into.

No, I *needed* to understand. So I could get Sam and myself safely out.

In the den, I slid a fingernail under a peeling edge. Blank plaster. Dining room—same. I crouched by the baseboard in the entry hall and picked at a seam. Still no writing.

Stairwell. Landing. Upstairs hallway. I peeled. Pried. Scraped. My thumbnail split, then tore halfway down. Blood welled beneath the nail bed of another.

That didn't stop me.

Please, Bessie. Please tell me what kind of monsters they are.

But every wall was silent.

I blinked. Looked around.

Wallpaper hung in curling strips. Ragged seams flapped like open wounds. My hands were shaking, flecked with plaster dust and smeared with blood.

Oh my God, I thought. *What have I done?*

I went to the utility closet—

They tell you it's forever love
this house
too late

—and fumbled around until I found an old bottle of Elmer's glue. The nozzle was crusted, but I bit it open—my fingertips were too sore to pick at it—and squeezed out a blob of stinky white glue. Room by room, I started sticking the wallpaper back down.

Smooth it. Hide it. Fix it.

Gregor couldn't know what I'd found out.

That afternoon at KinderWild, it felt like a mask had been ripped off the entire operation.

These weren't your run-of-the-mill earth mamas with their kombucha and felted wool clogs.

They were killers.

I pushed on sunglasses, even though the sky was murky and gray. They made me feel protected. Then I stepped out of the Mercedes like I was stepping onto a stage. Every nerve screamed *danger*. My face ached from how tightly I was holding it in neutral.

No one else was in the parking lot, but in the Gathering Place, there was Teacher Terra by the rope swing, laughing. Gwen crouched in the mud with her twin boys. Hildy's little girl clung to her like a baby koala. Kirsten wiped Alder's nose with a bandana. All of them smiling. Radiant. Self-satisfied.

They'd known all along who my husband really was. What I'd only just figured out. It made me want to scream.

I kept my head high as I scanned the clearing for Sam. But I could feel the burn of their eyes on me.

Did they know that *I* knew?

Was it written on my face?

"Sam!" I called, too brightly. I'd spotted him—and let out a breath I hadn't realized I was holding.

He dropped the stick he was waving and ran to me. His hair was damp, his face smudged, his little body warm and solid as he flung himself into my arms. I held him tighter than I should've. He squirmed.

"Ready to go, sweetie?" I said softly.

"Yeah. Why are you wearing sunglasses?"

"I have a little bit of a headache. Let's grab your backpack."

Just one more day, I thought. *Then we're out of here.*

I glanced back as I was buckling Sam into the car, to see who was watching.

Kirsten was walking toward her Volvo, holding her baby close, her two little boys straggling behind her like dirty ducklings.

She caught me looking. Smiled. Waved.

I forced myself to wave back.

Bitch, I thought.

Witch.

The biggest challenge was going to be acting normal around Gregor.

The girl with the rope around her neck. The rotting head in the ravine. The footage of him sneaking around in the trees, high and naked.

Yeah. *That* was my husband.

What exactly did my game face look like for that?

I checked on Sam, who was still hypnotized by the TV. I gave him another hug—too tight—and then I went into the kitchen to put together something for dinner. I came up with a box of penne and a jar of marinara, and then my eyes fell on the wine rack.

On an impulse, I grabbed a bottle of pinot noir and carried it with the pasta things into the kitchen. I uncorked the bottle, poured a large glass, and drank it down.

This, I thought. *This will definitely help with my game face.* I poured a second glass and got started with dinner.

A little later, the pasta water was boiling, the marinara was simmering, I was chopping yellow peppers for a salad, and a tray of frozen meatballs was circling the microwave, when—

"Hey there, beautiful."

I fumbled the knife. *Gregor.* I hadn't heard him come in.

He walked over. "Something smells good." He kissed my cheek, and the hairs on the back of my neck stood up.

"Hey," I said. My thoughts were a scribble.

He pulled back. "Whoa. Have you been drinking?"

"I had a glass of wine," I said, still chopping. "Is that a federal offense?"

His frown deepened. "You said you wanted to keep trying."

"I *was* trying. And now I've got my period. So I poured some wine." I gestured vaguely at the bubbling marinara. "Dinner's happening."

Gregor ran a hand through his hair. "I just mean . . . it's not over yet. We can't give up hope. The doctors said—"

"I'm tired, Gregor. Okay? I'm tired of being a . . . a *shrine.*"

"If you get pregnant—*when* you get pregnant—it isn't going to be just your body anymore."

My knife froze, mid-chop. I stared at him. Somehow, after all I'd seen that day, I still couldn't believe what I was hearing. "It'll still be *my* body."

Gregor was shaking his head. "Your body, and what happens to it, is determining the future of our whole family."

"What's that supposed to mean? I'm nothing but some kind of Himmel heir-making factory? Actually, that's basically what your mom implied, with her crazy talk about the 'Himmel nose' and—"

"Don't joke about that." His jaw clenched.

"I'm *joking* because your mom talked about our theoretical baby like she was playing eugenics bingo."

Why am I even arguing about this? I wondered. *I'm leaving tomorrow, and the next time I see my husband, it'll probably be in court.*

Gregor looked away. "Mother just wants to make sure the family line stays intact."

"Meaning what?" I said. I shouldn't have drunk all that wine. I was starting to feel woozy. "That the baby actually *looks* like a Himmel?"

"She has her preferences. And she's made it clear that there's a lot of money at stake."

I blinked. "Wait—Gregor. Did she actually say she'd cut you off if you didn't have a certain kind of baby?" I lowered my voice to a rough whisper. "What about Sam? He doesn't count?"

His eyes flashed. "I didn't say that."

"But—"

"I *didn't* say that." His tone shut it down.

I dumped the peppers into the salad. Mechanically tossed them with the tongs. My mind was screaming *Oh my God oh my God what is this messed-up family I married into?* but I kept my face still.

"Let me help." Gregor was reaching for the bowl, but then his gaze fell on my hand. "Jesus, Low." He grabbed my wrist. "What did you do to your nails?"

I jerked away. "Nothing."

"They're wrecked. You've got blood under the . . . what, did you *claw* something?"

"I was cleaning," I said. "I caught them on a drawer handle."

He didn't seem convinced. "You sure everything's okay? Because I need you, Low. Okay? I need you more than you can possibly understand."

I've heard that before, I thought.

51

Gregor took Sam to preschool before heading to band rehearsal the next morning.

I spent the morning tearing the house apart searching for our passports again.

Still nothing.

At this point, I was 99 percent sure Gregor had hidden them. It wasn't the end of the world, though. Sam and I could still leave. We just wouldn't be able to board a flight or cross any international borders. But we could drive and drive and drive.

My first thought was to head to Iowa and stay with Audrey's family until everything got straightened out. But when I took a deep breath and finally called her—planning to tell her almost everything—she'd answered with a gravelly voice and a stuffed-up nose.

"Harlow," she'd said blearily. "Hey. We have COVID—the entire family. Can you believe it? Is everything okay?"

I lied and said everything was great.

I couldn't bring myself to burden her when they were all sick.

Next, I texted Phoebe. Just a neutral Hey, haven't connected in a while, how's everything going? Neither of us had been great about getting back to each other over the past couple of weeks. I felt weird about coming right out with *SOS. I'm fleeing my psychotic husband.*

Phoebe got back to me with a photo of a huge diamond ring on her left hand.

Adi finally proposed?! I typed back. Congratulations!!

So yeah, maybe I'd wait a little bit before telling her what was happening with *my* marriage.

◆ ◆ ◆

Around noon, Anna showed up at the mudroom door with a canvas tote slung over her shoulder and wind-chapped cheeks. "Sorry," she said as I let her inside. "Ferry's off schedule again. You ready?"

"Yeah. Need a coffee or anything?"

"Nope. I'm fully caffeinated."

I led her to the library. When she saw the Winchester rifle hanging over the fireplace, she raised her eyebrows.

"It's purely decorative," I lied. I didn't need to freak her out any more than necessary.

I logged into the computer while she unpacked her gear—flash drive, portable hard drive, some cords and adapters I didn't recognize.

"Let's grab the files first," Anna said. "Then we'll clone the whole folder, just in case."

I clicked into the desktop, using Pauline's stupid password from the notebook in the drawer. The same mess of folders loaded like before. I opened the one labeled SECURITY and—

It was empty.

I blinked. "What the hell? It's gone."

Anna leaned over my shoulder. "Check the recycle bin."

I checked. Empty.

My stomach started to churn. "It was right here."

"Okay, don't panic." Anna plugged in her drive. "We'll search the system. If the folder was moved, renamed, anything—we'll find it."

She opened Finder and ran a system-wide search for any file created or modified in the past thirty days.

Nothing.

I felt like I was breathing through gauze. "He deleted it. Gregor."

"Who else has access to this computer?"

"I mean, no one . . . unless—could it be accessed remotely?"

"Sure."

"Well, then maybe Gregor's mom . . . or her boyfriend. He's an ex-Microsoft guy. I assume that means he has some technical skills."

Anna nodded. "Well, regardless of who deleted it, it might not be permanent." She tapped her keyboard fast. "I'm running a recovery scan. If it was just trashed, it's still on the drive. We can pull it."

A loading bar crawled across the screen. Anna chewed her lip.

The results popped up.

Nothing.

"Shit," she muttered. "Whoever did this used a secure wipe. That means the files weren't only deleted—they were overwritten. Erased beyond basic recovery."

I sat back in the desk chair. "He knows. He knows I saw the footage."

"You're sure it was Gregor who—"

"Who else?" My voice cracked.

"Maybe Gregor's mom saw someone was accessing the files and deleted it for, like, privacy. I don't know. Just calm down and listen, okay? There are forensic tools that might recover fragments, but they're expensive, and not exactly plug-and-play—"

"So I'm screwed," I said. My entire body was shaking.

"We'll figure something else out," Anna said, but she sounded uncertain. "We just need a new plan."

I nodded, but the gesture felt meaningless.

The footage—Sam's and my ticket to safety—was gone.

"Are you sure we should be talking in here?" Anna whispered. Her gaze flicked around the library like she was looking for something.

"You don't think—"

She stopped me by putting a quick finger to her lips. Then she headed for the door.

I followed her out of the house and into her Honda CRV. She got behind the wheel, and I got into the passenger side. It was very clean inside, and it smelled like coffee.

She swiveled to face me. A tiny muscle was jumping under one of her eyes. "Can't be too careful. If these people are into surveillance cameras, who knows where they've put them. Okay. What else do you have? For evidence, I mean. You said you saw footage of this shit going down in the forest that night, but have you gotten anything else that's concrete?"

"Like what?"

"I don't know. Documentation. Stuff on paper, or photographs. Voicemails?"

"No." I shook my head miserably. "There was the head, but then it was gone, and there must've been other stuff down in the ravine, too, but they dug it all up. Wait—" I lifted my head. "*Yes.* There was this guy at the KinderWild parking lot—an angry dad screaming at one of the moms, Hildy. She has a little girl. And the guy, the dad, he was saying stuff about Hildy's women's group, and something about him not being the little girl's father—I filmed it. Hold on."

I dug my phone from my hoodie pocket. Opened the camera app. Scrolled back until I found the video. I tilted the phone so Anna could see and hit play.

My camera work was unsteady, but when I turned up the volume, we could hear every word.

"—whore! Why am I paying child support for some other guy's kid? I'm gonna sue you and your whole psycho bitch group!"

"Psycho bitch group?" Anna said.

"He's talking about *them*," I said with a swoop of hope. "The women in the woods. I had no idea at the time, but now . . . it *has* to be, right?"

"You need to talk to him," Anna said. "He might know exactly how Gregor is involved. He might have more evidence. It's unfortunate that he seems like yet another unhinged whack-job."

"I don't even know his name."

"Sure, but you've got his license plate on camera. You'll be able to dig it up."

52

Anna had to get going so she wouldn't miss a work Zoom. She gathered up her equipment from the library and, telling me to keep her posted, she left.

I got my phone out again, pulled up the video of the angry dad, and selected the frame with the clearest shot of the retreating pickup.

I zoomed in on the license plate. Washington state. The number was clear.

I opened the web browser on my phone and went to one of those free license plate search websites. I typed in the license plate number, selected Washington state, and clicked "Proceed."

No result.

I found another website, this one requiring a five-dollar fee. I entered my credit card information, wondering what Gregor would think when he saw the charge on the statement next month.

This time, I got a hit. Toyota Tacoma 2018. Christopher Grasso. A local phone number and an island address.

I sent Anna a text: Got it. Thanks again for your help.

I thought about dialing Christopher Grasso's number. I imagined the man yelling at me and hanging up. I tried to think of what I could say in a voicemail message or text. *Hey, you don't know me, but I want to know all about your nasty divorce.*

No. I needed to talk to him in person. But it was Friday, and I'd be with Gregor and Sam nonstop all weekend.

Visiting Christopher Grasso would have to wait till Monday.

◆ ◆ ◆

I have no clue how I made it through that weekend.

Gregor was calm—making pancakes, playing LEGOs with Sam, working out on his mom's Peloton. Meanwhile, I was barely keeping it together. Images played on loop in my mind: rope, axe, girl.

Head.

But I did the Everything is Fine routine, too. For Sam's sake, yes. But also because, if Gregor didn't know I'd seen that footage? Then I had the upper hand.

Saturday night, he wanted to have sex.

I told him I was still on my period. Extra crampy. *Sorry, honey.*

"Are you okay?" he'd asked, brow furrowed. "Have you ever had bad cramps before?"

Is that all I am to you? I thought. *A baby incubator?*

Every time I went to the bathroom, I locked the door and checked the password-protected account I'd set up on Paternitrust.com. This account, according to the website, was where the results of the DNA test would show up as soon as they were available.

The Results tab was red every time I checked, though. When I clicked on it, nothing happened.

The website said to expect test results about a week from when you mailed it in.

By Sunday, it would be six days.

◆ ◆ ◆

Saturday's post from IntoTheWoodsWeGo: A shot of Kirsten in a white dress, standing in a grove of slender trees. The trees have silvery bark and yellow leaves, and they seem to glow in hazy sunlight. Kirsten's hands span her belly. Her head's thrown back, hair flowing, mouth open, eyes shut, as though she's laughing, and the hem of her dress twirls out.

> Before I found my faith, before I was Blessed by God, I was lost. I was empty. But I was led to the right place at the right time and my life was forever changed. One autumn day when the time was ripe, I found my God and my Calling in a beautiful grove of alder trees. I will never forget that day, or all the riches it has brought me since then. Ladies if you are struggling with fertility, know that there is hope. You were MADE FOR MOTHERHOOD. Don't let anyone tell you otherwise. #fertility #RIPLucy #blessed

Hashtag RIP Lucy? I thought. *Lucy, like the hen Kirsten slaughtered last week?*

Or like her husband's disappeared ex?

Sunday's post:

A shot from above of Kirsten's hands steadying the handle of an axe. Her fingernails are a freshly manicured, short, shiny peach. The axe-head rests on a round whetstone, and the whetstone sits on a tablecloth printed with pink-and-green sprigs.

> Old things have so much more soul than new things, especially store-bought things in this day and age. That's why I treasure the specialness of the antique items in my home. One of my most treasured items—and one that I get SO many questions about—is the axe we have hanging over our kitchen fireplace. My husband and I found it years ago in the woods, almost buried under the fallen leaves. The original handle was half rotted but the amazing thing was the blades were still super sharp! We made a new

handle for it out of maple wood, and every now and then I sharpen the blade the old-fashioned way, with a whetstone. There is NO substitute for doing things the way your grandparents did them. #autumnvibes #traditionalliving #blessed

Hashtag autumnvibes? I thought in disbelief. *Like sharpening her blood-sacrifice axe is some cute little seasonal activity?*

◆ ◆ ◆

By Sunday night, my nerves were shot.

Gregor was still acting like everything was normal. I still hadn't found our passports.

And I was praying Christopher Grasso knew something solid. Something I could use.

◆ ◆ ◆

On Monday morning, I dressed in jeans, a T-shirt, sneakers, and a trucker cap, no makeup. I didn't want Christopher Grasso to think I was trying to be cute when I paid him a visit.

I went downstairs and got Sam's bento lunch box out of the dishwasher. Lunch-box prep had fallen upon my shoulders ever since Gregor fired Emilia. I'd tried to be conscientious by packing turkey sandwiches, carrot sticks, apple slices—that sort of thing. But the lunches had come back untouched at the end of the day. Sam told me he didn't like what I packed.

Today, I put in leftover pizza cut into small wedges, Sun Chips, and a couple of Oreos. He would for sure eat that.

Then I started on breakfast. It was critical that everything at home seemed perfectly normal.

"Whoa," Gregor said sleepily, walking into the kitchen that smelled like pancakes and coffee and scrambled eggs. "This is a surprise."

"Good morning, honey," I said brightly, flipping over a pancake.

He came over and hugged me from behind.

The feel of his body on me made me want to scream.

"Did I ever tell you how sexy you look when you're doing the whole domestic goddess thing?" he murmured.

"I'm hardly a domestic goddess," I said with a forced laugh.

I didn't mention that the pancakes were from a boxed mix I'd found in the pantry.

53

After I dropped off Sam at KinderWild, I climbed back into the Mercedes and opened the map on my phone. I'd already typed in Christopher Grasso's address.

Before I set off, though, I sent Anna another text: Heading out to see the angry dad. Wish me luck.

She hadn't responded to my last text, but I figured she was the type to communicate on an as-needed basis.

Christopher Grasso's home was several miles away, down near the south-end ferry. I hadn't been to that part of the island yet, and I soon discovered it was even less populous than the rest of the island. I drove through steady rain along a forested road. My windshield wipers thudded.

I felt untethered.

Few houses were visible from the road. Instead, mailboxes marked driveways that twisted away into darkness.

I spotted the mailbox with Christopher Grasso's address, dented metal on a cockeyed post. I braked. A driveway, more dirt than gravel, extended into berry thickets and gloomy fir trees.

For the first time, the foolishness of my plan hit me. Anyone would consider paying a visit to some random guy with a documented history of aggressive behavior as . . . unhinged.

Was I unhinged?

Even if I was, I didn't care. I was doing this for Sam.

I felt laser focused. Maybe Christopher Grasso would make everything crystal clear.

I turned down his driveway. It was so potholed I bounced in my seat, and branches screeched against the car's sides.

I heard the dogs long before I reached the home.

Two dogs, I decided as I got closer. No—three. Big ones, with a shrill, frantic lilt to their barking.

My belly fluttered.

The home was a mossy cabin merging with the undergrowth. A black Toyota pickup was parked out front, and its license plate matched the one in my video.

I braked beside it.

I heard a slam, and a second later three muscular dogs were milling and sniffing around my car. One of them bounded up against the driver's side door, and I recoiled with a gasp.

Drool swung in glistening ropes from its jaws.

"Hey!" someone bellowed, and I saw the man from the video coming down the porch steps. A rifle hung from his hand.

What the hell had I been thinking, coming here? This wasn't detached research in a laboratory. This was my life. This was *dangerous*.

The man swore and kicked at the dogs, and they slunk away. He stopped beside my window. "Who the hell are you?" he said, his harsh voice muffled by the window.

I buzzed the window halfway down. "Hi," I said, trying to smile. It felt like a cringe.

He was thirtysomething, burly and black-bearded, in a T-shirt and jeans. The shirt said Come and Take It over the silhouette of an assault rifle.

"Who are you?" he repeated. "This is private property."

"Yeah. I know. Sorry. You're Christopher Grasso, right?"

His face went wary. "Who wants to know?"

"My name is Sarah." I'd decided ahead of time not to divulge that I was part of the Himmel clan. On the island, that meant something. "My son's at KinderWild. He just started."

Christopher's eyes narrowed. "That damn place."

"Yeah. Well, last week I happened to notice your, uh, your visit to KinderWild—"

"You one of Hildy's friends?"

"What? *No.* Not at all."

"Then what do you want?"

"I want to talk to you."

"About what?"

"About KinderWild. About the moms and teachers there."

Christopher looked surprised. Then hate flashed in his eyes. "Those crazy bitches?"

"I couldn't agree more."

"How did you find me?"

"I looked up your license plate on a website."

"Fucking feds," he muttered, and spat on the ground.

"I wanted to ask what you know about the KinderWild women," I said. "I think they might be dangerous."

He gave me a sharp look. "*Dangerous?* How?"

"That's what I'm trying to figure out." I took a breath. "Like I said, my son is at KinderWild—"

"Why the hell would you send your kid there?" Christopher said. "They don't teach them anything. They wallow in the dirt like animals."

"I'm trying to convince my husband to pull our son out. Listen, I'm sorry for just showing up here, but I didn't know how else to reach you."

"You don't just drive down people's driveways, you know. It's a good way to get a bullet in the brain."

I forced myself not to glance at his gun. "I know. I'm sorry. It's . . . I'm desperate. I'm really worried about my kid."

"Okay." Christopher's vibe was softening. "Well, I don't know much about the school because Hildy and Greta—you met Greta? Hildy's kid?"

I thought of Hildy's little girl with the matted corn-silk hair. "Yeah."

"Greta didn't start at KinderWild till after Hildy and her left."

"You mentioned a women's group when you, uh, when you visited the school last week."

"I did?"

My confidence wavered: *Maybe he doesn't know anything.*

"You said you were going to sue Hildy and the whole 'psycho bitch group,'" I said.

"That's what I said?" His lips twitched. "I think I had a few beers that afternoon."

"Does Kirsten Blakeley belong to the group you were talking about?"

"Kirsten goddamn Blakeley." Spittle flew from his mouth. "That bitch has them all hypnotized. Hildy and I moved to this island because of her, you know."

54

I frowned at Christopher Grasso. "What do you mean? Kirsten brought Hildy and you to the island?"

"Hildy was obsessed with Kirsten," Christopher said. "With her Instagram and shit—you know about that?"

I nodded. "Yeah."

"Well, Hildy couldn't get enough. It was almost like a religion for her, Kirsten's stupid posts about breastfeeding and roosters and shit, and—we were living up north of Spokane, everything was fine—but then Hildy started messaging with Kirsten online, and Kirsten told her we should move out here to the island, that things are so woo-woo magical here, and that if we did, Hildy would get pregnant. Hildy wanted a kid really bad, but she wasn't getting pregnant, which was fine by me, but she was, like, *fixated* on it. After that, Hildy would not shut up about it until I agreed to move out here. We ripped up our lives. I can't even buy a house here, all those Seattle soy boys are driving up the prices. I spend most of what I make drywalling just to rent this pile of garbage." He jerked his thumb in the direction of the cabin.

So that's how Kirsten recruits all these women, I thought. *With her Instagram account. She probably recruits the "teaching interns" that way, too. Women desperate for a baby, or desperate for a sense of belonging and purpose.*

"And . . . Hildy got pregnant," I said.

Christopher hacked out a humorless laugh. "I don't know what kind of voodoo shit they're doing, but yeah, after four, five months here,

Hildy told me she was pregnant. I thought Greta was mine." His eyes went watery, and he pinched the bridge of his nose. His eyes fell shut. I felt sorry for him. But when he opened his eyes again, they were so hot with rage that I drew back. "I thought she was mine even though she didn't look a thing like me—*look* at me. Us Grassos are pure Sicilian. But Hildy let me think Greta was mine. Last week, though, it finally hit me. Greta has that blond hair and blue eyes cause *she's not mine*."

"I'm so sorry," I said quietly.

"I had no idea Hildy was cheating on me. After we moved here, she barely even left the house because she was so wrapped up in all that homesteading shit. Pretty much the only place she ever went, besides the IGA and the farmers' market, was to her women's group meetings. She said it was just to get together and talk about babies and knitting. And I was an idiot because I thought it was great, because then she couldn't bitch about me hanging out at Sporty's with the guys from work. She'd come back from that women's group really late. Like, once it was when the sun was coming up. I could tell she'd been drinking, or maybe doing drugs. She'd always get right into the shower, but one time I woke up and saw her. She was covered in blood."

"Where do you think the blood came from?" I asked.

As if I didn't know.

"The blood? They were partying so hard that someone had an accident, maybe? How do I know? She'd always vomit a lot, too. Afterwards. But I figured that was from the drugging and drinking. She'd always be fine after a day or two. I tried to get her to talk about it because she was pregnant by the time I realized what was going on, and that shit isn't good for babies. But she acted like I was crazy, or imagining things, or like *I* was the drunk."

"What do you think they do? The women's group, I mean."

"Those whores get wasted together and have orgies."

I blinked. "You mean—are they gay?"

"I don't know. Maybe. But there are guys involved, too, because I think Hildy got pregnant at one of those orgies."

"Who are the guys?"

"Some horny assholes they like to party with. You know that chick Gwen?"

I nodded, picturing Gwen and her small twin sons getting out of a Subaru in the KinderWild parking lot. Gwen, bare breasted, slipping past the security camera.

"We went to her and her husband's place—this was before Hildy left, when she was still trying to make me behave myself—we went over there for some beers, and she showed us her artwork, and she was painting some dude with his dick out, like, over and over again. A whole shed full of paintings of this one guy. Crazy bitch. She said the paintings were of God, but as far as I know God doesn't stand around with his dick out. But I think that's one of the guys."

"Did you recognize him?"

"No."

"What did he look like?"

"You think I was standing there studying what this dude looks like when he has his dick plastered all over every single painting?"

"Sorry," I said. "I . . . thanks for talking with me. I really appreciate it." I tightened my grip on the steering wheel.

I really needed to leave. Christopher's anger was starting to freak me out.

He looked at me, for the first time focusing on me as a person rather than a sounding board for his rant. "Hey—what did you say your name was again?"

"Sarah." I turned over the ignition and gave him a little wave as I pulled forward.

"That's a real nice car, Sarah," he shouted after me. "Real easy to spot!"

◆ ◆ ◆

At first, all I thought about was getting away from Christopher Grasso.

But once I was back on the main road and I'd put a mile or two between us, I realized I needed to look at Gwen's paintings to see exactly what this orgy guy looked like.

Wake up, Low, a voice whispered in my head. *Wake up and smell the coffee. You're obviously knee-deep in the Himmel family's sicko traditions.*

I ignored the voice. Because no matter what things seemed like in the heat of the moment, I was *not* going to leap to any conclusions until I had all the data.

Hypothesis, experiment, analysis, one by one and never out of order—that was all that stood between me and madness.

I knew my next step was confirming who was in Gwen's paintings.

But I didn't even know Gwen's last name. A normal school would have an online, searchable parent directory, but this was KinderWild. Their website was bare bones.

However, Christopher had made it sound like Gwen was a professional artist. Maybe she had some kind of online presence.

I googled *gwen artist washington*. That took me to the island art center's website, where apparently Gwen taught at a summer art camp for children. And her last name was Lloyd.

Gwen lloyd washington I typed into Google.

A phone number popped up, but no address.

55

At KinderWild pickup, I collected Sam and got him in the car. Then I climbed behind the wheel and watched for Gwen Lloyd in the rearview mirror. I'd seen her in the Gathering Place, talking with Gilda.

Gilda had carefully avoided eye contact with me.

"Why aren't we going?" Sam said. "I want to go home."

"We are going home. But we need to do one little drive first, okay?" I was thinking that the easiest way to learn Gwen's address would be to tail her home.

Through the mirror, I watched KinderWild women arriving and leaving with their children. I saw Hildy, Kirsten, a few others come out of the woods—and then here came Gwen, on the heels of her twin boys.

She got the twins into the back seat of her blue Subaru.

My hands were shaking with impatience, my eyes glued to the rearview.

A rap on the window made me swing my head.

Teacher Terra stood outside my car, that habitual smile on her face.

I buzzed my window down. "Yes?" I said impatiently.

"Can I have a word?"

"Of course." My eyes darted to the rearview. Gwen was getting into her car.

"It's about Sam's lunch box," Terra said.

"Okay."

"Did you pack it?"

"Yes."

"Leftover pizza?"

"I liked it," Sam said in the back seat.

"And . . . cookies?" Terra said, as though she was saying *cocaine*.

My eyes were on the rearview again. Now Gwen was backing out of her spot. "What exactly is the problem?"

"Pizza and cookies aren't adequate nutrition. It would be wonderful if you packed him some fruits and vegetables." She was still smiling.

"Sam won't eat fruits and vegetables, so why pack them? It's a waste."

"We need to model good choices."

"I don't want my *kid* to be *hungry*," I snapped.

"You can't feed growing children all that processed junk."

I looked in the rearview to see Gwen's car rolling away.

Damn it.

"I'll be discussing this matter with Sam's father, of course," Terra was saying, "but I wanted to give you a chance to explain yourself."

"*Explain* myself?"

Terra gave me one last sad little smile and then turned and walked away.

Great. I had lost my cool—and Gwen had gotten away.

I sagged back in my seat and let my eyes fall shut.

"Can we go home now?" Sam asked.

"Yeah," I said, switching on the engine.

"What happened to the car?" Gregor asked when he got home that evening.

"What do you mean?" I said, trying to look innocent.

Sam and I were working on a jigsaw puzzle at the living room coffee table. I'd found the puzzle in a cupboard, and I'd been able to coax Sam to work on it by pointing out that the puzzle was illustrated with puppies in snowsuits, and he *loved* puppies in people clothes.

We were laughing so hard about how silly one of the puppies looked that we hadn't even heard Gregor arrive.

Gregor was flushed as he looked down at us. He seemed annoyed, and I didn't think it was only about the car. "The paint got scratched," he said. "Didn't you notice?"

"No. Really? It must've happened on that road to KinderWild. It's so overgrown in places."

"That's not what I think."

"Okay. And what do *you* think?" I couldn't keep the bite out of my voice.

"I think you've been going places you don't want me to know about."

Our eyes locked. Time seemed to stop.

I was the first to look away.

"Don't take this the wrong way," Gregor said, "but . . . are you sure you're okay?"

"What's that supposed to mean?"

"Well, the house is a mess, I got a call from the school about Sam's lunch—"

"I liked it," Sam said.

"—and the car's scratched and you don't know why, and—was that take-out Thai I saw in the kitchen?"

"What's wrong with take-out Thai?" I said.

"Nothing, only . . . I mean, what are you doing with yourself all day, Low?" He was watching my face carefully.

I shrugged. "Gentle workouts. Watching TV. Trying to chill. You know, like Dr. Zakarian said?" I hadn't meant for that last part to come out so bitter.

"Did you hear about Anna?" Gregor asked, flopping down onto the sofa.

My belly clenched. "What?"

Gregor lazily met my gaze. Held it. "You know, Ruby's girlfriend?"

I swallowed. "Yeah. What happened to her?"

Gregor propped one bare foot, then the other, on the coffee table—right beside our half-finished puzzle.

"Daddy," Sam whined.

Gregor ignored that. "I guess she had a pretty bad fall down their basement stairs this morning. She was airlifted to Seattle and went into emergency surgery. Sounds like she broke her neck."

I stared at Gregor, struggling to piece together his words in a way that made sense. "She . . . she *fell*?"

"Uh-huh."

"Is she going to be okay?"

Gregor shrugged. "I mean, I guess? Time will tell. Sometimes a broken neck just means a couple titanium pins or whatever. Sometimes it means you're paralyzed for life."

And sometimes you die, I thought, thinking of Sam's mom's skiing accident. *Oh my God. This is all my fault. I never should've involved Anna.*

I wanted to ask Gregor for Ruby's number, but I was too afraid of what that would reveal.

"Who's hungry?" Gregor said, flashing a grin. "Suddenly, take-out Thai doesn't sound half bad."

That night, I lay in bed next to Gregor like a hostage, eyes open in the dark, replaying the conversation about Anna's broken neck over and over in my mind.

I didn't know if he'd pushed her, or had someone else do it. Maybe it really had been an accident. But my gut was telling me Gregor was capable of anything.

The next morning, I spotted Gwen Lloyd unlocking her filthy blue Subaru in the KinderWild parking lot, her twins squabbling as they half tumbled out.

She's here, I thought.

I walked Sam to the Gathering Place, kissed his damp forehead, and whispered "I love you" like it was a goodbye.

Then I hurried back to the Mercedes.

By the time I got there, Gwen was already backing out.

I yanked my door shut, started the engine, and backed out, too.

Stay calm, I told myself, even as my heart jackhammered.

Her bumper bobbed ahead of me down the gravel road. Her stickers read SKYCLAD and THE GODDESS IS ALIVE AND MAGIC IS AFOOT.

I tracked her north, hanging back as far as I dared. Finally, she turned down a long driveway engulfed in trees.

I didn't follow but kept driving, memorizing the mailbox number as I passed: *9674*.

I took the next turn and rerouted toward Himmel Cottage.

56

Back at Himmel Cottage, I searched Gwen Lloyd's address on the Google satellite map.

I saw the private driveway disappear into a clump of trees and reappear again. It passed through what looked like a pasture and then ended at a freestanding garage or barn and a nearby house. Off to the side stood a smaller outbuilding with skylights.

That had to be the studio.

If I waited until after dark—until everyone was asleep—and if I was careful, quick, quiet, and lucky . . .

I could do this.

Anna was in the hospital. My evidence was gone. No one was coming to save Sam and me.

So *I'd* save us.

The paintings wouldn't be proof of any criminality on Gregor's part. Not legally. But if they looked like Gregor, it would mean I wasn't paranoid—*I was right.*

◆ ◆ ◆

Gregor slept soundly that night, after two beers and two episodes of *Reacher*. Good. I needed him to crash hard.

I hadn't slept at all the night before, but I'd had a coffee after dinner to stay alert.

When his breathing had slowed into that deep, heavy rhythm, I slid out of bed. Barefoot. Silent.

In the downstairs powder room, I opened the cupboard under the vanity and pulled out the clothes I'd hidden earlier—black leggings, a black tee, dark-blue hoodie. I peeled off my pajamas and shoved them behind spare rolls of toilet paper.

My fingers shook as I tied my sneakers. Every sound felt too loud. Every shadow seemed to move.

I crept through the kitchen, snagged the car keys off their hook, and slipped out the mudroom door.

The cold night air slapped me awake.

I didn't see a single other vehicle on the road. The entire island was still except for the yellow flash of raccoons' eyes. In the sky, an apricot-shaped moon glowed.

I was afraid. More afraid than I'd ever felt in my entire life. More than the day Dad left. More than the time a man followed me through a near-empty parking garage at night.

There was a well of fear inside me, flowing up like stale, freezing air.

But I couldn't put my finger on what, exactly, I was afraid of. Was it Kirsten and the other KinderWild women and their horrific ritual in the woods? Was it the impending arrival of the paternity test results? The unthinkable fact of my husband being a criminal?

Or was I afraid of *myself*?

Of how I'd crossed over into this upside-down version of my life, where nothing was certain and everything smelled like rot? Where I lied like it was breathing, peeled wallpaper off the walls till my fingers bled, and stalked women through the trees just to prove that the man I loved might be exactly as monstrous as I feared?

I'm just trying to find the truth, I told myself. *I've got to find my way out of these woods.*

I parked on the side of the road and walked to Gwen's driveway, using the flashlight on my phone to light the ground. My crunching footfalls seemed too loud as I turned by the mailbox.

It felt farther than I'd estimated when looking at the satellite map. It felt spooky, especially through the treed section.

Wind shuffled the branches.

Up ahead—a glow.

I killed my flashlight.

It was a porch light on Gwen's house. All the windows, though, were dark.

Here was the garage. I walked alongside it and peeked around the corner. There was the studio, across a stretch of lawn. Completely dark. Firewood stacked up against the wall.

I glanced again at the house. I felt watched by all those empty black windows.

I jogged across the lawn and circled the shed, stopping when I saw a pair of glass doors. Luckily, they were on the opposite side of the shed from the house.

The panes gleamed under my flashlight. I tried one of the doorknobs.

Locked.

Why had I assumed I'd just walk right in?

Each door had eight or ten little panes of glass. If I broke the pane closest to one of the doorknobs, maybe I could reach in and unlock the door.

I hesitated. Would the breaking glass be noisy? It wasn't like I'd ever done anything like this before. But I'd seen it on TV.

I set my phone down and stripped off my hoodie. With only a T-shirt on, the cold air sent goose bumps pricking down my arms.

I wrapped one of the hoodie sleeves tightly around my right fist. Took a breath. Punched.

My hand bounced off.

I punched harder.

With a crackle, the glass collapsed under my hand. Shards tinkled onto the floor inside.

I wriggled the hoodie from my hand and dropped it. I gingerly reached between glittery glass teeth.

Pain bit, and I gasped.

I kept going, because by now, I was blitzed on adrenaline. I fumbled around until I felt the button lock on the inside knob.

Maybe I should've worn gloves, because I was leaving fingerprints *everywhere*.

I twisted the knob. There was a little click as the button popped up.

I withdrew my hand.

Red flowed like a ribbon down to the crook of my elbow.

Blood.

Panic surged into my throat. You're not supposed to cut the veins in your wrist. I was no first aid expert, but I knew *that*.

I picked up my hoodie again and shook out any clinging splinters of glass. I wrapped it tightly around my wrist and then held the whole thing against my chest.

The door opened smoothly on its hinges. I stepped over the glass on the floor.

Skylights glowed dully on the vaulted ceiling. Odors of oil paint and turpentine choked the air. I skimmed my flashlight beam around the perimeter.

An easel with a large canvas, sketchy marks across it—perhaps the beginnings of a new painting. Dozens, possibly hundreds, more canvases of all sizes leaned against the walls in stacks.

The paintings were colorful and a little abstract, but they all depicted the same subject: a man. A man with a startling erect penis, outlandishly large and front and center in every painting.

At first, that was all I noticed. The penis. Because, I mean, it was preposterous. Christopher Grasso was right: Gwen was *obsessed*.

The second thing I noticed was that most of the paintings had the Inguz rune somewhere on them: Interlocked double X's furnished the hazy background behind the man, or they were scrawled across the man, or they floated amid splotches and dashes of color.

In one painting, buck's antlers branched from the man's head. The crisscross of the antlers formed two X's.

I looked more closely at the man's other features. Yellow hair, or green hair, or sometimes pink hair, bright blue eyes, and a muscled chest and abdomen.

I aimed my flashlight beam at one of the largest paintings.

My mind stuttered. My breathing stopped.

Of course it was him.

57

Despite the abstract quality of Gwen's paintings, there was no mistaking Gregor's high-bridged nose with its distinctive nostrils. His straight, dark eyebrows. The exact deep-sea blue of his eyes.

It was as though Gwen knew my husband's face as well as I did.

My entire body was shaking.

It all made sense now.

Now I knew why Kirsten's kids resembled Gregor: because over the years he had returned again and again to this island—even after we met—and impregnated her during bizarre, bloody, drug-fueled forest orgies.

And it wasn't only Kirsten's children Gregor had fathered.

The thought slammed into me so hard that I doubled over.

I crouched. I tried to suck in a little air.

I pictured Magni, Alder, and Barri. I pictured Hildy's tiny daughter Greta with her matted pale hair and bright blue eyes. I pictured Gwen's twin boys with their butter-colored curls. I pictured the sea of small blond heads at KinderWild. I pictured all the pale little faces turned toward me. All the straight little eyebrows. All the distinctive little noses.

It wasn't just that almost all the KinderWild students were blond. No, almost all of them looked like *siblings*.

"Freeze," someone said behind me.

I went rigid.

"Put your hands over your head." It was a woman's voice.

Still crouching, I set my phone on the floor and raised my hands. My cut wrist gave a sudden throb. Spots glittered behind my eyeballs.

There was a click, and garish light flared.

"Stand up and turn around."

I stood stiffly. I turned, squinting against the blinding white light.

"Holy shit," the woman said. "Harlow Sullivan? What're you doing in here?"

Still squinting, unable to see the woman—Gwen, presumably—behind her eyeball-searing flashlight, I hesitated. Was there a lie that could make any of this look even the slightest bit better?

Not that I could think of. I'd have to go with the truth.

"I wanted to see your paintings," I said.

She snorted. "I wish more people were that desperate to see my work."

"They . . ." I swallowed. "They look like my husband. All of them."

Gwen laughed. It had a scornful edge to it. "What? Your *husband*?"

"Yeah. Gregor Sullivan." I gestured to one of the paintings that depicted Gregor's facial features so perfectly.

"That's *not* your husband," Gwen said.

"What? No. It is. I'll . . . let me show you." I picked up my phone. I turned the flashlight off and pulled up the screen saver, the loved-up-looking selfie of Gregor and me on our honeymoon. I turned it toward Gwen.

She stepped closer, frowned at it, and then shook her head. "No. That's just a man."

"What are you saying?" I looked around at her stacked paintings. "That this guy you paint over and over again *isn't* a man?"

She laughed again, and her eyes looked weird. Wide, unfocused. "I understand why you came here," she said. "I really do. And it's okay."

"It is?" I wanted to leave desperately, but Gwen was blocking the door. I also had the vague idea that I should make sure she wasn't going to call the sheriff on me.

"You came here because you feel his pull, too."

"Whose pull?"

Gwen tilted her head. "He's why all of us are here."

"Where?"

"On the island."

"Who's *all of us*?"

"All of us mamas, of course," she said. "The Blessed."

"Okay," I said. "So all of you . . . you mamas, all of you came to the island to be close to . . . this man?" I gestured to the paintings.

"I told you, he's not a man," Gwen said. "He is the divine masculine, the divine phallus. He is seed and growth, male action and fertility."

My neck prickled. Why did this sound so familiar?

"He is the germ of potential energy that gets released in sudden bursts," Gwen went on. "He is letting go of the past. He is *sacrifice*."

Then it hit me: Gwen was echoing the description I'd read of that ancient fertility god. Inguz.

Hold on, I thought frantically. *Hold on. So Gregor isn't just doing forest orgies with these women and worshipping some pagan god. He's play-acting that he* is *that god?*

My peripheral vision was closing in.

"What about your husbands?" I said. "Don't you guys have husbands? Or boyfriends?"

"Some of us do."

"Don't they care that their wives and girlfriends are messing around in the woods with a . . . with a pretend god?"

"He isn't *pretend*, Harlow. And our husbands have failed to give us the children we long for." Gwen's tone was cold. "Kirsten is right. She says you need time."

"What?" My thigh muscles jumped with the need to run. "Kirsten talks about me? To you?"

"She brought you here, didn't she? It's okay, Harlow. Kirsten brought *all* of us here. To meet the God of the Grove. To bring ourselves as empty vessels. To bear fruit on this sacred green island. We are indebted to her."

"For—?"

"We're making the world a better place. Don't you see? Those children—those *children*. They aren't human."

"What?" I said flatly. "The children aren't *human*?"

"They're the children of God," Gwen said. "Don't you see? They're demigods walking this island. Picture it! An entire island populated with half-divine beings, and they'll grow up and have their own babies . . . It will be like when the world was new."

"It sounds like a recipe for severe inbreeding, actually."

Gwen looked surprised. Then her eyes narrowed. "Get out," she said, low and harsh.

I was momentarily paralyzed. Part of me didn't want to go yet. I needed to know more. And I couldn't bear the thought of going back home to my traitorous, lying, utterly *depraved* husband.

"Get. The hell. *Out,*" Gwen said in a scalding whisper.

I edged past her.

I went out the door and stumble-ran to the driveway, my smarting wrist in the balled-up hoodie clutched to my chest.

I ran all the way down the driveway through the darkness, not bothering to use the flashlight this time. I couldn't even see my own feet. I was floating in the blackness. Floating in pain.

I felt something building in my chest as I got behind the wheel of my car and started driving. A minute later, it erupted.

Sobs, smothering and rib-heaving. Hot tears that made my glasses slide down.

I could barely see to drive, but I somehow made it back to Himmel Cottage.

◆ ◆ ◆

The house was just as I'd left it, heavy and dark and seeming to slumber in its spot between the forest and the harbor.

I slipped into the mudroom and went to the downstairs powder room. I unwound the hoodie from my wrist, gasping with pain. There was a scary amount of blood, but when I examined the two-inch gash under the bright vanity light, I could see it had mostly stopped bleeding.

I found an extra-large Band-Aid under the sink, and after washing up, I stuck it on.

I had no idea how I was going to explain the cut to Gregor, but on the other hand, did I really owe him an explanation after all the messed-up stuff *he'd* been doing?

I hid the bloodied hoodie under the vanity. I'd take care of it tomorrow.

Upstairs, Gregor didn't stir as I entered the bedroom.

In the en suite, I swallowed one Ambien and, after a moment's hesitation, a second. I really needed to sleep.

God only knew what tomorrow held.

I crawled into bed to wait for the Ambien to kick in. I considered sleeping in a different room because I was so panicked, confused, and angry about what I'd pieced together about Gregor.

But until I had concrete evidence that would hold up in custody court, I needed to keep playing my cards close.

Or try to, anyway.

Who are you? I thought, watching his gently breathing silhouette. *And what do you want from me?*

58

I awoke groggy and with a low-grade despair that I didn't understand.

Then it all hit. Those paintings. What Gwen said about the God of the Grove who just so happened to look exactly like my husband. All the little blond kids who could be siblings.

No. Please, God, let it all be a bad dream.

Out of habit, I groped for my phone. On the top of my notifications list was a text from Gregor: Hey sleeping beauty. Took Sam to school because I couldn't wake you. Hope you're not overdoing the Ambien. xxo

With a start, I mistook the xxo for the Inguz rune. But then I took a breath, let it out slowly, and saw it for what it really was.

Kisses and hugs? It felt like he was taunting me. *That asshole.*

I went back to my notifications.

My stomach flipped.

I had a new email from Paternitrust Inc.

The DNA test results. Maybe.

I don't need to open it, I told myself. *It'll only make me feel worse than I already do, if that's even humanly possible.*

I clicked open the email.

Your DNA Paternity Report is available now.

Like a zombie, I clicked the link. I logged into my account. This time, the "Results" box, which I'd been checking so obsessively for the last few days, was green.

My hand shook as I tapped "Results."

A file opened. At the top it said DNA Paternity Report. It was a spreadsheet with a lot of numbers in boxes that I'd need a coffee to comprehend.

But at the bottom of the file it said, *Combined Paternity Index: 0. Probability of Paternity: 0%. The alleged father is excluded as the biological father of the tested child.*

I read it again and again, sure there must be some mistake.

But no. Those big fat zeros could mean only one thing.

Gregor wasn't Barri's father.

◆ ◆ ◆

I wanted it to be over.

If Gregor wasn't Barri's father, then everything I'd been thinking about him—*it wasn't true*.

Yes, the KinderWild women were up to some very weird stuff. But there was no concrete link between them and Gregor. There had to be some other explanation for Gwen's paintings and how they so closely resembled Gregor, that was all. Something simple.

Maybe he somehow hadn't seen the head. Maybe he had nothing to do with *any* of it.

Maybe I could love him again.

I thought of the babies I'd been dreaming of since I fell in love with Gregor. Golden, beautiful babies who looked just like him. My heart felt like it would explode.

Maybe that family was still possible.

Thank God I'd never voiced my suspicions to him. That was probably the one smart thing I'd managed to do over the past few weeks.

I showered—carefully keeping the water off my bandaged wrist and the thick scab on my scalp—and got dressed in jeans and a sweater with sleeves that hid the Band-Aid. I made myself a shot of espresso and gulped it black.

I texted Anna: Heard about your accident. Worried about you! Please reach out when you're feeling up to it.

And her fall down the basement stairs really must've been an accident?

I made myself another espresso. I tried to imagine interacting with Gregor normally again, after these terrible weeks of our marriage imploding in slow motion.

But the thing was, I couldn't stop picturing the man in Gwen's paintings.

The sea of little KinderWild children who looked like siblings. Magni, Alder, and Barri so much like Gregor's baby pictures.

Maybe I could've written off *one* of those things. But all of them?

It was too many coincidences. I wanted to let it go, but I couldn't.

Genes don't lie.

What if . . . well, what if *Kirsten* was related to Gregor? Like, what if she was his sister, for example?

I liked the idea. I liked it way more than an objective scientist should. Because if they were siblings, I wouldn't need to be jealous.

I pictured Kirsten and Gregor, their heads bent together, laughing. They didn't look alike, but that didn't mean Kirsten's DNA wouldn't make her kids look like Gregor. The visible expressions of genes can skip generations.

If Kirsten and Gregor *were* siblings—or even cousins—did they know it?

There was a lot of money at stake. That could be it. Something to do with the Himmel fortune and who would inherit it after Pauline passed away.

If Gregor and Kirsten were related, it would have to be on Pauline's side. The Himmel nose, with its high bridge and defined nostrils, was visible in Jakob Himmel's portrait upstairs, in Pauline and in Gregor, and all the way down to Kirsten's three children.

Now that I thought about it, *Kirsten* didn't have to be a Himmel descendant, either. The other possibility was that the father of her three children *was* indeed a Himmel—just not Gregor.

Gregor's dad had died when Gregor was a teenager, so he was ruled out. But was there an uncle, or a cousin, or even a half sibling I didn't know about?

It's none of your business, I told myself. *Just be grateful you have confirmation that it isn't Gregor.*

Yet I found myself in the library again, wiggling out volume IV of the Himmel family photo albums from the bookcase.

I thumped it onto the desktop beside the computer.

I was searching for something different this time around. Instead of pictures of Gregor as a little boy, I was looking for pictures of some other, as-yet-unknown-to-me Himmel man.

I paged through the album. I saw Pauline and Gregor's dad, Cubby, on their wedding day, and when Pauline was pregnant, and with Gregor from newborn to prep school student.

Nowhere along the way did I see a picture of a man who I thought might've fathered Kirsten's children.

Not that the photo album proved anything. Illegitimate kids don't usually make it into family portraits.

I turned another page to see Gregor's Stanford graduation photo.

I was pretty sure I'd seen it before, somewhere along the line. But I'd never examined it closely. I guess it seemed so generic: Gregor in a black gown and mortarboard, standing between Pauline and another guy in a gown. Gregor has his arms around both of them. Gregor and Pauline beam for the camera, but the other guy has his head turned. He's grinning at someone off camera.

Wait—what?

I grabbed the edge of the desk to steady myself.

Could it be?

I bent closer, studying the second young man. He had brown skin and thick dark hair in a bun. I'd seen him before. Only once, but I was certain it was him.

It was Dr. Zakarian.

59

I was sure it was Dr. Zakarian mugging with Gregor in the graduation photo.

Dr. Zakarian, the fertility expert—*my* fertility expert. From the fancy clinic in New York. Before he was a doctor, obviously. Young, fresh, in a man bun instead of slicked-back doctor hair.

He'd been in Gregor's class at Stanford? He was Gregor's *friend*?

Why didn't Gregor tell me?

Did he think that I'd be uncomfortable being examined by his friend? Sharing intimate details about my hormones, my body, our *sex life*?

I mean, *Jesus*.

Without thinking it through, I got out my phone and dialed the clinic where Dr. Zakarian worked. I wanted to ask him why he hadn't mentioned knowing Gregor. It seemed like a weird breach of doctor-patient trust.

But as it turned out, Dr. Zakarian was on vacation.

"I can schedule you for the week he gets back," the receptionist said. "That's—let me see—that would be in ten days."

I was about to agree to this, but then I thought, *If Dr. Zakarian is Gregor's buddy, he's not exactly objective. That's the whole reason I'm checking into this. So maybe I should get another pair of trained eyes on my lab reports.*

"Is there another doctor in the clinic I could see sooner?" I asked.

"Well, there's Dr. Solzniak. She has . . . give me a second . . . yes, she has availability next Tuesday at eleven if that works?"

Tuesday felt like a million years away.

"I'll take it," I said. "Oh, and this will be a telemedicine appointment, if that's okay. I'm on the West Coast right now."

"Oh, in that case—hold on. Yes, in that case I can squeeze you in at the end of the day."

"Today?"

"Yes. Dr. Solzniak just had her last telemedicine appointment cancel. It's at four forty-five Eastern."

That would be 1:45 Pacific. Plenty of time before Sam's pickup. "Perfect," I said.

"Wonderful. I'll send a link to the email address you have on file with us."

After that, I went for a run. There was nothing else to do with all the electricity zapping through my body.

Dr. Solzniak was two minutes late logging on to the telemedicine appointment.

"Hi," I said. "Hello." I was still nervous.

"Good afternoon," Dr. Solzniak said. She was a reassuringly older woman with rosy cheeks and gray hair. "Sorry I'm late—may I call you Harlow?"

I nodded.

"I've been looking over your records and your labs to get up to speed. Everything seems up to date. So, what can I help you with today?"

I had prepared for this question. "I guess I just wanted a second opinion on my labs," I said. "Dr. Zakarian told me I—my husband and I—have unexplained infertility, and we're working on that, sort of focusing on overall health, lowering my stress levels, things like that. But I wanted to get a second opinion before we start going the whole IVF and egg donor route."

Gregor and I had never discussed using an egg donor, but it seemed like the most efficient way to give Dr. Solzniak a sense of the urgency.

"Egg donor?" She furrowed her brow. "According to your ultrasound, your eggs look great. Your eggs are not the problem."

"Oh, okay," I said, playing dumb. I already knew this.

Dr. Solzniak said carefully, "Did you mean to say *sperm* donor?"

Now it was my turn to frown. "Sperm donor? No—I . . . that was never on the table." *Oh wow,* I thought. *Gregor would die if he heard her suggesting that he's the problem.*

"Harlow . . . the reason you aren't getting pregnant isn't because of you. All of your tests look great—hormone levels, egg reserves, vitamin and mineral levels, all of it. It's . . . well, this is a bit concerning."

"What?" I said. "What's concerning?"

"Were you led to believe there's something wrong with *you*?"

"Yes. No. I mean—sort of? Dr. Zakarian diagnosed me with unexplained infertility and said that if I could lower my stress levels—"

"Sonofabitch," Dr. Solzniak muttered.

"I'm sorry?" My heart was pumping hard.

She looked directly into the camera, meeting my eyes. "Harlow, your husband's medical records are his medical records, and he never signed a waiver permitting anyone here at the clinic to share them with anyone, including you."

"Okay," I said slowly. "So you're saying . . . you're saying my husband has a fertility problem?"

"I didn't say that," Dr. Solzniak said but, almost imperceptibly, she nodded. "If I were you, I would ask your husband about *his* health history. *His*, um, numbers. Even his history of childhood illnesses that might've impacted his fertility. You shouldn't be thinking there's something wrong with you when there isn't. You're a perfectly healthy young woman who should have no issues conceiving."

"What are you saying? Are you saying Gregor's sperm count is low?"

"No." Dr. Solzniak gave her head a firm shake. "I can't comment on your husband's medical records. All I can say is that *you* appear healthy, and none of your tests indicate that you should be experiencing trouble conceiving."

Okay, I thought. *We're playing a little guessing game so Dr. Solzniak doesn't technically break any rules.*

A horrible idea hit me. But no. No way could it be possible.

I drew a shaky breath. "Are you saying his sperm count is . . . are you saying he's *sterile*?"

"I can't comment," Dr. Solzniak said in a tone that said *yes*.

A tinny little whine started up in my ears.

"You should definitely ask if that's a possibility, Harlow," Dr. Solzniak went on. "Ask him about childhood illnesses, which can sometimes cause sterility in boys."

Mumps, I thought. Gregor *had* told me he'd had mumps because Pauline didn't believe in vaccines. He'd had mumps as a young teenager, and furthermore, hadn't he always seemed inexplicably angry about it? He'd even gotten into the topic with her over the dinner table on our first night on the island.

"Can mumps cause sterility?" I asked.

"Yes," Dr. Solzniak said.

"Do you have his—" I began, but Dr. Solzniak cut me off.

"I'm afraid HIPAA regulations don't permit me to discuss this matter any further," she said. "Is there anything else I can help you with today?"

"No," I said, shaking my head slowly. "No."

"Okay. Well, if you'd like to explore other doctors, I can email some recommendations for other fertility clinics."

"Okay," I said. "Yeah. That would be great."

"Best of luck with everything, Harlow."

She ended the call, leaving me staring at my own reflection in the computer screen.

60

So. Gregor was sterile.

He was sterile and never told me.

No, it was even worse than that—he let me believe there was something wrong with *me*.

What kind of man would do that to his wife?

All these months trying to conceive . . . the desperate hope, the waiting, the fear. He'd put me through all of that *knowingly*. And then he'd brought me here to this island for, well, for *what*?

What about Sam? If Gregor had been sterile since adolescence, Sam couldn't be his biological child.

Why had he lied about that? Was he ashamed?

And why hadn't I seen the signs sooner?

I had no clue. And I wasn't going to stick around to find out.

◆ ◆ ◆

I hurried upstairs and started stuffing clothes into suitcases—mine and Sam's. Pajamas, T-shirts, toothbrushes, socks. I'd never found our passports. We'd figure it out. I was done waiting.

We were getting off this island *now*.

I grabbed Sam's favorite books. His new stuffed orca. His LEGO fire truck with the ladder that extended.

In the pantry, I loaded a canvas tote with road snacks—apples, granola bars, a sleeve of saltines, a pack of the seaweed crisps Sam liked. Then my eyes caught again on the curl of old wallpaper beside the cabinet.

My hand froze over the tote bag.

Slowly, I reached out and pulled the wallpaper back.

I miss Mama. They say I'm crazy. Crazy Bessie. Nobody believes me, and so I'm all alone here in—

I felt a pang of grief for that poor woman. I pictured her face, mutilated by an axe. I could feel her loneliness.

What were you trying to tell me, Bessie?

I checked the time: 2:44.

I shouldn't. It was almost time to leave.

But her words tugged at me. *All alone.* I felt that in my bones. We were two women trapped in the same frightening place, different centuries apart. Both of us struggling to be believed. Both of us dealing with cruel Himmel men.

Maybe this was a waste of time. But maybe it mattered.

I went to get the toolbox from the utility closet.

They tell you it's forever love
this house
too late

I dug through until I found a claw hammer and carried it back to the pantry. I wriggled the claw under the edge of the cabinet, just below Bessie's writing.

The wood didn't budge.

I tried again. The cabinet groaned, then splintered.

With my arms shuddering from the exertion, I pried it an inch from the wall. Then another inch. Nails squeaked. The glass door swung open, and then—the cabinet lurched overhead.

I threw myself sideways just as the entire thing—wood, glass, canned goods—ripped free from the wall and crashed to the floor.

The slam of it echoed in the small room. Shards of glass skittered across the tiles.

I tossed the hammer aside and peeled the wallpaper back some more.

Now I could read the rest of what Bessie had written.

Nobody believes me, and so I'm all alone here in the past.

Wait. The *past*? What did that mean?

I kept reading.

I'm not crazy, I'm lost. My name isn't really Bessie. It's Liz Reed. I miss my home. I miss Mama. I don't think I'll ever make it back.

Crazy Bessie was Liz Reed? *How?* They didn't even live in the same century.

Maybe I was wrong about all this writing being as old as I'd thought.

I didn't have the bandwidth to think about this right now.

I checked my phone again.

2:48.

Oh no. Not again.

I hurried out to the Mercedes. I dumped the snack tote in the back seat, hoisted the suitcases into the cargo area, and slid behind the wheel, tossing my shoulder bag onto the passenger seat.

I turned over the ignition.

One last pickup. Then we were gone.

◆ ◆ ◆

It was smooth sailing until I came up behind a school bus.

There was no safe way to pass the bus, and it stopped every mile or so to let students off. Each time the bus's red brake lights flared and that little stop sign popped out on its side, I wanted to scream. I watched the clock creep upward. 3:05. 3:10. 3:15.

Finally, at 3:17, the school bus turned off the main road and I could pick up speed again. But by the time I bounced into KinderWild's parking lot, there was only one car left: a mud-streaked Prius. Teacher Terra's car.

I parked and jogged across the lot and into the forest.

In the Gathering Place, I didn't see Sam. I spotted Terra across the empty clearing, drinking from a steel water bottle.

"Where's Sam?" I called as I approached her.

She lowered the bottle and wiped her mouth with the back of her hand. She was looking at me with an expression I couldn't interpret.

"Where's Sam?" I repeated when I reached her. I was out of breath and sweating despite the cool air under the trees.

"He's gone." Terra screwed the cap back on her water bottle. "You're too late."

"Did Gregor pick him up?"

"When it was obvious you weren't going to show, I called his father—"

Oh no, I thought. *This is going to make things way more complicated.*

"—and he gave me the okay for Kirsten Blakeley to take him back home."

"Wait. Sam's with *Kirsten*?"

"He was happy to go with her."

"I doubt that."

"She's an amazing mama. You could learn a lot from her."

I was turning to leave, but fury spun me back around to face Terra. "What does *that* mean?"

"Well, if you had even the tiniest bit of maternal instinct you wouldn't make Sam wait for you to do whatever it is you do all day before you pick him up. You make him feel abandoned, you know."

"Go to hell," I snarled.

"Maybe when you give birth, things will change for you. It's all about biology—*you* of all people should know that. It's about *blood*."

"No, it's not," I said. "It's about love. Sam's my baby—I'd *die* for him—" I stopped. "What are you talking about? *When* I give birth?"

A flicker of confusion. Terra lifted her eyes to the circle of sky above us, then back to me. "It's your turn."

"What?" I said, my thoughts skidding and spinning out. "My turn for what?"

"You're lucky. Some of us have been waiting for *years*." Terra's eyes filled with tears. They lifted skyward again, and this time I followed her gaze.

She was looking up at the moon.

It looked translucent against the blue sky. It wasn't quite full, but its ovoid shape almost seemed to swell as I watched.

If I hadn't found that dead girl's head in the ravine, I thought, *what would've happened to us—to Sam and me? Is this why we're here? So I can ovulate on this island when the moon is full and join those delusional pretend-pagan psychos in their bloody fertility ritual?*

And then I thought, *Oh my God I need to get Sam and get off this island before the moon is full.*

I started running to the parking lot.

61

As I speed down the driveway to Himmel Cottage, I have no recollection of how I got there. I'm drunk, only instead of alcohol fuming through my blood, it's terror.

I don't understand how Gregor thinks a blood sacrifice in the forest is going to make him magically fertile again. I don't *want* to understand. All I know is, he lied to me again and again to bring us to this point.

I slam the Mercedes into park and get out. I walk toward the monstrous, bulky house.

Go away, it seems to say.

But Sam's inside, and I'm not leaving without him.

In the mudroom, I see Gregor's discarded boots and jacket. I can hear bottles clinking in the kitchen.

"Babe?" Gregor calls. "Is that you?" He appears in the doorway, holding a beer. "Whoa," he says. "Are you . . . okay?"

He doesn't move to kiss me, like he normally would. He stays right there in the doorway.

He senses something is off.

"Yeah," I say. I hang the car keys on their hook. "I'm just . . . I wish you would've told me you were having Kirsten give Sam a ride home. I almost had a heart attack when I got to KinderWild and he wasn't there."

"When you *eventually* got there. How late were you this time? Ten minutes? Twenty?"

"Where is he now?" I look past Gregor.

"Sam? At the Blakeleys'. The boys all wanted a sleepover."

I look back to Gregor, startled. "*Sam* wanted a sleepover?"

"Yeah." Gregor swallows some beer, never taking his eyes off me.

"But that makes no sense. Sam doesn't even *like* Magni or—"

"Low," Gregor says on a groan. "Stop. They're just little kids, working shit out. Look, why are we standing here?" He turns to the kitchen. "Come on. I'll make you a drink. Let's enjoy being child-free while we can."

I follow him into the kitchen, even though my body is shouting *run*.

He's looking in the fridge, his back to me.

I perch on one of the island stools. Dead flowers droop in a crystal vase on the island top. A bowl of bananas sits beside the vase, bruised and brown.

"Want a mocktail?" he says.

"A mocktail," I repeat. Rage bubbles up inside me. "Right. Because I can't have alcohol. Because I'm having such a hard time conceiving."

Gregor glances over his shoulder, brows furrowed, eyes sharp. "What's gotten into you?"

I shouldn't have said that, I think.

"I'm just . . . tired."

"How about a coffee, then?"

"Sure. Yeah. That would be great."

"Awesome." Gregor goes over to the coffee machine, inserts a pod, gets down a cup, positions it under the spout, and flips the switch. The machine grinds to life, making it impossible to talk for a few moments. We both watch the cup like it's the most important thing in the world.

When the coffee finishes brewing, Gregor carries the cup to the fridge and pours in some almond milk creamer, the way I like it. Then he places it delicately in front of me.

"Thanks," I say, and take a sip.

Gregor kisses my hair, whispering, "I know you're worried about Sam—"

His hot breath sends prickling voltage down my spine.

"—but you don't need to be. I love that your maternal instinct is finally kicking in, but save it for your own baby."

"What baby?" I say.

He takes a step back, frowning down at me. "You're not giving up hope, are you?"

"About what?"

"That you're going to conceive. It's going to happen, Low. It's going to happen soon. You're going to be a mother. I promise."

That's when it sinks in that he really, truly thinks I'm going to get pregnant at the ritual. Which means he believes in magic.

How did I, a *scientist*, marry a man who believes in magic?

Unless . . .

Oh my God.

Why didn't I think of it before?

Unless he plans for *some other man* to impregnate me.

The mysterious man in Gwen's paintings. The God of the Grove. The guy who is maybe one of Gregor's relatives.

I start to shake.

To hide it, I sip my coffee. Gregor didn't put in enough almond milk creamer after all, because it has a strange bitterness. I drink it anyway.

He watches me with unblinking focus.

"What?" I say, trying to sound light and undemanding, the way I always used to. I place the empty cup on the marble island with a clack.

"When I got home earlier, I noticed your toothbrush was gone," he says.

My belly drops.

"Then I saw that two of the suitcases were gone from the closet. So I checked the security program—"

"Wait—you said you didn't know anything about that program."

"—and when I looked at the footage, there you were, loading stuff into the car and driving away. Where were you going, Low?"

My mind scrounges around, weighing different responses, but it's all getting tangled up.

"I love that you're smart," Gregor says. "I really do. It's one of the high-quality traits you have that hopefully you'll pass on to our children. But you just *had* to be the dog with the bone. It's really too bad. It makes everything so much harder—for me, but especially for you. But I'm not going to let you screw this up for me."

I stare at him, only half comprehending what he's saying. Did his lips always have that petulant tuck at the corners? Were his eyes always so cold?

Part of me wants to jeer at him. To tell him I know he's shooting blanks. That I know he's scheming to have me impregnated—no, *raped*—by a stranger, some random Himmel cousin or uncle or half brother, just so I can carry on his precious bloodline.

But that would be dangerous.

I have to play dumb. Isn't that what we women do best? Play dumb? Men think we're stupid, and we go along with it just to survive.

I tip my head, pretending confusion. "Honey, I wasn't leaving. Why do you—"

"Stop lying. I saw the suitcases."

There's probably a clever way to explain the suitcases, but I can't think of it. A fog is seeping in around the edges of my brain.

"What did you find out?" he asks. For the first time I notice how he's pinching the beer bottle so tightly, it looks like it might crack. "You got into my mom's computer. You saw security footage from that first night. What did you see?"

"That? Oh." I lick my lips. "Nothing. Just . . . darkness?"

"Stop lying. And I know you went to Gwen Lloyd's place last night—"

I suck in a breath.

"—and that you broke into her art studio. What did she tell you?"

"Nothing," I say idiotically. "She didn't tell me anything."

"Bullshit."

Nausea swills through me. I slump over my elbows on the countertop, bile rising in my throat, its acid mingling with the taste of coffee and almond milk and that other bitter taste.

"What did you put in the coffee?" I say.

"It's already kicking in?"

"What is it? Are you . . . did you—"

"I'd never hurt you, Low. Don't you get it? I *need* you."

He's told me this before. Lots of times. Only now does it sound, not like a declaration of love, but like a threat.

So finally, at long last, I ask him what I—lovestruck and gaslit and blindsided—never asked before: "Need me for what?"

"Let's get you to bed."

"Need me for *what*?" I repeat shrilly. "For my genes? For my womb?"

"Come on," he says, reaching for me.

Something inside me snaps.

I lunge across the kitchen island and grab the crystal vase with the dead flowers. It's cold, and blessedly heavy.

I wind up with my softball pitcher's arm, as nimble and sure as when I was thirteen, and I smash it down on his head.

The thump is sickening.

I watch as he, in slow motion, crumples into a rag-doll pile.

I stand there, panting, with the vase dangling from my hand, and then let it slip. It hits the floor with a crash, spraying glittering shards and water and dead petals and leaves.

He doesn't stir.

"Gregor?" I whisper.

His eyes are shut. Blood is darkening his hair. A red string trickles into his ear.

I kneel beside him. Glass bites through my jeans, into my knee. "Gregor?"

He's breathing. That's good. I mean, I didn't want to *kill* him.

I sway. Whatever Gregor put in that coffee is pumping steadily through my veins now. Slowing my limbs. Thickening my thoughts.

Get Sam, I think. *Just get Sam.*

I get to my feet, stagger to the mudroom, and grab the car keys.

62

It feels like the car is flying down the endless driveway. Then I see the closed gates rushing at me before they spring open at the last second.

Easy, Low, I tell myself.

Then it's only a matter of turning onto the main road—*Okay, I've got this*—and then, a little way down, onto the Blakeleys' driveway.

The car jounces up the steep, curved gravel. At the top, I park sloppily and get out.

I walk carefully to the porch because the ground seems to be made of Play-Doh. I pound the front door with my fist.

Immediately, the door swings inward. Kirsten stands there in one of her ridiculous floral dresses and a lacy apron.

I see her surprise and then—could it be?—her panic. But she irons it all out. She's serene again. Blank. Ready for a selfie captioned with a few sanctimonious hashtags.

"Harlow," she says. "What are you—"

"Where's Sam?" I lean past her and shout, "Sam? Sam, sweetie, it's time to go!"

"You need to leave," Kirsten says, pushing the door.

I ram my sneaker against the jamb, wincing as the door smashes into my instep. I don't pull away. "I'm not leaving without Sam."

"He's just fine where he is. He doesn't need to be subjected to all your drama."

"All *my* drama?"

"I told Gregor you weren't a viable option. But he wouldn't listen."

"*Excuse* me?"

"I told him that if you get pregnant, it's going to be a disaster."

"You know what? You and your blond pagan-wannabe minions didn't *invent* motherhood. You don't *own* it. No matter how much you preach to your choir on social media about putting lentils into mason jars and breastfeeding your preschoolers and reassuring your insecure husbands that they're the boss of the household, you're just a big *fake*. There's nothing under there, is there? You don't even believe in any of this shit. You just want attention, and you'll do literally *anything* to get it. Am I right?"

"If you don't leave, I'm calling the sheriff," Kirsten says. But I've gotten to her. Her face is waxy. Lips pinched, nostrils flared.

"Be my guest," I say. "What're you going to tell them? That you're holding my son hostage?"

"Your *son*?" She smirked.

"Yeah," I said. "My *son*."

"Sam's father gave permission for him to come here for a sleepover. You have no right to take him."

"I'll tell the police all about your drugged-up orgies with a pretend god in the woods. I'll tell them how you're *sacrificing humans*."

"Really? You're going to tell that to Sergeant Marcus?"

From somewhere upstairs a childish voice calls, "Harlow?"

"Sam!" I shout. "Sam, it's me!"

"I want to go home!" he calls back. I'm not sure, but I think he sounds tearful.

"Come on, baby!" I call. "I'll take you home."

Now Kirsten is leaning her weight harder against the door, crushing my foot.

Instinctively, I yank my foot free.

The door slams shut.

"Hey!" I shout. I pummel my fists on the door. My cut wrist smarts under its bandage, but that doesn't stop me.

"I'm dialing nine-one-one," comes Kirsten's muffled voice. I hear the bang of a dead bolt.

Now the whole world is spinning and my feet are *way* too far away. I grab the porch railing and thump to a seat on the top step.

I just need to think, I tell myself, holding my head in my hands so it won't fly away. *If I can just think straight for a minute, I can come up with a plan for getting Sam out of there.*

I still haven't come up with a plan when I hear the crunch of tires on gravel.

A black-and-white SUV rolls to a stop beside the Mercedes. SHERIFF, it says on the side.

Two people climb out. They both wear dark-blue uniforms, and neither one is Sergeant Marcus. One is a Black guy, and one is a woman with dark hair and deep olive skin.

I sigh with relief.

Kirsten steps out of the house, hugging herself. "Oh my gosh, thanks for coming so fast," she calls to the officers, who are walking closer. "I've been so scared."

"She's not scared," I say, hoisting myself to my feet. The words are mushy in my mouth. "*She's* the scary one. *She's* the one who—"

"I think she's drunk," Kirsten says, talking over me. "She has a problem with alcohol. That's actually why her husband's son is here in the first place. He was planning on getting her checked into rehab this weekend—"

"Liar!" I shout, but it's garbled and I'm swaying, and the female officer takes hold of me before I fall sideways.

"Come on," she says. "Let's get you home."

"It's right across the road," Kirsten says. "Himmel Cottage? You'll see the driveway gates. The gate code is 6790. I know it because the kids go back and forth a lot."

"Gotcha," the officer says, and I'm being led to the SUV and funneled into the back seat.

Only when the door slams shut do I remember what's waiting at Himmel Cottage.

My husband. On the kitchen floor. Bleeding.

Maybe dead.

"You okay?" the female officer asks, swiveling on the front seat to look at me.

I open my mouth. I want to say *I don't know*, but I can't get the words out.

"Man, she's wasted," the male officer says.

At Himmel Cottage the officers guide me—one on each arm—up the steps and to the front door.

One of them raps the knocker.

"I can just go in," I say. "I live here."

They don't seem to understand me.

Then—footsteps inside.

The door opens.

Gregor.

My knees buckle. The two officers hold me up.

"Oh my God, Low," Gregor says. "Are you okay?"

"We picked her up at the neighbor's house," one of the officers says.

"She's pretty severely intoxicated," the other one says. "The neighbor indicated this is an ongoing issue?"

"Yeah. It's . . . sorry." Gregor is wearing a clean shirt and his stupid hipster fedora. I guess to cover up whatever I did to his head. "Come here, babe," he says. The officers release me, and a second later I'm in Gregor's arms. He reeks of stress sweat and fresh blood. "It's going to be okay."

"You got this?" one of the officers asks him.

"Yeah," Gregor says. "Thanks so much for your help."

"No worries."

The front door closes.

63

"Let go of me," I slur at Gregor, trying to arch away from his grip.

"The fuck I will." His fingers jab deep into my arms. "You tried to *kill* me. You're out of control."

"Let go of me!"

"Jesus. Calm down. Stress delays ovulation, you know."

"It's a little late for that, asshole."

He's steering me toward the staircase, and I have to stumble along with him or else be dragged. We go up the stairs, along the upper hallway, and to the stairs leading to the third floor.

"No," I say, whimpering. *"No."*

"Don't make this harder than it needs to be. You need rest."

"What did you give me? Was it poison? Am I going to die?"

"I told you. I'd never hurt you. How do you not know that?"

"You're hurting me right now!"

"This is for you. For what *you* want."

Up the steep stairs with their squashy carpet runner. At the top, the door to Pauline's bedroom stands open.

He thrusts me through the doorway and drops me. My hip, my elbow strike the floorboards, and I grunt.

"Oh," he says. "I almost forgot." He leans down and digs things out of my jacket pockets. My phone. The car keys. "Get some rest, babe," he says, straightening.

The door shuts and I hear the snap of a bolt.

I struggle to my feet and try the doorknob. Locked. Wait—how did he lock it from the outside?

"Gregor!" I shout, banging the door. "Gregor, let me out!"

I bang and shout till my voice goes raspy and I can no longer stand. Then I hobble over to Pauline's bed and lie down. The pillow stinks of Chanel No. 5. I set my glasses on the bedside table and shut my eyes.

But I don't sleep.

I'm slopping around in a tiny wooden boat, tumbling and corkscrewing on inky ocean waves. I hear my own frantic breathing like it's playing over a sound system. Faces surge toward me and sail past, terrifying black-and-white masks. Then there are the rats, skittering along the edges of my vision. They're the size of terriers, and if I nod off they'll eat me alive, so I use a big stick to beat them away, and they dissolve like ashes. Then the moon rises to fill the entire sky over me, glowing so round and cold that I feel its malice inside my skeleton. And then I'm a deer, leaping through pitch blackness, my hooves dinging the rocky ground as I go, and I'm panicked because I'm being hunted. My deer's heart is a bloody, pulpy plum inside my furry body, and it might burst because I have to get away get away get away . . .

I open my eyes. Daylight sears in. I squeeze them shut again with a moan. I try to sit up. Nausea shoves me back down.

I'm thirsty, *so* thirsty, and my mouth is sticky. All I can think about is cold water, tasting of crisp minerals and pouring down my throat.

I force my eyes open again. I cringe. It's bright. It has to be morning—no, afternoon, even.

I put my glasses on and climb off the snarled-up bed and go to the en suite bathroom. I'm still in my jeans and running sneakers and puffer jacket. I feel damp underneath my clothes.

I go to the sink and turn on the cold tap.

There's a gurgle in the pipes before a few drops of water drip into the basin. Then, nothing.

I crank the cold tap all the way, and then the hot tap.

No water.

I go to the bathtub. Same thing. The shower. Same.

Gregor must've turned off the water supply.

The toilet, I think. *Won't there be clean water in the toilet tank?*

I go to the toilet closet. My heart sinks. It's one of those toilets with the water tank built inside the wall.

I go to the window over the bathtub, undo the latch, and push the upper sash. It won't budge. It's painted shut.

I look out. It's a long, long way down to a stone pathway at the back of the house.

I go back out to the bedroom—moving more quickly now—and cross to the windows.

There are three windows in a row, overlooking the harbor. The first window I try is painted shut. So is the second. So is the third.

I could smash the glass, I think. *But the noise will alert Gregor, and if I jump out the window, onto the porch roof, I'd probably break my legs? Or my neck.*

Like Anna.

A spiral of nausea forces me into a squat. The arch of my left foot is starting to cramp like it always does when I'm dehydrated. I don't know how long I've gone without water, but it has to be twelve hours. No—maybe even twenty.

Has Gregor left me up here to die of thirst? Is that the plan? What would be the point?

I lie back down on the bed.

◆ ◆ ◆

I wake to the sound of footsteps on the stairs.

Now the room is dark. I touch my face. My glasses are gone.

Panicked, I pat around the bed until I feel them underneath a pillow. I sigh with relief as I slip them on.

I'm walking unsteadily toward the door when—*thunk*—it swings open.

Gregor fills the doorway.

He's backlit by light in the stairwell, and he's holding something.

A rifle.

Braced against his shoulder. Aimed at me.

64

"Don't try anything," Gregor says. He adjusts his hold on the rifle.

"Wow, this is a new side of you, Gregor," I say, but my voice sounds feeble. "Very macho."

Now that he isn't wearing the fedora, I can see the blood-matted hair above his ear.

"Yeah," he says, catching me looking. "Congratulations. You really screwed up my head."

"Clearly not enough."

Keeping the rifle aimed at me, he nudges something with his boot. A tray on the floor. He pushes it all the way into the room. I see a sandwich on a paper plate and a large plastic water bottle. "You need to drink," he says. "I don't want you to get dehydrated."

"Then why did you shut off the water supply?"

"When did you turn into such a mouthy little bitch? You're not the sweet girl I married."

"Yeah, well, believe me, I'm having a little buyer's remorse myself. What's in the water? More psychedelic drugs? You even drugged me the night I found the head, didn't you? With the food you brought to me in bed?"

"What am I supposed to do? Let you freak out—let you *leave*—when everything is coming together for us?"

"There is no *us*. Not anymore."

"You'll change your mind. When you hold our baby in your arms for the first time, you're going to realize—"

"I know you're infertile, Gregor."

I hear his jagged breath. I watch his face flush, and how he regrips the rifle.

"The doctor told me," I say. "Not your college buddy Dr. Zakarian. A different doctor. One who realized what you were doing to me."

"I didn't *do*—"

"You made me believe I was infertile," I say. "Why? Why would you do that? It's unbelievably cruel. Letting me worry all the time? Letting my heart break over and over, month after month? Do you have any idea how that . . . how it *shattered* me? And what about Sam? You never told me he wasn't your biological child."

"It was all necessary."

"*Necessary?* Why? To keep me broken, and to try to keep me feeling less connected to Sam so I'd go along with anything you suggested, no matter how insane? I know what you have planned, Gregor. I figured it out. You—"

"It's not like it isn't for you, too."

"I have no idea what you're—"

"My mother, Harlow. My fucking *mother*. Don't you get it?"

"Get what? That she wants grandkids? That Sam isn't good enough because she thinks that the precious Himmel bloodline is the greatest thing that ever happened to the human race?"

"Yes! Yes, exactly that! It's all she cares about, and she's going to cut me off unless I give her the grandchildren she wants, okay?"

I stare at him, panting. "Cut you off," I repeat.

"Yeah."

"You mean . . . financially?"

"The inheritance, the house in New York, the allowance, everything."

"Wait—allowance? I thought you had a trust fund."

"There is no trust. It's just . . . she just puts money into my accounts. I told you there was a trust fund so you wouldn't think I was being jerked around on a string by my mother."

"I never—" I stop myself. I was about to say *I never would have thought of you that way*. But it would be a lie, because now? Now, that's *exactly* what I think of him. "So this is all about money? You did all this to me—the lies, the gaslighting, the *imprisonment*—for *money*? I thought you cared about me. I . . . I thought you *loved* me."

"There are things I love about you." His gaze climbs me down and up, as though checking me out for the first time. "I mean, you're not really my type. But you keep yourself in amazing shape. And I love how much you love me. I love how flexible you've always made yourself. How accommodating you are. I love how you always back down and back off. Until recently, anyway. Why'd you have to go and change?"

"So you were never actually in love with me," I say.

"Not really, no."

"Then why did you choose me?"

"Because you were so *desperate*. Jesus. You told me you wanted kids on, like, our second date—"

"It was the third date. And I told you that so nobody's time would get wasted if that wasn't what you were looking for. I was only being honest."

"You were so needy and desperate—you were exactly what I was looking for. Oh, and your German and Norwegian bloodline, obviously."

I remember Pauline examining me that first day on the island. Pauline saying, *You'll have to do*.

"So I'm just a body to you?" I say to Gregor. "A baby-making machine?"

"That's how you thought of *me*. A sperm donor, and a bottomless ATM thrown in as an extra bonus. Face it, Harlow. We've been using each other. And frankly, I think *you* have the better end of the bargain."

"And when I got my period this month, you were *relieved*. I couldn't figure it out. You were relieved because it was confirmation that my cycle was still on track?"

"I don't think you're appreciating how tricky the timing has been," Gregor says. "Women with twenty-eight-day cycles—like you—only ovulate when the moon is full about once a year. We aren't going to have too many chances before you're too old to—"

"You asshole," I say, choking up. "You complete *asshole*!"

Ever since the moment Gregor approached me in that Brooklyn bar, I've been wondering *Why me? Why did he choose me?*

Well, now I have my answer.

He's infertile. His mother wants blond grandbabies with the Himmel nose. He'd wanted someone desperate enough, and enough of a doormat, and with the right kind of genetics, to go along with his plan.

He wants those millions of dollars far, far more than he ever wanted me. But he has a gun aimed at my ribs, so I have to at least try to convince him otherwise.

"I love you, Gregor," I say, forcing myself to meet his eyes. "I love you so incredibly much. Honey, we don't *need* money. We only need each other. And it's not like we'll be poor—I mean, I can start working again, and who knows, maybe you'll get a record deal. We could move, too, out of the city, to someplace where housing and the cost of living isn't so high, and you won't ever have to do what your mom tells you to do ever again. You'll be *free*."

I can almost see him picturing it, this alternate path I've laid out. A modest home. A weekly grocery budget. Economy airline seats. Everything *I* think is normal but that, as I watch, makes him twist his mouth with contempt.

He shakes his head. "Maybe that sounds okay to you, but I won't live like that. No way."

"Why?" I ask with a sudden bite of anger. "Why are you so special?"

"Because I'm a fucking Himmel." He's stepping backward, through the doorway. "It's fine. I get that you want something else. Once the baby is born, I'll cut you loose, okay? Then everybody wins." He gestures to the water bottle on the floor. "Stay hydrated."

"I'm not drinking that."

"You will. In the end, the body always wins."

The door shuts. The bolt clacks. Footsteps recede down the stairs.

65

I wait as long as I can. Twenty, maybe even thirty minutes. Then I snatch up the water bottle and unscrew the lid. The water is cool. Silky. It's like heaven.

It's also bitter, and I know what it's going to do to me. But I drink it down, every last drop.

At first, my thoughts are clear, now that I have enough fluid circulating in my veins. And my first thought is, *Wait. Once the baby is born, he'll cut me loose?*

That's the plan? I'm going to be raped by a stranger, and then Gregor will keep me locked up in this attic for nine months until I give birth? And then he'll take my baby away and—then what? What does that even mean, *cut me loose*?

If he keeps me captive and steals my baby, he won't just let me go. I'd tell people what he did.

No, he'll kill me. And it'll be so easy for him to get away with it, because he's a rich boy, and rich boys do what they want.

The drug, whatever it is, kicks in faster and harder this time.

I try to fight it, but Gregor was right: In the end, the body always wins.

I lie down on the bed and look out the windows.

There it is, the treacherous, almost-full moon. I imagine its pale beams reaching inside my body, coiling around my ovaries, whispering, coaxing, making my body do things I don't want it to do.

The ritual won't be tonight, though. The moon isn't perfectly full. It's safe to close my eyes . . .

Slippery phantoms rush forward to greet me. They grab me by both arms and whisper gibberish against my face. They drag me down deep.

◆ ◆ ◆

When I wake up again, it's because I feel like I'm being watched.

I'm sprawled sideways across the bed. Lips cracked, throat raw, veins begging again for water.

Daylight. Afternoon, judging by the slant of the sunlight.

Horrors still flash across my field of vision. Monsters. Witches. Human heads rotting into the moss.

The feeling of being watched isn't going away.

I grope around until I feel my glasses on the bed beside me. I slide them on.

My eyes toggle upward. They land on a face. The portrait of the great-grandpa. The German guy. The lumber baron. What was his name? Jakob. He looks so much like Gregor that my heart kicks into high gear.

I was wrong before. Gregor's face is every bit as cruel as this guy's.

I look at the round, painted moon in the sky behind him. The leaning axe. The dish of caramel-capped mushrooms. His arm drapes languidly on the chair, hand dangling, golden signet ring on his pinky finger.

I think of Crazy Bessie's fragmented words under the dining room wallpaper:

bitches
those witches in the moon

and old man Himmel
say
dances with them
frolics with
they made him rich

What did you do, Jakob? I think. *What kind of twisted traditions did you pass down to your descendants?*

Wait—there's something written on the ring.

I sit up and crawl closer to the portrait.

The signet ring is painted to look like polished gold. It's a flat rectangle with rounded edges, a little oversize even for a signet ring. Very delicately painted on the rectangular face, as though with a single paintbrush hair, it reads

VALCAMBI
SUISSE
1 g.
FINE GOLD
999,9
CHI Essayeur Fondeur
AA37567

A gold bar.

Which isn't *too* strange. Jakob Himmel transformed himself from a penniless immigrant to one of the wealthiest lumber barons in American history. It made sense that he'd flaunt his wealth, even in the peculiar way of wearing an actual gold bar as jewelry.

But . . . didn't I see exactly this kind of gold bar before, in one of Kirsten's Instagram posts?

they made him rich

And—hold on. When I looked up Valcambi on Wikipedia, didn't it say the company had only been around since the 1960s? If that was true, how could Jakob Himmel have owned a Valcambi gold bar? He died in the '50s.

None of this makes any sense.

I stand up on the bed and sweep the velvet curtain shut across the painting. I don't need that arrogant freak watching me anymore.

The sun goes down. The moon drifts up, ripe and round over the hills across the harbor. I feel a slight ache in my pelvis, like I always do at this time of the month.

It's all lining up perfectly, exactly how Gregor wanted when he put this plan into motion so many months ago.

Except for one thing. He never counted on me not being a doormat.

I put on my glasses and get up.

I make a methodical review of all the items in the bedroom. I assess each one for weight and how easy it is to hold.

There are the ceramic lamp bases on either side of the bed. Unplugged and with the shades removed, they could work, but they're unwieldy, and breakable.

I need something I can strike with over and over again.

There's the desk chair, dainty and wooden. That's a little better. I could hold on tight to the legs, and if it splinters apart, well, it might make an even better, sharper weapon.

The closet holds nothing very likely, although the heels on some of Pauline's shoes look sharp enough to pierce an eye socket.

I check the bathroom. The medicine cabinet is bare. Gregor must've had the foresight to empty it, probably assuming I'd try to overdose on Tylenol since he thinks I'm such a wuss.

He doesn't know me at all. He thinks I'm weak. But I guess people who are incapable of love think love is a weakness.

The truth is, love is keeping me going. Not for Gregor, but for Sam, and for myself, and for the idea of the baby Gregor wants to be violently brought into being inside my womb.

No.

Hell, no.

There can't be a baby. Not like that.

And I'm going to survive. And Sam and I are, somehow or other, going to get out.

I explore inside the cabinet under the sink.

It, too, has been emptied out. *Heaven forbid the doormat gets her hands on a bottle of Drano.*

I start to close the cabinet, but then I notice the curved part of the drain under the sink. The P trap, I vaguely remember it's called. Underneath its chrome plating, I'm guessing it's solid, heavy brass. It's attached to the other portions of the drain—the part coming down from the sink, the part going into the wall—with nuts that look like you'd need a large wrench to loosen.

Lefty loosey, I think. I try unscrewing one of the nuts with my bare hands. It won't budge. I try again.

It's stuck, and the skin of my palms burns.

Something makes me try turning it to the right.

I feel it give.

My heart leaps up. For whatever reason, this nut *isn't* lefty loosey.

I unscrew it all the way, and unscrew the other nut, too. The curved pipe comes loose in my hand. I pull it free. A little water dribbles onto my hand, and I lick it off.

The P trap isn't huge, but it's a solid, heavy hunk of metal that fits perfectly in my hand. You could shatter a mouthful of teeth with it. You could cave in a skull.

Not that I *want* to kill Gregor. But things have rearranged themselves in my brain. I've shifted into a primal gear. If it's my survival or his, then yeah, I'm picking *mine*.

66

I sit on the floor behind the bedroom door, leaning against the wall. I cling to the P trap like it's a life buoy.

Waiting feels like forever.

Outside, the white bubble moon continues upward.

I might've dozed off, because the next thing I know, I start with a gasp. My heart hammers.

What woke me?

I sit rigid, listening.

Footsteps.

He's trying to be stealthy. He's probably hoping I've fallen asleep so he can surprise me. But I'm wider awake than I've ever been in my life.

I get up stiffly. The arches of both my feet are cramping with dehydration now. I grip the cold pipe with both hands and will the cramps to pass. I crave freedom like I crave water.

I feel nothing at all for Gregor. No love. No grief. Not even anger. He's become a mere obstacle in my way.

The footfalls stop outside the door. I think I hear him breathing.

The latch slides.

My pulse hisses against my eardrums.

The door swings inward, a yellow fan of light spreading open across the floor.

There's a long pause.

I hold my breath. I can almost feel him trying to gauge where I am.

He takes a step into the room.

I lift the P trap and take a step, too. All I want is to sink that chunk of cold metal as deep as I can into his skull, but just as I set my foot down, my arch cramps up again hard. My foot can't hold my weight, and I thump to my hands and knees on the floor. My glasses fall off, and the P trap goes skidding across the room.

Blurry boots stop right next to my hands.

I try to get back up.

But before I can, he twists one of my hands behind my back and then the other. Something rigid is wrapping my wrists and pulling them together tight. A plastic zip tie, I guess. My cut wrist throbs with pain under its bandage.

"Get up," Gregor says. "It's time to go."

"I'm not going anywhere with you."

"Yeah." He's produced the rifle from the other side of the doorway. He digs its cold muzzle into my cheekbone. "You are."

"I can't walk without my glasses," I say.

"Fine." Gregor snatches up my glasses and pushes them crookedly onto my face. "Happy?"

"Not really," I say.

Outside, a dark landscape cowers under the moon-bathed sky.

My breath appears and vanishes in pale little puffs. Cold air wraps around my legs and stretches long fingers down the back of my jacket. My face is wet because in the kitchen, Gregor dumped two glassfuls of water messily down my throat.

He also pulled a beanie onto his head, the kind with a small built-in LED flashlight, which now casts its narrow, jostling beam in front of us.

I walk ahead of Gregor, the rifle's muzzle a steady point of pressure between my shoulder blades. My hands tingle from the too-tight zip tie.

I scan the dark edges of the driveway. How far could I get before he felled me? I don't doubt that he'd shoot. Not lethally, of course, because he has big plans for my uterus. But he probably wouldn't even flinch about maiming me in the arm or the leg or some other body part not required for pregnancy.

"We're hiking all the way up there?" I ask him over my shoulder. "To the grove?"

He doesn't answer, but the rifle's muzzle digs a little deeper into my back.

"Who's the guy who you want to rape me?" I say. "Who's *the God of the Grove*?"

No answer.

"I figure it has to be one of your relatives," I say, "because your mom is so hell-bent on getting the Himmel nose. Why not just tell her you're infertile? I mean, it's *her* fault. For not getting you vaccinated for mumps? It's almost funny, actually. She didn't vaccinate you because *survival of the fittest* and so she wiped out her entire precious bloodline. Here's to Charles freaking Darwin."

"Shut up," Gregor says, but I hear his voice waver.

"Aren't you sorry at all?" I say.

"For what?"

"For lying to me the entire time we've known each other?"

"You *chose* to believe me. You were so focused on what *you* wanted."

"Okay. And did you push Anna down the stairs because she was helping me?"

"She's a meddling little bitch."

My breath catches. "And *you're* a twisted freak. What about Kirsten? Why is she helping you?"

"Why do you think? For the same reason anyone does anything for me. Because I'm paying her."

"*Paying* her? How much?"

"I'm giving her the land they're renting. She's desperate to own the deed to the grove. I don't know how much it's worth. I don't really care. Once we have a baby, my mother will be willing to do anything I want her to do."

"I doubt it," I say. "She'll just think of another hoop for you to jump through."

"I'm done with this conversation."

We go through the driveway gates and cross the road. I pray that someone will drive past and see Gregor's rifle in their headlight beams. But this is a lonely road even in daytime, and now it's the middle of the night.

We walk up the Blakeleys' driveway. We circle their house. The kitchen windows are lit, but upstairs it's dark.

Is Sam asleep up there? Is he okay?

Sam, I think. *Sam, as soon as I figure out how, I'm coming back for you.*

Gregor steers me through the tall grass at the back of the house, and into the trees.

Into the woods we go, to lose our minds and find our souls.

67

It's a long way up to the ravine.

Much farther and steeper than I remember from the two treks I made before. Tonight, I'm exhausted. Hungry, still dehydrated despite the water I had back at the house, and coming down from back-to-back drug trips.

Maybe it's the lingering psychedelics in my system that make the forest seem otherworldly. Were the fir trees so girthy before? So black? Did their branches whisper so urgently in the wind? Did the undergrowth cling so tightly to our legs? Did the bird calls sound so alien?

Somehow or other we make it to the nettle patch at the top of the ravine, my horrible husband and I. My spine is sore from the prod of his gun. I'm sweating, and we're both breathing fast.

Moonlight washes the nettles to white, but the ravine is a black abyss. Across the way, though, I see light. Yellow light, dancing and muzzy, leaking through the trees.

I smell smoke.

This is really happening, I think. *There's really some kind of ritual happening over there, and I'm headed straight for it.*

"Let's go," Gregor says.

"Down?"

"Where else? Down is the only way across."

I squint down the slope. I see moonlight-edged ferns and fallen logs. I can't see to the bottom.

"It's really steep," I say. "I'll lose my balance with my hands behind me like this. I'll break my neck."

"Nice try. I'm not untying you. Let's go."

This could be my last chance, I think.

I step quickly to the side, and then back, and then I plow my shoulder into Gregor's and send him staggering down into the ravine.

"Fuck!" he shouts.

I hear thumps and cracks and crunching vegetation and then a scream of pain before everything goes quiet.

I turn and start back toward the Blakeley homestead.

"Sam's not there!" comes Gregor's distant shout.

I stop.

I go back to the edge of the ravine. "Where is he?" I shout down into the darkness.

"I think I broke my leg!"

Good, I think.

"Where's Sam?" I shout.

"I need help." Now Gregor is whimpering. "Come down here and help me, and I'll tell you."

Maybe he's bluffing, and Sam really is still at the Blakeley homestead. But maybe he isn't. I have no way to know.

So I start down the steep slope for the third time in my life, checking the strength of the soft soil before every shift of my weight. My hands are almost numb by this point, and my shoulders ache. I'm not fully in control of my body. I have to focus on every little movement.

Gregor lies in the dark at the bottom. His LED beam shines out at a diagonal. Once my eyes adjust, I see that one of his legs is bent at an impossible angle.

He isn't going anywhere.

"Where's the gun?" I ask him.

"I don't know. I dropped it. Is that all you care about? *Look at my leg!*"

"Where's Sam?"

"You *broke my leg,* you bitch, and all you—"

I smush my sneaker into the side of his face. *"Where. Is. Sam?"*

"Up at the grove," Gregor says, his words garbled by the pressure on his cheek.

"The *grove*? Why?"

"You know why."

To sacrifice him? I think. *What else?*

"You're a monster!" I scream at Gregor.

"Fuck you," he snarls into the ground.

I hate him so much it takes my breath away.

"I'm taking your hat," I say. "If you make any sudden movements, I swear to God I'll kick your face in."

Gregor grunts.

I crouch sideways and, with one of my bound hands, snatch the beanie off his head. I stand.

Not that I can *wear* the beanie. I can't reach up with my zip-tied hands. But if I hold it just so and walk kind of sideways, the LED beam will light my way.

"See you," I say to Gregor, walking away.

"You said you were going to help me!"

"No, I didn't."

I scan the other side of the ravine with the LED beam. It looks even steeper than the way we came down, plus it's covered with impassable-looking thickets. I don't think I can make my way up there with my hands behind my back.

There has to be a path, though. One the women use to get up there to their grove. I just need to find it.

I walk along the bottom of the ravine, searching for a way up.

There's the big, mossy rock I hid behind when Gregor—or whoever it was—shot at me that day. It glows ghostly in the LED light.

And then, in the outer reaches of the light, I see them again.

The holes.

The last time I was here, I didn't understand what I was looking at.

Now I know.

They aren't fresh anymore. Days of rain and wind have scattered leaves across them, softened the edges, but they're still visible: two dozen, maybe more. All different sizes.

How many dead girls did they dump down here? How many hacked-up body parts did they have to dig up again? What did they do with them? Burn them? Or simply dump them somewhere even more remote?

Fear wraps me like a shroud.

I need to keep moving. I need to get to Sam. If anything happens to him, if those insane, vicious women—

There—over there.

I spot a path, switchbacking up the far side of the ravine.

I climb up.

Slowly, slower than the adrenaline in my bloodstream wants, but I can't afford to fall. With my hands bound behind me, a fall could be deadly.

As I climb, the smell of smoke sharpens. I start to hear snippets of feminine voices—laughter, maybe. I see the glow of firelight in the sky above. I see the moon, cold and perfect and round.

You bitch, I tell it. *You controlling bitch.*

I'm at the top, on level ground again, sweating and panting, my wrists on fire. But I've made it. And over there—an opening in the trees. Firelight jumps and shudders. The smoke smells like cedar and animal fat and tar. The women's voices are definitely laughing.

I walk closer.

Then I freeze, because I've registered *human faces watching me.*

Fear zaps my mind blank.

No—wait. They aren't living human faces but faces carved on wooden poles, one on either side of the opening in the trees. They're like slender totem poles, ten, maybe twelve feet high, with men's faces crudely embellishing their rounded tops. Bulging, blank eyes stare, with rough pits gouged out for the pupils. Lower down, the poles have been stripped of every shred of their bark and all of their branches except for one each. The lone branches jut forward, carved to look like big, erect penises.

A figure appears in the glowing space between the poles.

Kirsten.

Naked and graceful, her long, pale hair hanging down over bare breasts. She's holding an axe by its handle against her shoulder.

"I knew you'd come for Sam," she says to me.

"Where is he?"

"Somewhere else."

"It's human blood you want to spill tonight, isn't it? I know Sam is—"

"You don't know anything, Harlow. You think you're so incredibly smart, but you have no idea what's coming. You're not high, are you? That means you're going to remember, and *that* means Gregor's going to have to keep you locked up for a very long time after this." She shakes her head. "I *knew* something would go wrong on his end. He may be a child of God, but he's *so lame*."

"You think he's a child of God?" I said.

"How else could he look the way he looks?"

"You're a sociopath."

She steps closer. Her hands tighten on the axe handle. "Thank you, I guess?"

"Where's Sam?"

"Sam doesn't matter anymore." Kirsten smiles her empty smile and lifts the axe.

"It was a trap," I say. Then the flat of the axe smacks the top of my head, and the world vanishes.

68

I can't open my eyes.

The lids are sealed-shut sandpaper. A fireball of pain throbs inside my skull. The ground is moist and hard. My clothes are wet and twisted around me. My feet are numb with cold because they are, for some reason, bare.

What's that sound? Not quite singing, not quite talking, but definitely women's voices.

Chanting. That's what it is. In a language I don't know, with lilting cadences and fibrous consonants.

I smell smoke, acrid like a kitchen grease fire. I smell the damp night air and fungal decay in the ground under my cheek. My mouth tastes of copper.

The chanting lifts up now, urgent and breathless, and it's enough to finally push my eyes open.

At first, all I see is yellow flame. My glasses are gone, but I can tell there's fire all around me and that treetops form a ring overhead. Inside the ring is a circle of gray-blue sky, and the moon, a cold, blank disk, floats in the middle of the circle. It's beautiful, actually. The symmetry of it.

I struggle upright. I'm swaying, and my head hurts so badly, and I think I'm going to vomit.

"Ah!" a woman's voice says.

"She's awake!" another woman says.

A tittering wave of excited voices.

The nausea boils up and I hunch toward the ground, gagging, but of course nothing comes up because I've drunk so little and eaten nothing for days. I'm empty.

I realize for the first time that someone has braided my hair.

I try to get onto my hands and knees, but my ankle is caught on something. I twist to see what it is.

That's when I realize I'm wearing a long white nightgown, soaked and muddied and snarled like a trap around my legs.

The nightgown. The braid.

Gregor was *grooming* me for this.

When I yank the nightgown up to my knees to free myself, I still can't get up. There are ropes around my ankles. And—I strain to focus my eyes—the ropes are knotted to a metal stake in the ground.

An animal sound comes out of my mouth, somewhere between a sob and a wail.

More tittering from the women.

"Let me go!" I shout. It's so cold out, I can see my breath in the air.

Laughter.

"How can you do this?" I shout. "How can you treat another woman like this? Like a . . . like livestock?"

"Mooo!" someone calls.

Shrieks of laughter.

I look around myself.

The grove is otherworldly—or at least, the impressionist version I can see without my glasses.

Torches on tall stakes flame orange and gold, puffing black smoke. Green moss, outrageously plushy like velvet furniture, carpets the softly undulating ground. The trees around the clearing have silver trunks as slender as human legs. Their heart-shaped yellow leaves shiver like a reflection on the surface of a pond.

And the women, they're slipping and darting around the grove like frolicking children, only they're naked and their long hair is flipping around, and their breasts and buttocks jiggle, and their movements are unwieldy, and the way they're chanting and humming and giggling, I think they must be drunk or high. Yes, very, *very* high, because their facial expressions are smeary—mouths stretched ghoulishly, whites of their eyes flashing. It's a party atmosphere, but it's also threatening. The fun is hanging by a thread.

Madness lies waiting.

I'm not thinking very clearly, and I know I've still got Gregor's drug in my own system, but I realize I might be the most sober person here.

That's an advantage.

I twist to examine the ropes around my ankles again. It isn't easy to do in the strobe-light flame and shadow. The rope is the cotton kind, I think, and it's wet. It's chafing me.

Thank God I'm free of the zip ties, though. That's one good thing.

I look around. No one seems to be paying attention to me.

I pick at one of the knots at my ankle. It's so tight, I bend a fingernail backward.

"Hey!" someone says, and they lunge at me and slap my hands away from the knot and shove me so hard, I fall sideways.

I struggle upright again.

It's Gwen, standing over me, naked, breathing hard. "What's the matter with you?" she says. "Why are you so ungrateful? The rest of us would kill to be where you are right now."

Someone else emerges beside her. Hildy, breathless too, but scowling. "We can't let her ruin this," she says to Gwen. "Not after the Gilda got away last time."

Gwen groans, disgust mixed with glee. "When she *turned*!"

Hildy nods eagerly. "When the axe got her in the face!"

"I wonder where she crawled away to die. We never found her."

Bessie, I think. *No—Liz.*

Liz was supposed to be last month's sacrificial victim, but she got away.

I can hear the KinderWild children's chatter in my head:

My mama says Old Gilda ran away 'cause she's bad. My mama said she ruined everything.

I can't possibly wrap my head around the physics of it, but Liz somehow escaped into the past . . . and survived a horrible axe injury to the face. She changed her name to Bessie, became the cook at Himmel Cottage, and penciled those lonely inscriptions on the walls.

Now someone is coming forward into the center of the clearing—no, two people. Terra, her hennaed dreadlocks unmistakable, and a slighter, younger woman with tiny breasts, a curved-forward spine, and stick-straight brown hair.

Gilda. The new one.

There's something wrong with her smile, though, and with the way her head lolls to one side. And it's weird how Terra is guiding her so carefully by the hand. All the women seem high, but I suspect Gilda has been drugged into a whole other dimension.

They stop exactly in the middle of the clearing. Terra lets go of Gilda's arm and Gilda twirls in a slow circle, stretching her arms up, her fingers caressing and plucking at the rays of the moon.

Terra, meanwhile, has sunk to a crouch. She picks up something from the ground—a hand broom, I think—and carefully, section by section, she sweeps a large stone on the ground. It's a flat stone, like a crooked little footstool made of rock.

She finishes sweeping. She stands again, takes hold of Gilda's arm, and pulls until the girl thumps to her knees in front of the stone. Gilda cries out, and Terra quietly scolds her.

A hush falls over the grove. For the first time, I can hear the sizzle of the torches and the leaves crinkling in the wind.

Someone is walking out from the dark behind the ring of torches. Kirsten again. Head high, still naked, carrying the axe in front of her with both hands.

Oh my God, I think. *They're really doing this.*

69

I give one of my ankles a jerk, but of course it's still tied tight.

I can't just sit here and watch a murder, though. I have to *do* something.

Something flashes in the corner of my eye. I turn. It's . . . oh my God, yes, it's a pair of glasses, maybe *my* glasses, discarded nearby on the ground.

Maybe I can reach them, I think. *And then . . .*

I glance up at Gwen. She's still standing over me, but her attention is on Kirsten, her face rapt.

Sicko.

I crawl slowly, slowly, toward the glasses.

I stretch my arm as far as I can, and my fingertips graze the frame. I stretch a little more and—*got them.*

With the glasses in my fist, I return to a seated position just before Gwen sends me a sharp look.

Kirsten walks slowly to the center of the clearing and stops beside the stone where Gilda kneels.

Kirsten tips her head back, gazing up at the sky, the moon. Then she speaks, her girlish voice as sharp as glass. "In the Before time, I walked this sacred grove by moonlight, searching for my love."

A murmur ripples through the circle of women, appreciative, almost soothed. I get the sense Kirsten is retelling a well-loved story.

"I was lost," she says. "I was empty. But the ancient gods had led me to the right place and the right time that night, to be forever changed and blessed."

"Blessed," a woman murmurs, and then another and another—*"Blessed." "Blessed."*

I spot a golf ball–size stone in the wet leaves nearby. I pick it up. I punch it down hard on the glasses and feel the crackle of breaking glass.

Beside me, Gwen shifts her weight.

Kirsten is holding up a hand for silence. The women go quiet again.

I see what's going on here. Kirsten is these women's priestess, and this is her sermon. And she isn't high. She doesn't need to be because she's batshit crazy.

"In this sacred grove," Kirsten says, "the gods revealed to me Light-bringer Lucy, preparing to debase herself on the dirt with the mortal man, Benjamin. In the very same moment, the gods revealed to me this sacred axe." She lifts the axe skyward, both hands wrapped just under its double head. She starts to speak louder and more quickly. "By the light of a single moonbeam, I drew out this axe from the leaves—"

Excited murmurs undulate through the clearing.

"—and, guided by the moonbeam, I took this sacred axe and spilled Lucy's still-virgin blood into the soil, and then . . . the God of the Grove appeared."

"Yes!" a woman cried.

"Bring him!" another shouted. "I want him—I *need* him!"

I feel around in the shards of the broken glasses. I choose a piece of lens that's large enough to keep a firm pinch-hold on but that also has a sharp edge.

I inch one of my tethered ankles closer to my hand. I start sawing at the rope.

It takes a few seconds to breach the rope fibers. But I finally feel them giving way, and then one of my ankles is free.

I start on the second rope.

Kirsten is saying, "We offer him gifts of gold and we offer him the precious gift of pure blood so that He will come to us. So that He will love us. So that He will bless us with his sacred phallus and his eternal seed, so that we will bring forth his golden children and make this terrible, filthy world clean and new again."

The second rope goes quicker than the first, and I'm scrambling to my feet, taking lurching, swaying steps toward the center of the clearing.

"Gilda!" I scream, hobbling on my cramped-up feet across the moss.

Gilda's head turns.

"They want to kill you!" I shout. "See the axe? You need to run!"

She's blinking at me.

"Run!" I repeat. "Run, run, run!"

Her gaze snaps to the ring of torches and naked flesh. To the darkness beyond.

"Run," I cry. "Run, now, or they're going to kill you!"

She gets to her feet. Lithe and nimble, she darts past the ring of firelight before any of the other women have time to register what's happening, and she's gone.

"Get her!" Kirsten shouts. "Go get her!"

A few of the women straggle after Gilda.

"Run, Gilda!" I shout. *"Run!"*

And now I'm face-to-face again with Kirsten and her axe. Only this time, she doesn't want to capture me.

She wants to kill me.

Face contorted, she swings the axe.

I dodge it, displaced air brushing my cheek.

She swings again with a grunt, and this time the heavy blade sinks like a scream into my shoulder.

I totter for a few crooked steps. The axe handle is jutting out of me in a way that's hard to understand.

I drop.

My head bangs the ground, but that's nothing compared to the yawning void of pain down my side. I see the axe handle sticking up. The blade's in deep.

I think about pulling it out, but I'm afraid that if I do there'll be too much blood. And there's already *so much*.

"He comes," someone is saying, and someone else says, *"He's here, he's here,"* but it's all muted by the giant mosquito whine in my ears.

I turn my head. Everything is ground level and sideways.

Over there, where all the women's bare legs are clustered, I see two hands emerge from the blood-soaked dirt like the hands of a surfacing swimmer. The hands scrabble around, fingers hooked, searching, and then they catch on to the firmer ground on either side of the blood—*my* blood. The top of a head rises up. Ears that stick out. Fair, muddy hair plastered to a pale neck. Muscular shoulders.

And then this man, whoever he is, this visitor from underground, he lifts himself out of the dirt like he's climbing out of a swimming pool. I see his back, his buttocks. Now he's kneeling, now he's getting to his feet. He's bloody and muddy and stark naked.

He turns his head. I see his profile against the throbbing torchlight.

Gregor, I think.

The women whisper and chant and coo. They step back to give him more space.

I don't know how it's possible, but somehow Gregor has crawled out of the ground, and his leg must not be broken anymore.

He's seen me.

Seen me in the long, white, bloody nightgown and the braided hair that he thinks are so damn sexy. He comes toward me, his penis jutting, his mouth an expressionless line.

It all clicks into place.

This isn't Gregor.

None of these women know who he is. But I do.

He's no god.

He's just a German boy from the logging camps who likes to eat strange mushrooms and frolic with witches in the woods.

That's what Liz had been trying to say, scrawling her secrets on the walls of the house. And that hole in the ground . . . that must've been her escape route.

By some accident these women figured out how to open up a tunnel through the earth that leads to the past. Maybe it's the moon. Maybe it's the blood-soaked dirt. Maybe it's the axe. I don't care.

All I know is, I think I can make it stop. I can undo all of it. All the killing, all the spilled blood. I know how to get rid of Gregor, and Pauline, make it so that they were never even born. Maybe even the dead girls might be spared somehow, all the Gildas, and Liz, and Anna, somewhere, in the folding and refolding helixes of time.

Jakob Himmel, a young, virile version of the great-grandfather, the traveler through time and blood and dirt, advances toward me.

And what kind of monster is he that he can look at me with undisguised lust when my life's blood is pumping out of my shoulder and into the ground?

I'm glad he's a monster, though. It'll make this so much easier.

I crouch laboriously, drunkenly. The fingers of my good hand curl around the axe's slick handle. I stand up, stagger sideways, and right myself.

I tighten my grip on the axe handle and seesaw it free, and I hear screaming. It might be me. And the axe is free, and the life is flowing out of me—

Jakob is four strides away.

Three.

Two—

I lift the axe as high as I can.

It's *so heavy*.

But I summon all my strength and rage and grief that I have to die so soon, and I channel it into that axe blade and hurl it into the side of Jakob's skull and—

70

I've always loved Central Park in autumn.

There's something so romantic about the late October foliage all rusty and pink against the white sky. And the perimeter of high-rises around the park looks just like a Broadway backdrop.

Or maybe I was feeling romantic because I was holding hands with the love of my life, both of us bundled up in coats and walking shoulder to shoulder, footsteps perfectly in sync. In his free hand, Theo was holding a steaming paper cup with a plastic lid, the almond milk latte we're sharing.

Decaf, I thought happily, and with my own free hand I couldn't resist touching the firm dome of my belly, no longer disguised even under my roomiest coat.

The morning sickness had faded like a bad dream, and in its place bloomed something golden. Now, every breath felt like a promise. And I was also finding myself narrating my days aloud so the baby wouldn't miss anything important, like which flavor of yogurt I picked.

I felt happy, happier than I'd ever felt in my life, and, more than anything else, hopeful.

My sister Audrey said it was because I forgave our mom when we went to visit her grave over the summer. She said there was something about Theo's love for me, or the fact that *I* was going to be a mother, that shifted my thinking about Mom.

"Penny for your thoughts, my love," Theo said.

"Oh, I don't know. I guess I'm just thinking about families."

He gave my hand a squeeze. "In a good way, I hope?"

"Yeah," I said. "Definitely in a good way."

We walked in silence for a few minutes, simply enjoying the peace of each other's company.

That's one of the things I loved so much about Theo—he was so easy to be around. I didn't have to be fun, or cute, or whatever. I could even be snarky.

I could simply be myself, the best version of myself.

He wasn't very tall, and he wasn't what a random person on the street would necessarily consider handsome, but I adored his open, honest face and his geeky professorial vibe. I mean, he came by it honestly—he was a professor of constitutional law at NYU.

Every day I thanked my lucky stars that I met him that day in the stuck elevator at Bloomingdale's.

Then we were strolling past a playground. Children shouted and laughed and streaked this way and that. A ring of adults on benches watched with bored expressions.

There was only one adult amid the playground equipment. A young, smiling woman, dark-haired and with brown skin, pushing a little boy on a tire swing.

"Faster, Mama, faster!" the boy shouted gleefully.

"Sam, baby, if I push you any faster, I'm afraid you'll go flying away to the moon," the woman laughingly replied.

"I *want* to go to the moon," the boy said. "You can come with me."

There was something about that little boy. I don't know what it was. He seemed . . . not familiar, exactly, because I was sure I'd never seen him before. Nevertheless, something about him tugged at my heart in an almost painful way.

"When you get it right," Theo said to me softly, following my gaze, "that bond, the one between moms and their kids, it's really something, isn't it?" He gave my hand another squeeze. "It's like the backbone of the world."

"Yeah," I said. "I mean, it kind of freaks me out, the idea that I have zero experience being a mom and I might mess it up—but yeah. I think you're right."

We started walking again.

Acknowledgments

First off: Dear reader, thank you. You could've been doing literally anything else, but you chose to spend hours with this book, and I'm wildly grateful. To my editor Laura—thanks for rolling the dice on this story. To my agent Stephany—thank you for never giving up on me. To Tegan, Nicole, Jon, and the rest of the editorial team: You made these pages tighter than I thought possible. To the art and marketing crew at Thomas & Mercer—your magic made this book look far cooler than I ever hoped. My brother Tom, my perennial consultant on all things that go bang or grow antlers in the woods—you're the best. Tamara, our tradwife chats cracked this whole thing open, and you, Jennifer, and Zach as beta readers gave me sharper eyes when mine went blurry. And finally, to Zach, and to Henry and Aesa—you three are my everything, my engine, my chaos, my home. I love you.

About the Author

Maia Chance writes addictively creepy domestic thrillers with a supernatural twist, including *The Body Next Door*. She's also the author of the quirky and humorous *Discreet Retrieval Agency*, *Fairy Tale Fatal*, and *Agnes & Effie* mysteries. Every story she writes starts with a house she's obsessed with—whether it's a New England farmhouse or a castle in the Black Forest. She loves to bake, read, and walk her dog (a terrier with an incredible moustache) while secretly gawking at other people's houses. Maia lives in the Pacific Northwest with her husband and two children, and you can connect with her at www.maiachance.com.